Dangerous Spring

Dangerous Spring

MARGOT BENARY-ISBERT

✦   ✦   ✦

Translated from the German by James Kirkup

PETER SMITH
GLOUCESTER, MASS.
1990

The historical events in this book are based on my own and
my husband's diaries of this period. This is exactly how we
lived through the last days of the war. So, as an historical docu-
ment, it has the positive truth of personal experience, along
with the possible bias of personal feelings. The story, however, and the characters are entirely fictional.

Dangerous Spring

✦ *Chapter One* ✦

Easter Monday, the second of April, 1945, a day with a gray-blue springtide sky, over which a harmless flock of white lamblike woolly clouds was drifting. At least, that's how it started out.

We've come through another night, thought Karin Lorenz. Father had just telephoned from the hospital, where he was on emergency duty two nights a week. He still had two patients to see in the clinic and one in the town; then he'd be able to come home for breakfast. Mother was seeing to her milk-ewes and her fowls. During the war she had started a miniature farm in order to keep her family reasonably well fed in the long years of rationing. In the waiting room and dispensary in the basement, Karin could hear Nurse Ottilie making cheerful tinkling sounds with glasses and instruments.

During the past weeks, the early morning hours had always been the quietest in the day. You could fairly safely count on having no air-raid warning before ten o'clock. You had time to take a bath and put on clean clothes after the long night spent in the cellar, to put the house in order and prepare for consultations. Dr. Lorenz's first patients always turned up about eight o'clock.

Young Till was still in the bathroom. Bluebeard, the family dog, was sitting at the bathroom door waiting. The shower had now been running for at least five minutes. Till sang, a

9

little out of tune but with enthusiasm; this morning it was a marching song popular with the members of the Hitler Youth Movement, called the H.J. He was the only unmusical one in the family, and the only one who could muster any enthusiasm for the H.J. The boys had a group leader for whom they'd go through fire and flood. They played all kinds of sports with him, and he was outstanding at all of them: riding, skiing, swimming, and tennis—Karl could do everything. In summer they went for long hikes and canoe trips. They had wandered all over Germany, from the Bavarian mountains in the south to the bays and beaches in the north. They stayed overnight in hostels set up in ancient castles, sang around their campfires in the evenings. They practiced night patrols and army maneuvers. And of course Till thought it was just great. Besides, as long as you had good marks for athletics and for your activities in the H.J., you weren't expected to wear yourself out with boring old schoolwork.

"Haven't you finished yet?" his sister shouted at him through the bathroom door.

"Wait a sec! Don't rush me! Cleanliness isn't a luxury."

"You're not the only one who wants to be clean, though."

He came out of the bathroom with a wet towel clutched around his middle, his body pink from the cold shower. A lanky-legged thirteen-year-old, fair-haired and fair-skinned like his father and, in spite of his mother's valiant farming efforts, still as lean and sinewy as a greyhound. "Heil, sister!" he cried. "All clear! Heil, Bluebeard, King of Dogland!"

"Get yourself dressed and go and help Mutti. She's tethering the sheep in the garden. Tell her Father'll soon be home for breakfast. And then make a start with your Latin verbs. You won't always be able to get away with being in high favor with the H.J."

"What d'you mean?"

"Poor innocent lamb! Even the German news is admitting

now that the Americans have reached central Germany, the British are in Westphalia, and the Russians are on the outskirts of Breslau."

"So what? Wait till they've had a taste of our gigantic new secret weapon. The enemy must be held back until then. Karl explained it all to us yesterday. This afternoon he'll be showing us how to sling a hand grenade. He says our garden wall would be, strategically speaking, a wonderful defense position. They'll have to come down the road from Castle Hill, won't they? So all I need to do is to make my stand behind the wall —not a soul among them'll be able to see me—and then, bang goes the leading tank!"

"Yes, and bang goes Till!" his sister retorted, seizing him by the shoulder and giving him a good shake. "Till! You who could never hurt a fly! Just remember there are human beings inside those tanks."

Till bit his lips and wrinkled his forehead. Thinking was not his strong point. "D'you think I like it?" he said. "But a soldier has to carry out the orders he is given; that's all."

"We'll see about that," replied Karin and shoved him out the door. Then she got under the shower.

The water was icy cold. For the last three years there had been hot water only once a week, except for the dispensary, where Nurse Ottilie kept guard over her hot-water heater against all comers. But this was a family that liked to sing under the shower, whether the water was hot or cold, whether it was peace or war. A year ago Karin had been in the habit of humming a waltz tune; but now she always sang a hymn. Today it was her favorite, "Oh, for a thousand tongues to sing. . . ." The rivulets of cold water poured down her slender, long-legged body and dripped from her dark, close-cropped hair. The stinging cold made her glow all over in a few seconds. Oh, how good it was to be alive! Reason enough to give thanks with tongues, for wasn't it like a miracle, to be alive in the midst of so much death, to know that there was someone like Helmut Lobelius in the world and that it was spring again: that the earth, soaked with blood and tears, should be bringing forth fresh blades of grass once more and cherry blossoms and fields of grain . . . to know that the war could not last much longer now. That was what her parents said; it was what the English radio was saying. They listened to it every evening, with doors and windows tightly shut and with the telephone muffled under the tea cozy, in case it might have a hidden microphone built in. They would wait, with bated breath, for the first bars of Beethoven's *Fifth Symphony*, which opened the program. Then: "This is London! This is London! This is London!" And then came the voice from a world of freedom, a world that would perhaps be theirs again, some day.

It was now simply a matter of endurance, of living through the final days of the Third Reich.

Pastor Wolf said they were all in God's keeping. But hadn't Lore and Elsbeth also been in God's keeping? Now they were lying dead under heaps of rubble with their parents, sisters, and brothers. And what about the young men, still boys really, with whom they had danced the year before? At that time the boys had just become soldiers and had been trained here in the barracks. Hans and Robert and Paul, and all of them; they were only a year or two older than the girls—and now so many of them had been killed or crippled, or taken prisoner in Russia, in France, in the Balkans. And they had all loved to laugh and to dance. They had wanted to live, and their mothers had prayed for them.

Karin thought: I *must* live! In August, I shall be seventeen. She rubbed herself fiercely with the coarse bath towel. I'm almost seventeen. I'm a grown woman; only my family haven't noticed it yet.

In February she had passed her final examinations at school;

her age group had taken them a year earlier, because of the war. So on the first of May she would be drafted for a women's labor camp. Only now it would not happen. The end of the war was too near. Since she had finished school, Karin had been helping her mother with the housework and her father with his dispensary and his practice. Kornelia, nicknamed Korr, the Dutch housekeeper who had come to Germany in the spring of '43 because there was more to eat there than in occupied Holland, had suddenly gone home at the end of January. She said she was sorry to go, but if the Allies found her in Germany, she might possibly be accused of collaboration. She came from Groningen, and Groningen folk are as stubborn as mules. It would have been hopeless trying to persuade her to stay. Since her departure, they just had a cleaning woman three times a week.

Housework was not one of Karin's favorite occupations, but for some years she had been passionately interested in her father's practice; always in the holidays she had been eager to help him and Nurse Ottilie. Her parents assumed that she would go to Heidelberg to study medicine as soon as it was practicable. Until quite recently, she herself had thought that was what she would do.

After she had put on fresh clothes in her bedroom, she sat thinking for a moment on the bed that had not been unmade, because they slept in the cellar. It was a pretty room, decorated in muted pastel shades, made comfortable with a few pieces of good furniture given to her as presents at Christmas and on her birthdays. On the walls she had hung beautiful reproductions of Old Master paintings and of the French Impressionists; these she was especially fond of. How important all this had seemed to her formerly! It wasn't so very long ago either . . .

In 1939, automatically she and her classmates had joined the German Girls' Movement, the B.D.M. But her distrust of

the high-sounding and meaningless phrases that were dished
out to them at meetings had very soon become evident, and
military drill for girls hurt her aesthetic sensibilities. She liked
books, music, and art. As her group leader warned her, she
was an individualist, and that was something deplorable. Then
she had decided to become confirmed in the Protestant church,
instead of attending the Nazi Youth Consecration, perhaps
more as a protest against coercion than out of a deep inner
conviction.

In the spring of 1942, she found a mimeographed sheet of
paper on her desk at home one day: it was a copy of one of
the sermons with which Count Galen, the Bishop of Münster,
was trying to arouse the conscience of the German people.
The copies were passed around secretly. A little later, Karin
heard about Hans and Inge Scholl and their friends, those
young students who died for the cause of freedom in Munich.
"Is it true?" she asked her parents one evening after Till had
gone to bed. She knew that it was her father who had placed
the bishop's sermon on her desk. That night they had a long
discussion. She had heard nothing of the terrible things that
had been happening. Even her parents, who from the very
first had been against the new rulers of Germany, had only
realized in November, 1938, the total decline of justice and
humanity in their country—through the experiences of their
Jewish friends, those few who were still left in the town at
that time. Three years later, the husband of a woman patient
had come to see Dr. Lorenz during his leave from Poland,
where he was stationed with the army. He had spoken to his
wife's doctor, as if to a father confessor, about what he had
seen there. "Now I have put my life in your hands, Doctor,"
he had said on leaving. "But I had to talk to someone or I
should have gone mad." Karin's father and mother spoke about
all these things with her, and ever since that talk Karin had
associated herself more closely with the youth group at the

14

church run by Pastor Wolf who had confirmed her. It was one of those small circles of young people, such as existed everywhere in Germany at that time, that strove with great seriousness to keep alive the ideas of freedom and truth and the spirit of Christianity. Now at last, Karin thought, she had found the place where she belonged.

They met every Wednesday evening not only to read the Psalms and the Book of Job and the New Testament, but also some of Plato's dialogues, Guardini's *Augustinus*, and George Bernard Shaw's *Saint Joan*. They would talk until late into the night, and if there was an alert, they went on with their discussions in the crypt of St. John's Church that before the Reformation had been a Catholic mendicant friars' church. They were ablaze with faith and enthusiasm; they were firmly convinced that one day they would build a new Germany out of the ruins of a godless period; that then, out of devastation, what Shakespeare calls the "glassy essence" of man would arise; this was something they never doubted, even though ". . . an angry ape plays such fantastic tricks before high heaven as make the angels weep."

It was in this group that Karin had gotten to know Helmut Lobelius. One rainy evening early last summer he had made an appearance in the crypt during an air raid. Karin still seemed to see him as he was then, at their first meeting—a slender, slight man with a boldly modeled face that seemed to have been carved from wood, almost ugly when he was not speaking or laughing. He wore a black patch over one eye and limped slightly. His hatless head, his wind-tangled hair, and his gray-green tweed coat were dripping wet; but he didn't seem to notice. A button on his coat was hanging by a single thread. One of the girls had gotten up, taken a spool of thread from her sewing kit, and sewn it on firmly for him. He was the sort of man for whom girls sew on buttons.

"Good evening, Helmut!" Pastor Wolf had cried out joyfully. "How nice to see you once again! I think you know everyone here except Karin Lorenz. This is Pastor Helmut Lobelius, Karin, another of my confirmation students, but many years before you youngsters."

Karin had moved to make room for him, and Lobelius had sat down beside her on the gravestone of a former pastor of the church. After that he had come more often to the meetings, and finally almost every week. Karin gradually learned from the others, who had known him for a long time, something more about him. After being wounded in the Flanders campaign, and after a long period of pain and sickness in a military hospital, he was demobilized with a missing left eye and a lame hip joint. In the autumn of 1942 he had taken charge of the Protestant community in Eberstein, a small country town north of Erfurt. Since the previous spring he had also had the care of two neighboring rural parishes.

After a while Karin took him to her parents' house, as she had always done with her friends. He seemed to like the family and the small circle of trusted friends among whom one could speak one's mind. Karin's parents liked him very much. The thought that their daughter might fall in love with a man so much older and outwardly so unattractive was so improbable that it was quite a while before Karin's mother began to feel seriously worried about it.

Meanwhile, Karin had been twice with the youth group to visit Pastor Lobelius's old country church in the little town of Eberstein to look at its painted galleries and fine altarpiece. Once she had spent a weekend there to hear him preach. And what a sermon that had been! Full of deep faith, spirited, manly, devoted to the cause of truth at a time when lies prevailed. And then the old parsonage! The garden running down to the river, the kitchen courtyard with its tumble-down outhouses, and in the house itself an absence of all luxury, which gave an impression of almost saintly poverty. Karin saw this as the "simple life," the only possible spiritual life in those dark days. Aunt Ulrike, a sister of Lobelius's dead father, was living with him, an old lady who seemed to have stepped out of the pages of *The Gentlewoman's Magazine*, with a white frilled collar and turns of phrase belonging to the last century. Her real home was a foundation for the spinster daughters of clergymen, but she had given up the secluded life in this convent-like place to keep house for her nephew until he should marry.

While Karin dreamily dusted the smooth surfaces of the furniture in her father's room, she was inwardly rebelling against the ideas of her mother, who wanted to keep up a certain amount of gracious living as long as possible. What was the use of dusting when at any moment the whole house might be a heap of rubble? Now if she were living in Eberstein, instead of dusting and cleaning, she would discuss theology with Helmut, go for long walks through the meadows along the river, visit members of the congregation, help Lobelius in the drafting of his sermons. The charming little town lay untouched by the war among green hills and woods in a narrow valley. It had not yet had a single air raid.

Karin kept waiting for the telephone to ring. Every morning about this time Helmut rang up to ask if they had survived the night. He was anxious that the Lorenzes should come and stay at his house. As a matter of fact, many of their friends had already left the city, if they had relatives or acquaintances in the country who could put them up. But Karin's father said that a doctor could never leave his patients in the lurch, and her mother refused to leave without him. Karin had not dared yet to suggest that they should let her go alone to stay in Eberstein. Her parents thought that in times of such great danger the family should stick together. Besides, their house lay a long way from the center of the city and even farther from the factory districts, so they had been spared so far, and it was only reasonable to hope that in these last days of the fighting they would also be in comparative safety. Karin's suggestions had met with success in one way, however: she had persuaded her parents to send a truckload of beds, trunks, and chests last February to the parsonage in Eberstein. "Just in case," she had said reassuringly. "Every sensible family now is storing some things in the country for safety."

The Lorenzes' house lay on the western outskirts of the city, on the far side of the bridge across the swiftly flowing mill-stream. Dr. Lorenz had inherited it seventeen years ago and fitted up his consulting rooms in the basement. It was a low house lying behind a gray stone wall that enclosed a large garden. When the ancient trees were in leaf, only the red-tiled roof of the house could be seen from the street. But at this time of the year the chestnuts were only just beginning to unfold their languid leaves, like soft pale-green fans. The branches of the linden tree were still bare and black. Over the birches with their shivering catkins lay the violet shimmer of early spring. On the lawn there were already a few patches of bright yellow crocuses, and in the rock gardens along the wall the first wild tulips were making a festive show of brilliant red. Karin looked out of the window and watched her mother cutting a few of them to place on the breakfast table under the linden tree. Not far from the crocuses two large sheep were grazing, both freshly clipped and evidently pregnant. They were Holstein ewes, which had been providing the family with rich milk and warm wool since the outbreak of war. Somewhere behind the house, the hens were cackling.

Karin had finished her dusting and was taking out the patients' files in the consulting room in order to make a number of new entries when at last the telephone rang. Without beating about the bush, Lobelius came straight to the point, and his voice sounded more worried than usual. He had heard that the city would be defended. "You must all get away, Karin!"

he urged her. "Please speak to your parents about it once more. If your father can't go, at least he should send your mother and Till and yourself to me. We've got your beds all ready for you, and there's ample room here for your sheep and hens; you know that."

"I'll see what I can do, Helmut," Karin replied. She would have liked to tell him that Till had been ordered to receive the American tanks with hand grenades: that at least would be one good reason for her parents to get him out of the way. But it was impossible to mention such a thing on the telephone.

"You'll be a lot safer out here," Lobelius went on, as he had already said a dozen times before. "Eberstein is far too insignificant to be worth defending. But there's no time to be lost, Karin! In a day or two it will perhaps be impossible to leave the city. Aunt Ulrike sends her regards and is looking forward to welcoming you all."

When Karin at last laid down the receiver, she saw Bluebeard jumping and barking around her father as he came into the garden. Her mother placed a cushion on a garden chair.

"Good morning, Franz!" Carola Lorenz said. She was always relieved when he came back home after a night spent at the hospital. Being separated made the raids all the more disquieting. "Is it too cold to breakfast out of doors?" she asked. "We ought to enjoy the fresh air and the sun as much as we can when we've a chance."

"By all means! The air in the underground operating theater was awful."

"Many casualties?"

"Yes, from the northern suburbs again," Dr. Lorenz replied. "Sit down. I'll bring the coffee."

Franz Lorenz leaned back wearily in his chair. If only he could get a good night's rest, he thought; he would like to sleep right around the clock. But then he gazed with eyes red-rimmed by tiredness at the tulips on the white linen tablecloth, at the delicate Berlin porcelain breakfast set, at the peacefully ruminating sheep on the once-so-well-tended lawn, and at his wife Carola coming out of the house in her blue cotton dress, carrying the steaming coffeepot, and once more he marveled how every day women managed, in a crumbling world, to conjure up a sense of security and comfort. Mrs. Noah must have done just that in the Ark, he thought.

"Where have the childen got to?" he asked as his wife sat down beside him to pour his coffee.

"Till has already had breakfast with Nurse Ottilie, but that won't prevent him from putting in another appearance at the breakfast table," she said. "Karin has had one of her interminable telephone conversations. It seems that Lobelius won't take no for an answer; he insists that she'll be safer there than here."

"He may well be right. And it might be a good opportunity for Karin to find out just what life in a country parsonage means. She's seen everything through rose-tinted glasses on her few short visits there."

"Of course. And nothing's more dangerous, at her age, than those confusing, romantic notions. All the same, I find it very touching that in order to have Karin in safety, Lobelius is willing to take on the whole family, sheep and hens and Bluebeard and all."

"There *is* something touching about him," Franz Lorenz said reflectively. "I'm inclined to think that he's a truly good man."

"Oh, Franz, even a truly good man should brush his hair a little more often, shouldn't he? And remember that until quite recently Karin had distinctly aesthetic leanings."

"I think you're taking the whole thing much too seriously."

"It *is* serious, dear! Just look at the situation—a child like Karin, only sixteen, and this man who is almost twelve years her senior! There's nothing funny about that, is there?"

"I wasn't laughing, only smiling," he answered defensively. "It just struck me that when you were a young student, you too had a weakness for older men. If I remember rightly, the difference in age was even more than twelve years. Didn't you intend to free the professor who gave the wonderful lectures on the Trecento from his ancient, boring wife (she must have been at least forty!) and fly with him to some romantic country where the lemons bloom?"

"You have a distressingly good memory. Anyhow, he wasn't the least bit interested in me."

"I wouldn't have advised him to be!"

"Oh, I still hadn't met *you* then. Besides, we're talking about our daughter, not about me. If we won't go, then she'll cycle over to Eberstein alone; I heard her telling him that on the telephone."

"And if we stop her, she'll hold it against us all her life for standing in the way of her happiness."

Carola fell into such deep thought that she forgot to drink her coffee. What had become of her family? Karin had retired behind an impenetrable barrier of reserve. She regarded every little question as an unwarranted intrusion in her private affairs. Till, too, was no longer the confiding boy he had once been. What his adored youth leader said meant more to him than his own parents' advice. Even between herself and Franz, things were no longer the same. They hardly ever had time for each other and for the children. All their energies were devoted to the daily struggle for a bare existence. They were all so weary, so exhausted from work and lack of sleep, that there was hardly a chance for a quiet talk, still less for the readings and the music that the family had once so much enjoyed together. They had all become touchy and irritable. Under the surface of formal politeness crackled the flames of easily fanned anger: between brother and sister, parents and children, herself and Franz. In all this, Nurse Ottilie stood as firm as the Rock of Gibraltar; she had no nerves, but precisely this lack of nerves in her made Carola nervous.

The house itself, after five years of war, was still peaceful and unharmed. But Carola knew only too well that this peace, which was being threatened from within, stretched no farther than the garden wall—for beyond the wall lay the great east-west road, the ancient imperial highway, along which Napoleon's troops had marched, and before them the Swedish infantry, and much earlier the Roman legionaries. Now this highway was a roaring river of vehicles of every description. There were ambulances full of wounded; camouflaged tanks and heavy artillery; six-wheeled trucks laden with girls from the labor camps or with soldiers; private cars carrying officers; rickety horse-drawn carriages dug out of barns, the cobwebs still trailing from their wheels; farm carts drawn by cows, which were so slow that they got in everybody's way; hand-barrows stacked high with bedding and kitchen implements; and among all these, people on foot carrying whatever they could of their belongings. The traffic went on pouring into the city and out, in an inextricable confusion: it was impossible to see any kind of pattern or system in these wandering masses of people and vehicles. Those coming from the east brought with them terrible tales about the Russian invasion; those from the west said the American tanks were at their heels. In fact, for the last few days, American artillery had been heard in the west. Every night the sky was hung with "chandeliers," those dreaded flares that led the enemy bombers to their targets. Then the sirens would go and the refugees would run pell-mell for the nearest house or shelter. In the gray dawn they went on their way again. On the basement floor of the Lorenzes' house there were always a couple of mattresses ready for strange guests. The family had been sleeping for the last three weeks in the consulting room and Nurse Ottilie on the couch in the X-ray room.

Karin came out of the house and sat down beside her parents. Her mother cut her a slice of rye bread. "Will you have jam or margarine on it?" she asked. "There's a piece of Easter cake left also."

"No, thank you," said Karin. "I don't want anything to eat. I want to talk to you."

Carola heaved a sigh. Karin would go on about Eberstein again, she was sure.

"Erfurt is going to be defended," Karin said. "Helmut heard it from a reliable source. And this afternoon at his H.J. meeting, Till will be learning how to sling a hand grenade. The great god Karl, his leader, has spoken; apparently our garden wall would be an ideal defensive position."

Carola shook her head, as if by doing so she could rid her thoughts, and the world around her, of these nightmares. "Turning an open city into a strategic defense point. How utterly impossible!" she cried. "And Till with his hand grenade . . . it's all a madman's dream. Please, say something, Franz!"

"It can't be denied that our garden wall would make a good strategic position. I hadn't thought about it in connection with Till, however, only with a Blackshirt division that might set up a resistance point there. We would not be the first open city to be defended by force of arms. There were all sorts of rumors going around this morning. I didn't want to worry you about it until I knew something more definite. But now it really seems to me essential that you and the children should go to Eberstein."

"We must start today, Father!" Karin urged him. "As there's no gas, we must find someone who'll take us there with a horse and wagon. Perhaps that farmer at Hocheim—what's his name —Krummbein—you delivered his wife of an eight-pound baby boy the other day, you know . . ."

"Nurse Ottilie is waving to you, Karin," her mother said. "She must have a job for you."

"I just wanted to tell you," Karin said in an unusually gentle voice. "We haven't much time to waste on talking. It would be a good thing if we could get away before Till has to go to his meeting this afternoon."

When she had gone, Carola looked at her husband. "Do you seriously believe that I would leave you here alone?"

"I believe we must do what is best for all of us."

"What about you?"

"I have to stay with my patients as long as I can. As it is, there are not enough doctors in the city. If at the last minute I have to clear out, that'll be no problem. There are plenty of people who would hide me for a few days; that would not be possible with a whole family at my heels. In any case, the children *must* leave, and you can't let them go alone. Try to see that, please."

She didn't answer; he gave her hand a quick caress. "Think of what Till's intending to do! Lobelius is quite right about Eberstein: it's far too unimportant a place to be thought worthy of defense. It's only for a few days, Carola. It can't go on much longer. As soon as it's ended, I'll bring you back here, and we'll start our lives all over again."

"Telephone, Father!" Karin called from the house. She came out as he was going in, sat down beside her mother, drank the stone-cold coffee, and distractedly crumbled a bit of cake. Till was also there now.

"I just heard the news!" he cried, his face radiant with confidence. "The Americans have been driven back. Shall I clean the chicken coop for you, Mutti? If you don't want that piece of cake, Karin— Thanks!"

It was some time before Dr. Lorenz came back into the garden. "That was Arthur," he said. "It's quite correct that we're going to be defended. All doctors have been put on emergency schedule. I've just rung up Krummbein. He's coming here as soon as possible with his wagon."

24

"Krummbein? Who's that?" Till asked.

"The farmer who's taking us to Eberstein," Karin explained.

"Not me. I have my H.J. meeting this afternoon."

"Now listen, son," his father said. "You're going to Eberstein with your mother and sister. There's no time for a discussion now."

"But I must defend our town!" cried Till.

"Don't go getting it into your head that you're a soldier just because somebody puts a hand grenade in your fist. You'll do as I tell you."

Till went scarlet. Impatiently, he thrust his plate away from him with the rest of the cake uneaten. Not for the world would he have admitted that the idea of throwing a hand grenade at a fellow human being filled him with horror. But Karl had said that it was his duty, so he must do it, whatever his own private feelings about the matter were.

His mother put an arm around his shoulders, but that was the last thing he wanted just then.

"I know I can depend on you," said Dr. Lorenz.

Till stood up and pushed his chair back so roughly that it fell over. He picked it up again. "Then Bluebeard must come with us," he said as gruffly as he could.

"All the animals are coming with us, all except the ram," his mother replied. "I don't know what we should do without you to help us with them. Just go and see if the feedboxes are still full."

Karin silently cleared away the breakfast things and carried them into the house. When both children were gone, Carola stood up. Her husband took her by the shoulders and tried to look into her averted face. He said persuasively, "Now, we're a sensible family, aren't we?"

She gave a brief nod and walked away. She wanted to be alone for a few minutes. So far she wasn't feeling very sensible.

Sitting on the bed in her room, she tried to put her thoughts in order. Of course Franz was right, she told herself. They mustn't be in his way if he found himself in danger at the last moment. And this was quite likely. He was the only doctor in the city who was not a member of the Nazi Party. A Jewish grandmother, long since dead, had given him a plausible excuse not to join, one that many of his colleagues secretly wished they had themselves. For this reason, and for others, too, he was not in favor with the Party. The local leader, who brought the ration cards to the house every month, had once denounced him because the doctor had not greeted him with "Heil Hitler." In any case, people were in no doubt about his opinions. And it was rumored that if the enemy went on advancing, all Party opponents would be liquidated.

And Till! That carefree, radiantly happy boy, who believed piously in all the big, empty, high-sounding phrases that were handed out to him in the Hitler Youth Movement. Doubt and suspicion were quite foreign to his nature. Obviously he would think of himself as a knight of the Holy Grail doing battle for innocents in distress if he stood on the garden wall lobbing hand grenades at enemy tanks. That *must* be prevented, Carola realized. But this realization didn't make things any easier for her, especially as an obstinate voice in her heart kept telling her that Franz apparently could do without her.

After a while she washed her face, dabbed her nose with powder, and went downstairs to get out the suitcases.

Nurse Ottilie came up to her with the forced brightness she found so successful with women expecting their first child. "Now there's no need for you to worry, Frau Lorenz; I can look after the doctor."

No, thought Carola, not the slightest need to worry! Nurse Ottilie could ask for nothing better than to have her adored employer all to herself. She would spoil him and fuss over him and anticipate his every wish. For the last fifteen years she had been his right hand. She was as strong as a horse, and her energy seemed inexhaustible; one of those women who, though possessing no physical charms, gradually make a place for themselves in a man's life by their efficiency and unquestioning devotion. And of course all men enjoy being treated as if they were gods, even one with as little vanity as Franz Lorenz.

"Just help me to get this straight, will you, Ottchen?" said Carola. "I'm taking the sheep with us, but I'll leave the ram behind. . . . I don't think he'll be much trouble to you. Where's Bluebeard's leash? The bag of dog biscuits? What about the hens? The coop they were brought here in must still be lying around the barn somewhere. Till must see to it at once. The more we keep him occupied, the better."

But it was not only Till who was lucky to be busy all the time. The suitcases had to be packed: a few provisions, the travelers' ration cards saved for a long time, without which it was impossible to buy anything out of town. Bluebeard kept prowling around the luggage with distrustful growls, his eyes full of sadness and bewilderment. He'd already had some dreadful experiences with these things; everybody had to keep patting him and assuring him that he was going with them. Till packed his rucksack. Nurse Ottilie was upstairs and downstairs, in every hole and corner, fetching this and that; she found time to stroke her darling Till's blond mane with a consoling hand, to put a pan of pea soup on the stove to heat, and was, as always, indispensable. She also showed patients into the doctor's consulting room, took blood samples and handed them on to Karin, made X-rays, and noted entries in the files. There was such a shortage of doctors that they had to work even on Easter Monday.

Karin sang to herself in a low voice as she worked in the laboratory; she would stop, suddenly shocked at herself, but after a few minutes she would be quietly singing again.

Meanwhile, the sky had grown overcast. That was good.

In cloudy weather, at least you were safe from low-level attacks by planes.

When the last patient had departed, Dr. Lorenz, wearing his white coat, came out of the consulting room and quickly packed a box with champagne and wine. During the last fatiguing months, alcohol had been useful as a sedative during air raids, just as coffee had helped their chronic sleepiness.

The Lorenzes were fortunate; in the spring of '45 they still had a good supply of coffee beans left. A grateful woman patient, who had emigrated with her husband to Brazil, had sent two sacks of coffee beans to her former doctor just before the war. For six years Frau Lorenz had carefully stored them, measuring them out with scrupulous exactitude every day. There was only one difficulty: the green beans had to be roasted at home, with all doors locked and curtains drawn, in the greatest secrecy, so that no traitorous fragrance could alert the outside world.

The pea soup was served, but today even Till did not do justice to it.

"Have you heard anything new from your patients?" Carola asked her husband.

"Frau Berger and Frau Liebenau left yesterday with their children," Dr. Lorenz reported. "A colonel and his staff quartered themselves in the City Hall during the night and are making preparations for the defense of the city. Trenches are being dug in the southwestern and western suburbs."

At last, about two o'clock, the wagon arrived, pulled by two hefty plow horses. The ewes, with much difficulty and many encouraging words, were loaded, tethered, and provided with straw. Till shoved together the feedboxes and suitcases to make a pen around the sheep and spread his tarpaulin over the top. He was competent at all practical things, and he knew how to handle animals. Bluebeard at once jumped up on the wagon and was defending it valiantly, with excited barks, against the "attacks" of Herr Krummbein, the farmer, who was helping them to load. A seat was made for the ladies on one of the boxes.

The doctor jumped on his bike, since gas had to be saved for visiting his patients. He wanted to ride ahead of the wagon through the streets of the city. There were detours everywhere to avoid streets that had become impassable because of rubble or fire or danger of sinking. If once they got clear of the town, Krummbein knew what to do.

There was feverish activity at the center of the city. The big wagon could barely make its way along streets blocked by people and vehicles. They were caught in one traffic jam after another, but finally they made it and stopped for the last time on a hill on the northern outskirts of the city, not far from a farmyard.

"Get there safe," Dr. Lorenz said. "I'll try to call you this evening. Give Lobelius and his aunt my kind regards. Three or four days and we'll be together again."

As the horses began to move forward, the sirens started wailing again from the city. "Go on, go on, Herr Krummbein," Dr. Lorenz urged. "Don't you worry about me, Carola. I'll go across to Wienerts' until the warning's over. They've got a good cellar at the farm. Good-by! *Auf Wiedersehen.*"

In his old leather coat, he went along the field path, pushing his bike beside him. He stopped to look back once more, waved his hand in farewell, and gazed after the rumbling wagon as it rolled away into the distance. The women waved in reply. Then the horses broke into a trot.

The highway, a third-class road, was remarkably empty after the swarming streets of the city. The road passed through meadows, fields, and villages. Playful children kept running after the wagon, screaming with excitement. "Look at the gypsies!" they yelled. The sheep baaed plaintively, the hens cackled, and Bluebeard barked frenziedly at the running children. The road went uphill and downhill, through a wood; then uphill once more and down again into a small valley. The warm brown of plowed fields and the still muted gray-green meadows alternated with absinthe-green patches of winter wheat. In the distance, the rising mountains swam hazily in a lilac mist.

"Don't be sad, Mutti," said Karin, now a little uneasy herself. Her mother nodded. "I'm glad you will be happy, Karin. You wanted it so much."

"It's not as simple as all that," Karin replied. For a moment her shoulder leaned against her mother's, but perhaps that was just because the wagon had jolted a bit.

"It looks as if we're riding into a rattling big cloudburst," Till shouted down at them from the driver's seat. "Keep Bluebeard dry for me."

Herr Krummbein seemed to have the same grave doubts about the weather. He clicked his tongue at the horses. If they wanted to get to Eberstein in daylight and before the storm broke, they would have to get a move on.

✦ *Chapter Two* ✦

"We'll soon be there now," said Karin, as they passed through the industrial suburb that had attached itself to the peaceful little town of Eberstein as an outgrowth of the war. There were a few rows of dismal workers' houses; the barracks of the foreign labor camp; the munitions factory that reared its tall smokestacks over the camouflaged roofs of sheds and hangars as if to beckon to enemy bomber squadrons. But this extraordinary hybrid, half armaments center, half medieval walled country town, seemed to be protected by a cloak of invisibility. Every day and night the birds of ill omen droned high above, and not a single bomb fell on the place—one of those inexplicable coincidences that war brings with it.

During the last half hour the heavens had opened their floodgates. The road the wagon was traveling was like a mountain torrent. The hoofs of the horses sent up spurts of mud and water at every step. Again and again the women had to haul the tarpaulin back over the wretched sheep, and again and again the excited animals struggled from under it. Carola and Karin sat close together under the umbrella, with an unusually quiet Bluebeard crouched between them. Herr Krummbein had draped a horse blanket around Till's shoulders and his own. Till was sitting up straight as a die on the coach box, a Spartan youth who refused to be intimidated by any second flood.

Beyond the factory came a stretch of sodden fields to right and left of the road, then a stone bridge across the narrow river, and a little farther on the turreted medieval gate that led into the town proper. Here the houses didn't stand in long, boringly regular rows but were jostled together in charming disorder, each one different from its neighbor; some had their upper stories hanging out over the street; others were set well back from the road; some were low and crooked; others high and narrow; still others of a portly prosperity, with the date of their construction and the first owner's initials carved on the half-timbered fronts.

Carola felt she was entering another world, a world that no longer really existed. The broad market square, with its ancient chestnut trees, slumbered behind the gray veils of falling rain. There wasn't one tile missing from the roof of the stately gothic town hall, and along the streets that led down to the river the farmhouses stood solid and prosperous, just as they had done for the last two or three hundred years.

"Isn't it like an old picture!" cried Karin, entranced by the scene. Wet strands of dark hair clung to her forehead, little rivulets were running down her face and neck, but her eyes sparkled as she shook the drops from her ears and chin, for all the world as if being soaked with rain were the greatest pleasure.

"Just a few more minutes," she said to her mother, "and we'll be there. Next turning, Herr Krummbein, and along by the churchyard; the parsonage is right opposite the church. Look, Mutti, you can see it now."

The parsonage lay surrounded by farm buildings in the rural part of Eberstein. It was a relic of that period in which parsons had time to farm their own land as well as tend their human flock. The broad front of the house had two windows on each side of the door, to which a small flight of stone steps led. On one side of the house was a covered driveway, shut off from the road by a massive gate. Barns, byres, and sheds lay behind the house, cut off from the garden by yet another gate. The cart stopped. Herr Krummbein gave Till the reins, clambered down from the driver's seat, shook the water from his hat and shoulders, rattled at the closed gateway, and then looked up at the two women, shrugging his shoulders. But help was soon at hand. Opposite the parsonage, built against the churchyard wall, stood the ramshackle little cottage in which lived the gravedigger, Krischan Möller, Pastor Lobelius's factotum, who now also had to perform the duties of sexton. He and his wife, peeping out—one through the left-hand, the other through the right-hand window—of their cottage, inquisitively observed everything that happened around the church and the parsonage. So they hadn't missed the arrival of the horse-drawn wagon. Lanky-legged Krischan came across the square with the unmistakable rolling gait of a former seaman, swinging a large key. His wife followed him like a smaller, broader shadow.

"The Möllers!" Karin whispered to her mother. "In Eberstein she is known as 'the Voice of the People.' He's a grumbler but efficient. Everything will be all right now."

Herr Möller had opened the heavy door in a trice; the wagon drove in, and now at least they were out of the rain. "Good evening!" said Karin sweetly. "What a good thing you saw us arrive! The pastor apparently hasn't heard us coming. We must unload at once and get the animals dry and cozy. This is my mother and my brother Till, and Herr Krummbein, who was so good as to bring us here. He naturally wants to get back home as soon as possible."

"Pleased to meet you," said Frau Möller. She flattered herself that she had picked up genteel manners in the parsonage. Krischan just grunted something or other by way of acknowledgment. He was already busy helping Till and Herr Krummbein unload the cart. This gave his wife an opportunity to bring the guests up to date with the news. "The pastor's gone to the confirmation over at Schwerta. Never told us nothing, he didn't, about you all coming here today. Pastor Bendix from Weimar has gone with him to Schwerta an' all—there's always a good feed at these sort o' dos. And his mother, Frau Bendix, the Frau Kirchenrat, is sitting upstairs with her housekeeper at Fräulein Ulrike's."

"Stop babbling, Stina! Help!" Krischan ordered. It was one of the unsolved mysteries of Eberstein how he, who had sailed the seven seas, had finally been washed up in this small Thuringian country town.

"Many thanks for your help!" Frau Lorenz said, holding Bluebeard firmly by his lead, for one couldn't be sure he would not mistake Herr Möller's help for an attack on the Lorenzes' private property. Karin, helped by her brother, struggled to get the sheep down from the wagon. Schwerta? she was thinking to herself. Schwerta, and the pastor from Weimar here, with his mother? What's the meaning of that? But she had no time to waste in idle speculation. The animals must first be seen to; her mother was quite firm about that. Pulling, pushing, and coaxing, they got the sheep down, soaking wet and baaing pitifully. Till held on to them with either hand while Karin walked across the stable yard to a ramshackle outbuilding that, on her last visit, Lobelius had pointed out to her as suitable for their sheep.

"Look, Mutti, isn't that a good living room for our expectant mothers? Two boxes, two cribs—what more do you want? If I remember rightly, the chicken coop is next door."

She strode determinedly toward another door. But at that moment Bluebeard began to bark furiously, for out of the back door of the parsonage shot a female figure in a blue-striped apron who planted herself threateningly in front of the alleged henhouse.

"No foreign fowls in *my* chicken coop!" she stormed. "In

here are *my* birds! Can't a poor bombed-out woman keep a few hens for herself? The pastor didn't say nothing to me about somebody bringing strange hens into the place, nothing, he didn't."

"Next thing, he'll be asking your permission to walk in his own yard," retorted Krischan Möller. The argumentative female was his stepdaughter. Stina, widow of the former gravedigger, on her marriage with Krischan several years before, had presented him with this stepdaughter as well as with her late husband's job. After that, the daughter had got married herself and gone to live in the Rhineland; but two years ago she had been bombed out and had then taken refuge in the parsonage, where, by dogged tenacity, she had succeeded in snatching more and more privileges.

"Hush, Wanda!" her mother hissed, poking her belligerent daughter in the ribs. "Go on, make yourself scarce, and stop bothering the ladies."

How frightfully embarrassing, thought Carola Lorenz. If Karin had so much as breathed a hint that there were other people here with a claim on the accommodations for the animals, nothing would have persuaded me to bring all this livestock with us.

But now they were here, the wagon was unloaded, and fate must take its course. It would only be for a few days, anyway.

Herr Krummbein took his leave. The Möllers, too, whose help was no longer required and whose curiosity had for the moment been satisfied, said good night. "And if you get any more lip from *her*," said Krischan, "just give us a shout, will ye?"

"She's a bit hot-tempered, is our Wanda," Frau Möller explained, to smooth things over. "A mouth like a machine gun, but don't mean no harm." Upon which Krischan Möller and his better half took their departure.

Carola and Karin set themselves to drying the wet sheep

with straw. Till brought in the coop with the hens and let out the flustered birds.

"Well, they're still alive and scratching," he said. "We'll give them a handful of oats, and they'll soon cheer up."

"They'll have to stay here with the sheep for tonight," said Karin. "In the morning we'll find more suitable quarters for them."

All this time Carola had not said a word. After a while, she remarked, as she rubbed a sheep's back, "I thought we were expected."

"So we are," Karin reassured her, despite appearances to the contrary. "Perhaps they didn't expect us quite so *soon*. And if Helmut had to go off to a confirmation ceremony in another village, naturally he couldn't stay at home to welcome us. The job comes first; you know that from Father."

"Yes," replied her mother. "Till, be a good chap and get out some hay for the sheep. You may give them some oats, too, after their upset. Then dry Bluebeard thoroughly; we can't take him into the house like that, all wet and muddy. If only we could put on some dry, decent things before we meet Fräulein Lobelius! We look like drowned crows."

"And I'm so starved, my belly's sticking to my back!" declared Till.

"Now, Till, please try to be as nice as you can," said Karin. "Aunt Ulrike's such a sweet, old-fashioned darling. Come on now, Mutti. Try to keep smiling, and don't feel disappointed because we haven't been welcomed with drums beating and trumpets sounding. And please, the pair of you, don't be critical of Helmut! Someone like Helmut can't be judged by ordinary, conventional standards of behavior."

As no one showed any signs of beginning a discussion on ordinary conventional standards of behavior, she remarked casually after a short pause, "Did I mention to you, Mutti, that there were a few evacuees and refugees in the house?

That needn't concern us, of course. And you mustn't expect to find the house as spick-and-span as ours."

Carola nodded, resigned by now to putting a good face on whatever lay in store for them. She smoothed her wet hair and took Bluebeard's leash. Each of them picked up a suitcase, Till humped up his rucksack, and then, with Karin leading, they marched through the back door into the parsonage.

They found themselves in a wide hall, onto which several doors opened. "These were formerly Helmut's offices," explained Karin. "That is the parish hall, now split in two by a wooden partition. In one half of it lives Frau Merkel, that mad hen-wife, with her little boy Josef; in the other half the Lübzins, a family from Pomerania—Grandmother, Mother, and one child. To the right of the entrance is an old couple from Potsdam, the Dünsings; their home was totally destroyed by bombs; the husband was a general in World War I, I think. On the left of the entrance are two aunts of the baron's. One day last autumn they turned up from East Prussia, and there's certainly room enough for them at the big house. But the baron thought they wouldn't quite fit into the manor and asked Helmut if he couldn't take them in at the parsonage. And then there's that small room giving on the yard; a single lady lives there, from Berlin, who plays the organ in church, Frau Wöllner. Well—I think that's all."

"What sort of a place *is* this?" asked Till. "A refugee camp or what?"

"Shush!" whispered his mother.

It was obvious that they were being watched. Three of the five doors were standing slightly ajar. Bluebeard had been the first to notice it. He growled, and his hackles rose.

Along the walls of the hall were benches piled with trunks, chests, and cardboard boxes. There was a smell of boiled cabbage, little children, and suds. At the rear of the hall a staircase with a baroque balustrade curved up. They went silently upstairs into another hall, crammed with cupboards, filing cabinets, and a writing desk. Apparently it now served as an anteroom, for two benches had also been placed here to accommodate those who had to wait for an interview.

A door opened, letting through a shaft of light, and there stood a small lady clad in black, straight as a ramrod, with narrow white frills at throat and wrist and a silver crucifix hanging around her neck, the canoness, Ulrike Amanda Lobelius, in person.

"Karin, my dear child!" she cried, trying in vain to repress a start of embarrassment. "So this is your family! Welcome, Frau Lorenz. And this must be Till, your little brother." She shook hands with everyone. Till clicked his heels together.

"How glad Helmut will be to see you! He didn't really expect to before tomorrow morning, though, but of course you are welcome here at any time. What a delightful surprise!"

"Helmut told me it was urgent to get here as soon as possible," Karin said. "Maybe tomorrow it would have been too late."

"Not another word about it. First of all you must get into some dry clothes," said Fräulein Lobelius. "You're shaking with damp and cold. See, the new parish help has her worktable out here now. This, as you remember, was once the living room—now it will be your quarters. Your beds are all ready—well, more or less— In the meanwhile, some unexpected guests arrived. But we can see to that later. The gentlemen will be back now at any moment. We'll all have supper then, but I'm going to prepare a cup of tea for you straight away."

When the door had closed behind her, the guests looked around. "Isn't it good of them to have made room for us here?" Karin remarked. In the corner a partition had been made with two cupboards; behind it stood a camp bed with a sleeping bag on it for Till. An old-fashioned iron washstand holding a china basin must have been brought down from the attic.

"Aha!" said Till. "This must be my billet." And like an old campaigner, who at once makes himself at home anywhere, he began unpacking his things. But first he looked around for a nail on which he hung the treasured picture of Hitler he had won last year as a riding prize.

Between the two windows, which gave on the yard and the garden, hung a pastel drawing of a very young girl gazing out at the world from a pair of large eager eyes, radiant with a kind of touching trustfulness. "Christel" was inscribed in a round, girlish hand at the bottom of the attractive portrait.

"Helmut's grandmother," Karin explained. "She was married at seventeen. Isn't she charming?"

Just then she discovered on a chair a carefully folded dimity nightgown, the bodice scalloped in red half-moons. "Oh," she said. "This obviously belongs to the Frau Kirchenrat. Well, everything will get put right when Helmut returns."

They changed, dried their hair, and then went across to the pastor's room, where they hoped to find Aunt Ulrike. But she was apparently still busy making the tea. The tile stove was lit, giving out a most welcome warmth. Bluebeard jumped with a happy yelp onto the red-cushioned seat next to the stove and made himself comfortable.

"Bluebeard!" Carola hissed and with a sweep of her arm made him jump down again.

Two ladies were sitting there gazing at the intruders: the mother of the pastor from Weimar, the Frau Kirchenrat, and Fräulein Lina, her housekeeper, both industriously knitting. They could do it without looking at their fingers. At the back of the room a tall girl stood up and bowed in greeting to the newcomers.

"Good evening," Carola and Karin said in unison. "I am Frau Lorenz," Carola continued, "and these are Karin and Till, my children." Till smartly clicked his heels together.

"Good evening," chorused the two elder ladies.

"This is Frau Kirchenrat Bendix and Fräulein Lina," said the tall girl, pushing forward an armchair for Carola and seats for Karin and Till. "And my name is Martha Born."

"How do you do, Miss Born," Karin said. "The pastor's new helper, I suppose?"

"Yes." Karin gave her a good look. She had high cheekbones and wide hips. Blond braids of hair were arranged in a crown around her head. She must be fairly old, thought Karin; at least twenty-five. What a nice smile she has! The girl went back to her seat beside the pastor's writing desk and bent her head over the men's gray socks she was darning. When Fräulein Lobelius came in with the tea things, Fräulein Born relieved her of the teapot and poured. "I've already introduced the ladies to each other," she said.

The little spoons tinkled on the china; the tea was amber-golden in the cups, giving out its refreshing, pleasantly bitter fragrance. There are not many difficulties in life that cannot be lightened by a cup of fresh tea.

"How sweet!" Fräulein Lobelius said, as her eye fell upon Bluebeard, who had once more jumped up on the red-upholstered chair behind Carola's back. "Oh, what a lovely gray poodle! I never knew there were gray poodles."

"He's a Kerry blue terrier," Karin replied, and quickly sat down beside him, so that at least he would not be scolded for having a chair all to himself.

"They come from Ireland," Till explained. "The coat is blue, not gray. His kennel name is Blue Boy of Limerick; both his parents were champions. We call him Bluebeard, because he's got such a long bluish beard and has had as many wives as Bluebeard in the fairy tale."

Frau Bendix pushed forward her lips as if she were going to say "Oh," but the sound stuck in her astonished throat.

"Really?" the canoness inquired, rounding her eyes and

making no attempt to conceal her surprise. "Bluebeard—now how did the story go, exactly?"

"Till, will you please bring me a handkerchief from the bedroom?" his mother asked him.

"Here, you can use mine. It's quite clean. Because of his first-class pedigree, Bluebeard's in great demand for breeding. . . . Ouch, Karin! That was my shin you kicked!"

"Sorry," said Karin, and a silence fell upon the company, long enough for an angel to fly around the room. Carola gazed about her. There was a writing desk across the window, a piano, a set of simple bookshelves, three straight-backed chairs. On the whitewashed wall hung a smoothly polished wooden crucifix, a reproduction of Dürer's praying hands, and portraits of four clerical gentlemen in gowns and bands. These were all obviously the furnishing of Helmut Lobelius's bare, monastic study. But now the not very large room had to accommodate also the living-room furniture, which had been squeezed in here to make room for the Lorenzes' belongings. All these things belonged unmistakably to the period just after World War I, when Helmut's parents, newly married, had moved into *their* first parsonage: the balustraded sofa, the plush-upholstered chairs adorned with fringe, the glass-fronted cabinet with the carved borders, over which hung the enlarged photograph of a married couple, probably in the 1880's. The husband had the burning eyes of an apostle or a prophet; the wife looked weary and wan. The furniture reminded Carola of the time when she and Franz had married in the early twenties, both of them as poor as church mice; Franz a young intern in a hospital, she a student of the history of art. The inflation had swallowed up the remains of their small capital, so that she worked as a night nurse at the hospital and was thankful if she could manage to get half an hour free for study. With a few period pieces from Carola's parents' house, they had set up their first small home and covered the hideous, grease-spotted wallpaper of the seedy lodging house with beautiful reproductions and photographs. Later, when Franz started his own practice and things slowly began to look up—she helped him in his office in order to save the cost of a nurse—they had, after much deliberation, acquired one good piece of furniture after the other, saving up for each one with grim determination.

"Do you know this recipe?" Fräulein Lobelius's voice broke into Carola's meditations. "We call it mock liver-sausage, but unfortunately you need plenty of yeast. That's almost as rare as liver now."

"Mock liver-sausage," said Carola. "Yes, we used to make something like that in World War I."

But now men's voices could be heard on the stairs. Karin lifted her head to listen, and under her arching eyebrows her eyes sparkled like those of a child waiting to see the door open to reveal a Christmas tree. The door did open, but instead of a Christmas tree, there stood Pastor Helmut Lobelius in his black Sunday suit, and on his plain, strong face Karin's own quiet radiance was reflected as in a mirror. His colleague from Weimar, standing beside him on the threshold, didn't look so radiant; in fact, he looked somewhat startled.

"How wonderful!" cried Lobelius, and no one could doubt that he meant it. "Greetings, and welcome, Frau Lorenz! I hadn't dared to hope that Karin would have brought about the exodus quite so soon. Bravo, Karin!" He took both her hands and held them for a moment, unconcerned by the fact that all eyes were upon them. "*Grüss Gott*, Till. How did the sheep survive the trip?"

"First-rate," said Till. "Had a bit of bother about the old hens, that's all. A queer sort of woman came out and swore at us like a trooper. We had to put the hens with the sheep for the first night."

"We'll see to all that in the morning," said Karin pleasantly.

The pastor from Weimar handed Aunt Ulrike a parcel. "From Frau Haller with best wishes. Confirmation cakes, homemade sausage, and a piece of bacon. She says your nephew often leaves such presents behind, so she gave them to me to give to you."

Lobelius smiled. "Let's have it all for supper, Aunt Ulrike. The starved city dwellers can take back with them tomorrow morning whatever's left over."

"We don't want to deprive you!" said Frau Bendix, but even her severe features brightened up at the prospect of such a nourishing meal. Her son was still looking rather worried, evidently concerned about sleeping accommodations for the night.

Frau Lorenz also thought the moment had come to broach this subject. "I suggest that my daughter and I sleep in here tonight on the sofa and two armchairs put together," she said. It was a heroic proposition when one looked at the hills and hollows of the old sofa. "Naturally we couldn't think of taking the ladies' beds."

"You mean *our* beds," said Till. "Not that it matters to me. I can easily lay my sleeping bag in the barn."

"Many thanks!" Frau Bendix said, with an annihilating glance at cheeky young Till. "I wouldn't dream of accepting your kind offer, especially as they are really your beds. No, Fräulein Lina and I will content ourselves with the sofa and chairs."

"That's out of the question, my dear Frau Kirchenrat," Carola said.

"We certainly shall."

Pastor Bendix had relied upon the well-known hospitality of the parsonage at Eberstein when, after the Easter Monday service, he and his two ladies boarded the one and only train from Weimar to Eberstein, hoping to enjoy a night's rest after the heavy raids of the preceding week. And now of all people, the lawful owners of the extra beds had turned up, people of whose existence he had been quite unaware.

"We'll manage somehow," said Lobelius, who was not going to allow anything to cloud his happiness. He exchanged a quick glance with Martha Born. More than once he had found that she was able to cope with the most complicated situations. Without a word she nodded to him and vanished.

The evening meal was a rather silent affair. Only the two men talked about the burning questions of church reorganization after the end of the war.

Karin had barely cleared away the dishes when Martha Born appeared with the information that she had found accommodation for the Weimar guests in the neighborhood—two beds for the ladies and a sofa in the kitchen for the pastor, if that suited him.

"Perfectly!" Herr Bendix assured her, greatly relieved.

"Then I shall wish you all a very good night," said Fräulein Born, and went off to the relatives' house where she was staying.

"She is worth her weight in gold," said Lobelius when the door had closed behind her. A person who could cope so easily with all the problems of daily life was a constant source of wonder to him.

The others, too, were obviously more at ease now that the question of accommodation had been answered, and when Frau Lorenz had the good idea of bringing a bottle of wine out of one of her boxes, there arose, finally, an atmosphere of restrained conviviality.

About nine o'clock the guests took their departure. They wanted to enjoy to the full the benefits of a night's rest in the country, for next morning, at the crack of dawn, they had to return to Weimar on the workmen's train. Pastor Bendix could not leave his flock untended for any longer period of time.

Till took Bluebeard for a walk in the garden, then went to bed. Soon after, Aunt Ulrike asked to be excused. "Since girlhood I have suffered from insomnia," she explained. "Therefore, my doctor insists that I must spend eight hours every night and one hour after lunch each day in bed, though for the most part I never get a wink of sleep. My nerves were never very strong, you know. Good night! May you rest well under our humble roof."

"How can she stay eight hours in bed?" said Karin in amazement, when she and her mother were alone with Lobelius. "Don't you ever have to go down into the cellar during raids?"

"We are a bit careless because there have still been no bombs dropped here," said Lobelius. "Only when we hear planes flying directly overhead, do we go downstairs. At such times, it is far from easy to rouse Aunt Ulrike! As for myself, I enjoy the peace in the house when all the others are in the cellar and I have a chance to study undisturbed or make a draft of my next sermon."

"I can't understand why my husband hasn't phoned yet," said Carola, as it got later and later and no sound came from the telephone. "Would it be possible for us to call him from here, Herr Lobelius?"

He went at once to the telephone. "We'll see what we can do, Frau Lorenz." He had to wait a few minutes before getting long distance. "What?" they heard him exclaim. "No private calls? But, operator, I put a call through to the city early this morning. . . . Ah, since this afternoon? Thank you, Fräulein."

So Franz had not been able to phone; this last line of communication was closed, and now they would not hear anything more until . . . until when? Karin cast a worried glance at her mother. But Lobelius was not so easily discouraged. "It was a strange operator on duty," he said. "From eleven onwards a girl I know is working on long distance; we'll try again then."

Carola gave him a grateful smile. Karin felt it would be better to change the subject. "How did you manage to get hold of the new parish help, Helmut?" she asked. "I know they took the one before for war service last fall, and when I was here at Christmas, you still hadn't found a replacement."

"Yes, I had a dreadful time without any help at all. You know how hopeless I am at office work, and everything had got into a frightful muddle when Fräulein Born turned up, like a guardian angel. And she was delighted to find the job vacant here when she arrived from Berlin at the beginning of February."

"From Berlin? Didn't you say she was a minister's daughter from East Prussia?"

"So she is. But she had gone to Berlin to take her examinations as a parish helper. At that time conditions in East Prussia were in such a state that she couldn't get back home. By letters, she had arranged with her father to come to Eberstein and stay with a cousin of her mother, who is dead. Her father was to accompany his flock on their flight westward and then join her here. But since then she has heard nothing more from him, and since last fall there has been no news from her brother, who is fighting in the Balkans."

"Poor girl!" said Carola. "I hope her relatives are nice to her?"

"More or less," Lobelius said hesitantly. "She had no idea that her uncle was our local Nazi group leader and her aunt a great force in the Women's Movement. Naturally they are not exactly enraptured by the niece's church connections. Well, anyhow, I'm glad I've got her. She's put all my church accounts in order at last, so now we can devote ourselves completely to the care of souls and to theology, Karin."

"That will be wonderful, Helmut!" said Karin, beaming.

The rising and falling, wailing note of the air-raid siren interrupted their conversation, but no planes were to be heard. "We can let Aunt Ulrike and Till sleep on and stay up here," said Lobelius. "I'm not needed down below. Krischan Möller has taken on the job of air-raid warden in the cellar of the parsonage, and it's already a bit cramped down there with all the lodgers of this house, without our going down to swell the numbers."

The alarm lasted one hour, two hours. Carola was finally almost dropping with weariness, but determined not to go to bed without first having made another attempt to get through on the telephone. She had unpacked one of her books but could not bring herself to concentrate on what she was reading. Karin was sitting with Helmut at the writing desk, and judging by the words that reached her, Carola guessed that they were reading a chapter from the Apocalypse. A very suitable theme for such a time! "Alas, alas that great city!" Lobelius was reading. ". . . For in one hour she is made desolate."

A shudder ran down Carola's spine. The great city, and Franz was there, Franz whom she loved, even though she had not told him so for a long time now. Why, after twenty-two years of marriage, does one give up saying such things?

It was almost another hour before the all clear sounded. Lobelius at once broke off his discussion with Karin and went to the telephone. "Ah, good!" Carola heard him say after a while. "Thank you, Lenchen!" He held out the receiver to Carola.

"Franz!" she cried into the receiver. "Yes, there are no private calls from here either, but Herr Lobelius managed to get me through to you. How is everything at home? . . . Tomorrow, do you think? If only it were over as soon as that! . . . Just a moment, operator, please. Good night, my dear. Karin and Lobelius send their greetings. Till's already asleep. Oh yes, he's behaving reasonably. . . . Yes, operator, I'll be finished in one moment. . . . Oh, Franz . . ."

She was cut off and laid down the receiver, staring at it as if trying to recapture the voice she had just heard.

"Now to bed," said Lobelius. "In about three hours the gentlemen will be flying back again, and one never knows; they may have a few bombs left over. I would advise you not to undress completely, Frau Lorenz."

"Undress? What an idea!" said Karin. "We haven't undressed at night now for I don't know how many weeks."

As Carola lay in bed, she reckoned things out this way: if the Americans take Erfurt tomorrow, they can reach Eberstein the day after tomorrow. Obviously we'll have to wait then another two or three days before Franz can come and fetch us. Anyhow, by the end of the week we should be back home, if all goes well.

Despite her tiredness she was a long time in getting to sleep. The air in the room was oppressive; the windows were shut and covered with blackout material, so that not one chink of light could be seen from the street.

The great city, thought Carola. "In one hour is she made desolate." She had heard of other cities wiped out in much less than one hour. A bomber squadron could do the job in fifteen minutes. Mustn't think about it. Keep a grip on herself, as Franz had told her. In the faint illumination of the bedside lamp she looked across at Karin. She was already sound asleep, breathing quickly, her red lips slightly parted. Long eyelashes cast bluish shadows on the soft curve of her cheek. How young she was! As young as the bride up there in the photograph, thought her mother, and her heart contracted. Carefully she stroked one of the dark strands of hair that lay loosely on the pillow. Then she put out the light.

✦ *Chapter Three* ✦

Wearing his bathing trunks and carrying a towel under his arm, Till crept down the stairs in the first morning light with Bluebeard tugging at the leash. The house was still asleep; its inhabitants had finally been able to go back to bed just an hour ago, after the last warning of the night. Only the members of the pastor's household had stayed upstairs all night.

The stable yard lay bathed in the pale, milky light of early day. There was that special stillness in the air that can be felt only in the hour before sunrise. Someone was standing beside the pump already: a tall, slim woman who was filling a bucket with water.

"*Grüss Gott,*" Till greeted her; he had approached her quite noiselessly on his bare feet, and he had the impression that she had started; grownups were often nervous these days. Should he perhaps have said "Heil Hitler?" In his own home there was an unspoken understanding that the old, familiar greeting, "*Grüss Gott,*" should be used as long as they were within their own four walls. The greeting "Heil Hitler" was reserved for public occasions, when even his parents could not always avoid using it.

"Good morning," the woman answered, somewhat reluctantly.

"Can I carry your bucket for you?" asked Till. She shook her head. "No, thank you; it's not heavy." Then she saw

49

Bluebeard standing beside Till, with cocked head and body trembling with eagerness to be off and doing. For a second a faint smile lit her face, and she seemed to be going to say something. As nothing came, Till and Bluebeard betook themselves into the garden.

The little stream at the bottom of the parsonage garden was still veiled in silvery mist. A wooden bridge led to the meadows and fields on the opposite bank. Till stood there for a few minutes, weighing the strategic capabilities of the place. A narrow path, bordered by bushes, led up through the meadows, visible even in this uncertain light. One branch of this pathway turned left toward the main road from the south, on which they had traveled yesterday from the city. The other branch twisted away toward the hills in the west. On the approach of the enemy the bridge must be dynamited, thought Till, enlivened by the prospect of perhaps being able to do something useful even out here. Luckily there would be no need to spill blood; he had something against shedding blood.

"Bluebeard!" he shouted. "One, two, three!" And together they jumped into the dark water underneath the white mist. They swam upstream, the dog paddling energetically, holding high up out of the water his long beard and lively, sparkling eyes, Till swimming with soundless strokes. The morning stillness was too mysterious to be broken with a splashing crawl.

"Wonderful!" said Till, meaning the cool dawn that was just beginning to color the April morning's sky. He was completely given over, like a healthy young animal, to the enjoyment of the water, the smell of weeds and wet earth, the slow, rippling light that was now casting all the colors of the rainbow across the heavens. The glorious morning sky, pearly tinted as the interior of a mussel shell, filled his young soul with so much happiness that, for the moment, there was room in it for nothing else.

They climbed out on the bank and shook themselves. The water had been warm compared with the sharp morning air. Bluebeard dashed up and down the bank, showering water all around him, to dry himself. Till stood gazing around him. Where was he? Next to a neighbor's garden, apparently, separated from the path by a brown wooden fence. In the field behind the fence about a dozen cows were pasturing. "Quiet, Bluebeard!" Till warned him, for the dog had run back to him and was showing a desire to investigate the source of the animals' strong smell. The cows were black and white, with shining coats; their udders, recently milked, swung beneath their bellies. Just then the last of the small herd came out of the milking shed in the background, led by a girl who was going to see if the gate was properly shut.

"Well?" she said mistrustfully, when she caught sight of Till, dripping wet, with goose pimples all over him. "Watch your dog there; I don't want him chasing my cows."

"Are they yours?"

She nodded. "And who are you?"

"Till Lorenz. We're living at the pastor's. And you?"

"Dorle Franke. Oh, so you must be the brother of the girl who's going to be the pastor's wife."

"Ha ha! Someone's been fooling you!" said Till with all the unsuspecting innocence of a younger brother.

"Everybody knows about it!" she retorted, rather saucily Till thought. "Is it true that you've brought sheep with you?"

"Holstein milk-ewes," replied Till, now rather condescending in his turn. "They're not in milk just at the moment because they'll be lambing soon."

"Will you be selling the lambs?"

"Not for money, anyhow. Have you anything to swap?"

She raised her eyebrows, disregarding the barter question

for the moment. She was almost a head shorter than Till, but broad and sturdy. Her rounded face was tanned to a ruddy red like a russet apple, the nose slightly turned up, the chin firm. She now stuck it out combatively. "You mean you can milk them like a goat?" she said. "Never heard of such a thing. How could you get your hands around an udder shaped like a cannon ball?"

"Shall I show you?"

"Not important. It's only that sheep's milk doesn't have to be delivered to the collecting depot. I'm more interested in the wool. Last winter I learned to spin at the B.D.M. And if I had a sheep of my own, I could spin enough wool for a sweater and stockings. Later on I want to learn to weave."

"They bear a lot of wool," Till said boastingly. "It's the largest-size sheep you can get. They have a pedigree and everything. Your cows are a mixed breed, aren't they?"

"East Frisians!" she snapped. "Every one of them in the herd book. Kathi over there has already won prizes for her milk yield. And we have two horses as well. So there!"

Till gave a whistle. Two horses; better be nice to the girl. "I'm keen on riding," he said.

"Pooh! Riding? Our horses aren't used for suchlike city pranks. They work."

"A little ride never hurt any horse yet," replied Till. "Only you need a horseman who knows what he's about." This was meant to impress her, but in his shivering, goose-pimply state the effect was rather comical. "Well, I may have a look at them one of these days. Heil Hitler!" he said with stiffly raised arm, and dived into the water again.

"Your dog's a joke," the girl shouted after him. "A cross between a bedside rug and a mop!"

Till lifted his head and spat out a mouthful of water like a face on a fountain. This was one of his special tricks that never failed to impress people. He gurgled and spat again.

"You know as much about pedigree dogs as you do about milk-ewes!"

The Angelus sounding from the hospital on the other side of the churchyard wakened Karin. Six o'clock. She stretched luxuriously in her bed. It was a long time since she had slept so soundly, wakened only once or twice by sirens. But then, as Lobelius had not knocked on the wall, they had not stirred.

I'm here, she thought. I've done it!

Her mother was still asleep in the other bed, next to her own. Karin got up and went to the window. Carefully, in order not to disturb her mother, she drew the blackout aside, peeped out into the pearly gray, misted morning, and gazed with the same rapture as Till had half an hour earlier at the soft radiance of the eastern heavens. She could see a bit of the garden between the gable of the barn and the tumble-down roof of a wooden shed. The meadow was a wilderness of long grass, golden-tinted and withered with frost, among which fresh green blades were already sprouting. By the gray wall of the barn stood a few still almost bare elderberry bushes, an old apple tree with gnarled, mossy boughs, and a table made of an old millstone. A little pond lay in the middle of the meadow, covered with duckweed and with a garland of water-lily leaves that looked like eyelashes around a great dark eye. Frogs were croaking. In the night, whenever Karin had been awakened by the sirens, the monotonous chant of the frogs had sounded like distant bells. On the farther edge of the pond, toward the river, a big weeping willow trailed its lovely yellow-green wands over the water; a bench ran around its trunk. On the side of the pond nearest the house four young fruit trees were planted. One of them bore a few timid blossoms, like touches of snow left from winter. Right along the northern wall, a broad stretch of lawn had been dug over. Seed packets were spiked on sticks in an orderly fashion.

Karin drank it all in like something long desired, even before she ever met Helmut. Perhaps she had once read somewhere in a book about such an enchanted and enchanting place. On the ridge of the barn roof a blackbird was perched, preening his feathers and smoothing them with his beak; after a moment, he let the silvery cascade of his song trickle out in the early morning stillness.

Finally Karin's gaze returned to the bedroom. On the washstand was a flowered basin with a water jug to match; and the small vessel that was discreetly hidden under the bed had the same flowery pattern, too. Good gracious! She smiled to herself, touched by this simplicity and innocence. To think that such things exist! Technical progress had evidently by-passed the Eberstein parsonage. There was no running water in the bedrooms, no bathroom in the house. The only water tap was in the kitchen. The tenants on the ground floor drew their water either from the washhouse or from the ancient pump in the yard. If you wanted a bath, you had to heat water in the great copper boiler down in the washhouse and scrub yourself in one of the wooden tubs.

While Karin was washing—and this she did slowly and thoroughly, because this kind of early-morning toilet was fun— a small lake formed on the floor. The simple life was obviously not as simple as one thought; it had to be learned.

She did some exercises and began to brush her hair. A hundred brush strokes every morning were all part of her program, just like the knee bends, and programs meant a lot to her. But suddenly she laid the brush aside and went to look at the young girl's picture between the windows. Christel. A pretty name and a pretty girl, and how radiantly happy she looked! *Her* parents had made no difficulties when she got married at seventeen. Not that Karin's parents had exactly made difficulties; the possibility of her marriage was simply not discussed. Karin sighed and leaned across the washstand to look in the mirror hanging above it. Two days ago Helmut's face had still been reflected there, the face of an apostle hewn from a block of limewood, the black patch over the left eye, the hair that always looked a bit disheveled. Naturally he had no time for a hundred brush strokes every morning. She examined her own face in the looking glass, frowning critically. Her hair, dark brown like her mother's, was as shiny and smooth as a chestnut freshly sprung from its horny green shell. The mouth was still too soft; nothing special about her nose and chin. The forehead was smooth and broad. Life had not yet written a single line on it. The eyes had a greenish tinge. Turquoise, her friends used to call them, finding it terribly attractive to have such blue eyes with such dark hair. But in dull weather or whenever she was feeling melancholy, Karin's eyes looked more like obsidian—bottle-green, impenetrable. Her best features were her immaculate skin and her long dark eyelashes. She gave her nose a little smack in the glass. "Middling, Lorenz, middling!" That was what her math teacher used to say about her work, and as far as her math was concerned, he was certainly right.

She did the rest of the hundred brush strokes, poured the used water into a bucket, slipped into her rose-flowered morning coat, a relic of better days, handed down from her mother, and went to the kitchen to fetch clean water.

There was still no one astir in the house, but when she came out of the kitchen carrying the jug of fresh water, she met Aunt Ulrike, already dressed in a gray house robe. The canoness gazed with unconcealed pleasure at the young thing in the flowery robe.

"Good morning, Fräulein Lobelius. Did you sleep well?"

"As usual, hardly closed my eyes all night. Good morning, my dear. Our Weimar guests have already departed. The workmen's train leaves at a quarter to seven. Helmut has gone with them. As soon as he comes back, we'll all have breakfast together. Then he must go into town to attend to his professional duties. Many of his flock are ill; others need consolation and guidance. How ravishing you look, Karin! Like a dewy rosebud."

Karin took up the water jug for her mother. She had brought with her a floor cloth to mop up the mess she had made at the washstand. If it started to drip on Frau Merkel in the room below, she'd kick up a nice row. Her mother blinked sleepily at her.

"Good morning!" said Karin. "Just look at me: a dewy rosebud."

Carola yawned. "Rosebuds were already out when I was a girl. What's got into you?"

"The spirit of the place. It's seven, darling, and in half an hour breakfast will be ready; then I'm going to accompany Helmut when he attends to his professional duties."

"Professional duties," repeated Carola, giving her daughter a worried look. "You might just see what Till's doing; tell him he's got to get up."

Karin looked behind the cupboard wall. "Gone, and Bluebeard too," she announced. "Vanished, evaporated. Obviously off to size up the strategic capabilities of the region."

"Heaven forbid! He'd better be seeing to the hens. They simply must have perches, a ladder, and some sort of nesting box, wherever they're going to be. We must talk to Lobelius at once about their accommodation."

"I doubt whether he could cope with hen roosts and so on; they scarcely form part of his professional activities. Now hurry, Mutti; I'm going to the kitchen to help Aunt Ulrike with the breakfast."

"Take some of our coffee beans along," her mother called after her.

Later, as Carola stepped out into the hall, the sound of song, with pianoforte accompaniment, came to her from the pastor's room:

> "Oh, for a thousand tongues to sing
> My dear Redeemer's praise,
> The glories of my God and King,
> The triumphs of his grace! . . ."

A fine hymn, sheer jubilation. Only Carola wasn't feeling exactly jubilant. She had dreamed all night about Franz and had seen him in frightful danger. There must certainly be street fighting now in the city. Or the enemy guns were bombing the narrow streets of the old town. Or a fighter or bomber squadron. . . . She pulled herself together. She mustn't let her imagination gain the upper hand!

With the others she sat down at the breakfast table. The text for the day was read, and then came grace, after which Aunt Ulrike poured out the coffee. "It smells like nectar and ambrosia!" she cried delightedly, and Carola wondered what kind of smell, if any, nectar and ambrosia had.

Till made his appearance in shorts and open-necked shirt.

"When and where did you wash?" his big sister demanded.

"I went for a swim in the river, if you want to know," he replied, swelling with self-satisfaction.

"In the river!" exclaimed Aunt Ulrike, clapping her hands together. "Oh, those young Spartans!"

"It was nice and warm," Till assured her. "Bluebeard thought so too. Just think, at the farm next door they have horses! I must go and have a look at them today."

"Perhaps they'll allow you to ride the horses if you promise to groom them," said his mother.

"Rely on me to do the trick," he said confidently. "Herr Pastor, are you aware that the bridge outside your garden leads directly to the main road from the south? We must blow it up when the enemy draws near. Or perhaps it could be dismantled. You don't want the U.S. Army trampling all over your garden, do you?"

"Blow it up, of course," Lobelius said. "Do we still have a bit of dynamite in the kitchen cupboard, Auntie? Anyway, we can talk about it when the need arises, Till."

Bluebeard, still moist, was trotting around the table, looking soulfully up at each person in turn and begging a little morsel from each one.

"I've also been seeing to a place for our hens," said Till, who wanted to show that there were not just warlike thoughts in his head. "Behind the sheep's stall there's an old hut for storing fodder or something, with straw all over the place. May we use it as a henhouse, Herr Pastor? If you could perhaps scrape together a few old sticks and bits of board, I'll soon fix it up."

"You'll probably find old bean poles and loose boards in the wooden shed. That is, if my other guests haven't used them up for firewood," replied Lobelius. He seemed to be relieved that no one expected him to bother his head about the internal architecture of the henhouse. Karin had already hinted at plans on the part of her mother. "Of course you may use the hut for your hens, Frau Lorenz. Please do just as you would at home."

"Many thanks!" Carola said. "Fortunately Frau Merkel's hens are Italian Leghorns, and mine are Rhode Island Reds, so they can't get mixed up. But I would be grateful, Herr Pastor, if you would speak to Frau Merkel and tell her that my hens, too, may have the run of the yard so that everything is quite clear from the beginning."

"Naturally your hens have the same rights as Wanda's. It would be better if Fräulein Born spoke to her about it; she can do that sort of thing much more competently than I can. And now let's be off, Karin, for you can be sure that as soon as she arrives, she'll have dozens of questions to ask me and will be wanting all sorts of papers that I shan't be able to find, and heaven knows what else. She's most awfully strict with me." He gave a good-natured laugh. "Apparently it's just as well she is."

"Wait!" Carola called after her daughter. "Take our traveling ration cards with you and try to get as much as you can on them. They might not be worth anything soon. Bacon, sausages, bread, oatmeal."

"And potatoes, Helmut; we're nearly out of potatoes," pleaded Aunt Ulrike. "We've only got enough to last today."

"Take no thought for the morrow," replied the pastor, seized Karin's hand, and the pair of them were off through the door, as happy as two children on a half-holiday.

Aunt Ulrike and Frau Lorenz cleared away the breakfast things. When they carried the crockery into the kitchen, Stina Möller was already at work there, examining closely the pastor's black Sunday trousers, which bore traces of yesterday's mud and rain almost up to the knee. "Really, the pastor should be a bit more careful," she grumbled. "Why did he lend his motorbike to the baron? If the likes of *him* can get enough gas, then a pastor with three parishes to look after should have a right to some, and him wounded in the war and all. It's not fair, it isn't."

"Ah, yes," said Fräulein Lobelius with a sigh. "He takes too much upon himself, but not for the world would he complain."

"What he wants, if you ask me, is a wife!" declared the Voice of the People, shaking the clerical nether garments as if they were a couple of puppies that had misbehaved themselves. "A good strong wife, that's what he wants; someone as'll get him to pay more heed to things and not be leaving the key o' the door lying around where he can't remember he's put it, and as'll make him look after hisself a bit."

Aunt Ulrike blushed. "Yes, Frau Möller," she said. "He should indeed be entering into the holy state of matrimony.

It is not good that man should live alone. Think how awful it would be for your Krischan if he didn't have you!"

"Him?" retorted Frau Möller. "If it weren't for me, he'd not be in the land of the living, not with his melancatholic ways when there's a bit o' fog about and he gets to hearing of his voices. Voices of all his drowned mates, he says they are, and then there's only one thing as'll put a stop to 'em: he has to take a drop hisself, and when he's like that, I can tell you, he needs me by his side, he does that."

"I know how heartily you pray for him," said Fräulein Lobelius. "Yes, a good wife is worth her weight in gold." The good, pious soul had no idea that Stina's help in Krischan's drinking spells was a very active one.

Meanwhile, Carola said nothing but busied herself with the coffee cups.

The shops in the town were still closed as Karin and Lobelius walked through the streets. The butcher and baker and grocer weren't going to sell good stuff for doubtful money. Who knew how long the meager supplies would last? It was no longer worth while for the shoe shop and the department store to take down their shutters; for weeks now there had been no more clothing coupons issued.

Everywhere groups of women were standing about, discussing things that just a short while ago they would have dared to mention only behind their own closed doors. The pastor stopped here and there, and each time he was soon surrounded by people asking him questions. The closer the enemy came, the greater became the respect paid to the church.

There were strikingly few men in the town. It was difficult to say how many had joined the home guard or how many had simply hidden themselves away. The grown-up sons had left years ago for the army. Many had been killed; many were

60

missing or prisoners of war or wounded. In January the fifteen- and sixteen-year-olds had been taken away from school to dig trenches in the west or to serve in antiaircraft batteries. The excited women told the pastor that next morning members of the Hitler Youth born in 1931 and 1932 had to gather in the market place, and it wasn't very difficult to see what they were going to have to do.

"Till would also have had to go if we'd stayed at home," Karin whispered to Lobelius. "We must tell Mother, and then she'll see how right we were to come away."

The angry voice of a mother was raised as if in reply.

"We mothers can take a lot, but this is beyond all reason. Taking school kids for soldiers, what next?"

Was it true, then, that every larger town would be forced to offer resistance, they asked the pastor? But he couldn't tell them, for he knew less than they did. When last winter the local Nazi group leader had several times visited his house and asked the tenants if perhaps the pastor listened to foreign radio stations upstairs, Lobelius had decided at once to deliver up his ancient wireless set to the authorities. If he wanted to hear foreign news broadcasts, he went to one of his trusted friends in the neighborhood.

As they walked on, they were met by a few Russians and Poles who were returning from some sort of work and going back to their camp. They nodded to the pastor. "How did you get to know them?" asked Karin.

He replied, "I often go to the camp to visit someone ill or dying. The Poles are all Catholics, and in their case it was natural that the Catholic priest should look after them. But I was astonished to find that many of the Russians, after twenty-five years of Bolshevism, should still want the services of a priest when they're in a bad way. And as there are no orthodox priests of their church here, I pay them visits, pray with them, and also bury them in the churchyard."

"And what does the Party say about that?"

"Once, on the occasion of the burial of a Russian, I had a difference with Martha's uncle, and the baron also spoke disapprovingly to me. He likes to act the lord of the manor, the baron does, and at first he tried to treat me like one of his employees. It's no wonder that he has difficulties with his Polish workers."

The air-raid siren sounded once again, but they paid no attention to it except to walk a little closer to the walls, so that they could slip quickly inside a doorway if they saw an air-raid warden coming. They visited a few sick people, then a woman who had recently had news of her husband's death, and then a grandmother whom they found in her bed in the cellar, surrounded by a swarm of noisy children. Human destinies were laid open for them like the pages of a book. And everywhere, so it seemed to Karin, Helmut was able to enter into these lives and to ease troubles and worries.

When the all clear finally went and they could move about a little more freely, they knocked at the butcher's bolted shop door. The proprietress looked cautiously out of a peephole at them and hurriedly let them into the shop through the half-opened door, which she bolted again behind her. Lobelius asked if they could get anything on the traveling ration cards; he was obviously embarrassed to be asking for a favor. "Gladly, if it's for the Herr Pastor's guests," the woman said and whetted her knife, whose great size made a comical contrast with the tiny pieces of meat she handled.

"And how are things in the city, Fräulein?" she asked. "They say that there's been an artillery bombardment going on since yesterday. Is it true?" It didn't seem to give her much comfort when Karin said no, that when she had left the city yesterday, there had been no artillery bombardment. "What will become of us, Herr Pastor?" the woman asked Lobelius, as if he were an oracle. "What on earth will become of us?"

Lobelius could have said that not a sparrow falls without God's will. But in the past years he had seen so many sparrows fall, and he knew all too well that for the afflicted it was no great comfort to learn that it was the will of God.

They purchased some sausages, a piece of bacon, and a pound of meat, which presumably had been part of some old nag, for making soup. But what did it matter! "Aunt Ulrike will be delighted," said Karin. "And now for the potatoes, Helmut."

"Oh, they can wait until tomorrow. There are enough for today. I have to pay another visit now, and this time I should prefer you not to accompany me. A third party would make it unpleasant for the woman to whose conscience I must make an appeal. Her husband is in the army, and she has been behaving herself in a most unsuitable way. It won't be an easy business . . ."

Karin sat down on one of the green benches under the chestnut trees of the market place and waited for him. A swarm of children had rushed out of the basements and cellars the moment the all clear went. They were playing and singing a song that Karin had often sung as a child. Her eyelids felt heavy. When you were not actually on the move, you suddenly noticed the weariness accumulated over all those weeks with too little sleep. She surrendered herself contentedly to the quiet, happy and relaxed in the knowledge that Helmut would soon be back with her again. And before she expected it, there he was coming across the market place toward her. "Come on," he said, "we'll go home by a roundabout way, through the meadows. I must enjoy having you to myself for a little."

They crossed the northern bridge to the other side of the little river that encircled Eberstein. The meadows were still wet from yesterday's rain, but the morning mist had disappeared. The grass stood fresh and green. The fields were spread out like a fan, in brown, pale yellow, and green stripes. A mild spring sun was shining, and at the edge of the towpath the sweet golden stars of the coltsfoot were bright.

They sauntered along, hand in hand and at last alone together. It was good now not to speak when Lobelius had had to do so much talking all morning; good to be silent, like the earth around them that was also silent and waiting. Karin thought: If only we could go on forever like this, just the two of us, with the world and the war far, far away. The war that gave warning of its approach with a constant sullen, grumbling sound. They forgot completely that they should be back home for lunch at one o'clock.

As they reached the wooden bridge that led to the parsonage garden, Lobelius said, "It would be quite easy to dismantle the bridge. But I hope Till will forget about it. I like it. In a way, it is my door into a world of dreams because you see, by taking the meadow path, we could be over in the wood within ten minutes and spend hour after hour wandering under the beech trees. At the edge of the pinewood on the hill, a little farther to the right, the broom will soon be in flower."

"But *that* dream world is surely easily enough reached, Helmut. Or have you really never been for a walk over there?"

"Only in my daydreams. Strange that I never have time to satisfy such desires. But isn't it wonderful to know that you can, if you want to?"

"Wonderful, but not enough," she said. "We shall go there together, you and I. And as for Till, we must hope that he'll find a more useful occupation here than pulling down the little bridge. Perhaps he'll be able to get one of the Frankes' horses from time to time for riding, and if they will let him groom the horses and clean out their stalls, he'll forget about everything else. Last year, when they had to do farm work for the Hitler Youth Movement during the summer holidays, he was completely happy."

"There'll certainly be enough work for him at the Frankes'. The farmer was wounded in the arm, and their only son is posted as missing in Russia. They are all busy from morning till night with only a Polish worker to help. I am sure they would welcome another helper."

"Perhaps you could have a word with them," said Karin.

The frogs were croaking with undiminished enthusiasm. Not even the air-raid siren could interrupt their nuptial cantatas. The optimistic plum tree had unfolded a few more blossoms. "Did you plant the fruit trees, Helmut?"

"Yes, I did. Last autumn, I suddenly got the idea into my head. Franke helped me; I couldn't have managed it alone. We must have lots of fruit trees—plum and cherry, apple and pear."

"Mirabelle plums," Karin added. "And of course currant bushes. Is that dug-up piece along the wall going to be a vegetable garden?"

"The tenants have gradually taken it over for themselves. Every week they annex a little more. The two old ladies from East Prussia are the most enthusiastic gardeners; I often wonder where they get the energy. The only ones who don't take part in this agricultural project are the Dünsings and Frau Wöllner. The others have boundary disputes every few days, sometimes accompanied by considerable uproar."

"If you're not careful, they'll be crowding you out of your own house and garden!" Karin frowned and laid her hand for a moment on his threadbare sleeve, as if to protect him from crafty onslaughts of the wicked world.

"That's what Martha Born says," he replied. "But why should they have less right to this big garden than I have? They've lost their own homes and gardens, and so a little patch of cultivated earth may help them to regain their faith in life and a sense of security."

It was after two o'clock when they finally sat down to

partake of an almost boiled-away potato and carrot stew. The atmosphere at table was not exactly blithe to start with, for about noon Frau Möller had popped in to tell them that the radio said the British and the Americans were making a new offensive. Aunt Ulrike was crushed. "The poor Führer!" She sighed. "What he must be going through!"

Karin opened her mouth to say something, but her mother gave her a warning sign. Who would have thought that the pious canoness had a passionate admiration for Hitler!

"Dearest Aunt Ulrike," said Lobelius, "I can only hope that what he is going through now is as bad as he deserves."

Aunt Ulrike gave her nephew a look of worried sweetness. "Of course, you understand all that better than I do, Helmut. We are all loyal patriots in the foundation and have always agreed with what it says in Romans 13:1: 'Let every soul be subject unto the higher powers. For there is no power but of God: the powers that be are ordained of God.'"

"But when the powers that be are *against* God, then we must be on God's side."

"Oh, Helmut, surely you don't believe all those bad things people are saying?"

"What sort of bad things?" asked Till. "It's bad when people drop bombs on women and children, as our enemies are doing. Do you think Divine Providence will give them victory, then?"

"Certainly not! His Excellency also is convinced that Germany can still be saved," said Aunt Ulrike. "He says that they should call in the old, experienced officers. He's working on a great plan of campaign."

"What excellency's that?" asked Till.

"General von Dünsing, who lives downstairs. He was the leader of an army in World War I."

"World War I?" cried Till in amazement, as if she had

been talking about the siege of Troy. "Are there generals still living from those times?"

"Oh, yes. And his wife is working on a horoscope for the Führer. She claims that his astrologers don't tell him the truth. I don't understand all these learned things. I know only one thing, that the Führer always had the best intentions."

"Let us give thanks for our food," said Lobelius, folding his hands.

Scarcely had the women, deep in their own silent thoughts, finished washing the dishes than the warning sounded again, and this time the whole sky was suddenly throbbing with bomber squadrons flying overhead. Lobelius thought it best that they should all go down to the cellar, even Aunt Ulrike had to go with them, though she would rather have lain down for her midday rest to soothe her nerves.

The parsonage cellar was deep and solidly built, but it was not intended for any lengthy occupation by large numbers of people. Krischan Möller as air-raid warden kept everything in good order, according to regulations: the sandboxes and the water-butt were filled; gas masks, first-aid chests, axes and shovels were all in their appointed places. But he had no objection to having the two perambulators brought down the narrow cellar steps during each alert, though they blocked the way. Bluebeard, however, who had come down with them for the first time that afternoon and was sitting as good as gold between Till and Karin, aroused the animosity of Frau Merkel, who declared that a dog in an air-raid shelter was a danger. If anything happened and panic broke out, then the dog would go mad and attack all and sundry. Frau Lübzin and her mother-in-law, usually the sworn enemies of Frau Merkel, this time agreed with her.

"You've just got to look at him to see he's got a wicked temper," complained Frau Merkel. "This morning in the yard he snapped at my little Josef."

"Your little Josef pulled his ear!" retorted Till. "I saw it."

"Till!" his mother warned him, but too late. The sluice gates of Frau Merkel's remarkable gift for words were opened, and a flood of abuse broke over Till and his dog.

"Quiet, please!" The low but penetrating voice of the general came from the corner where he and his wife were bent over maps and papers. On the table, which they had installed between two wicker chairs, a candle was burning. The two old ladies from East Prussia were not far away. Till gave Bluebeard into his mother's charge and crept over to Their Excellencies' corner; he couldn't resist the fascination of the general's campaign plans. After a while the latter looked around at him. "Who are you, my boy?" he asked.

"Till Lorenz, at your service, Excellency!" said Till, saluting smartly. The general nodded. "Glad to make your acquaintance. We must see if we can't do something to save the fatherland."

"Please, oh please, do!" Till said imploringly.

The general's wife, a neat little lady with whalebone stiffeners in the high-necked collar of her blouse, looked up for a moment and gave her husband an adoring, anxious look. Then she turned again to her calculations.

The last one to come down into the cellar was the woman whom Till had seen at the pump earlier that morning. Lobelius signaled to her to come over to the corner reserved for him and his family and guests. "This is my organist, Frau Lorenz," he said. "Karin, I don't think you have met Frau Wöllner?"

Carola looked at the stranger and thought: I have seen her somewhere before. Where can it have been? The woman was noble-looking, no longer young, but with a magnificent face under a broad forehead. It looked like the face of a mathematician, and Carola supposed she must have met her years ago at Berlin University.

"We haven't met before," said Karin, shaking hands with

Frau Wöllner, "but I heard you playing when I was here during the Christmas holidays."

Till had stood up to make room for her, and Frau Wöllner thanked him with a slight inclination of the head; she sat down beside Bluebeard, whom Karin was carefully holding by the collar. Frau Wöllner put out her hand to him, and he gave it a long, thorough sniffing. Then he waved his little stumpy tail in courteous greeting. "Well look at that; he likes you!" said Till. It was the greatest compliment he could pay to anyone.

"I like him too," said Frau Wöllner. "I once had one that might have been his twin."

When they finally came up from the cellar, they found Martha Born at her desk. "I must ask you to stay at home for the rest of the afternoon, Herr Pastor," she said. "There are some things here which I cannot deal with on my own."

With a slight sigh, Lobelius sat down beside her. Carola asked Karin to go for a short walk with her. They took Bluebeard with them, for Till had gone to the Frankes' farm to look at their horses, and he thought it was wiser to go without his dog, as Dorle's opinion about him hadn't been too favorable.

That evening Martha stayed to dinner at the parsonage. She had told Lobelius that her relatives were in a completely desperate state. Her uncle, the local Nazi leader, was preparing to leave; he had ceremoniously burned the Führer's picture and the swastika flag; nothing must fall into the hands of the enemy. Martha, who knew she was a thorn in his side, had no wish to provoke him at the last minute and preferred to slip quietly back into her room that evening as late as possible. When she had gone and Till and Aunt Ulrike had also retired for the night, the other three sat together in the living room. Conversation flagged. Today the Book of Revelation seemed to have no appeal for Karin or the pastor; the world around them was frightening enough without the addition of such prophetic texts. Carola was glancing through her books—the *Tao Te Ching*, which formerly had always been able to release her from the cares and complexities of life, and the *Shan Shui*, an illustrated volume devoted to Chinese landscape painting that had recently come out in Vienna and that Franz had given her for a birthday present; but however hard she tried, she couldn't succeed in concentrating. So they all felt relieved when Lobelius proposed that they should go to the movies. It would be at least a diversion, though not a very profound one.

It was an insignificant but high-spirited picture. They sat marveling that things had once been like that: this gay, happy world without the gloomy background of war; elegantly dressed people, brightly lit streets, restaurants with long menus from which you could choose anything you liked, and shops in which you could buy anything you had a mind to. And at the center of all this was a good-looking pair of young lovers who had obviously never heard of such things as death and separation. The whole thing was not very well made, but the music was light and infectiously gay, and when the two young people whirled through a brilliant ballroom in an intoxicating waltz, the girl in a cloud of white chiffon, her eyes starry as she gazed up at the partner bending tenderly over her, Karin was seized suddenly with a great hunger for life and an excrutiating longing to dance to that tune once again, as she had danced to it last year. Then she had completely surrendered to the moment, enfolded in the shy ardor of her youthful partner. They had been just a little in love, not enough to be painful. . . . And yet all that had happened at a time when things were already bad enough . . .

What's the matter with me? she thought, frightened; then she felt Helmut's hand pressing her fingers.

Just then something happened that brought them back with a jolt into the present. When the newsreel started, the audience stood up and left the theater. They were sick of being stuffed with war propaganda. Perhaps many of them had been fed up with it for a long time, but never before had they dared to show it in public. It was a silent revolt, and the strange thing about it was that the movie audience was suddenly no longer an anonymous mass that could be worked up and led by the nose in whatever direction the leaders wished, but an assembly of rational individuals who felt a deep compulsion at last to think and judge for themselves.

Outside an icy April wind was blowing. Showers of rain lashed the dark streets where not a ray of light was to be seen. It was a phantom town they were walking through; dead, sinister, forbidding. That night no one seemed to be in bed. They sensed, rather than saw or heard, people whispering, waiting, waiting for something beyond the power of their imaginations but which would be the end of the war. In the middle of the market place a small fire was glowing red like a Cyclops' eye. From time to time a shadowy figure would cross the square and swiftly throw something on the hot ashes. "The Twilight of the Gods!" said Karin, but Lobelius thought it should be called the twilight of the idols.

In the distance heavy thuds could be heard. Behind the black silhouette of the gable roofs the night sky was red.

"That's the northwest, Frau Lorenz, not the south," Lobelius reassured her. "Must be near Northeim or Sondershausen, I would say. They seem to be having a bad raid over there."

"Is there no way of getting reliable news?" Carola asked anxiously.

Lobelius, whose great quality was his ability to put himself in someone else's position, proposed that they should visit his friend, Kern the baker, and listen to the news from England.

They turned into a side street, and Lobelius knocked in a prearranged way on the door under the cast-iron pretzel sign. The door opened halfway, a hand guided them inside, and they found themselves in the friendly radiance of a warm room behind the shop, where the baker greeted them in his floury apron. Frau Kern, who had let them in, put a plate of biscuits in front of them and brought a jug of homemade cider up from the cellar. There was a good smell of freshly baked bread. The miller, Herwig, like Kern a member of St. Peter's Church council, sat beside the baker and spoke about a meeting of men called up for the home guard, which he had attended that evening. They were all good townsfolk who loved their country. For that reason precisely they didn't want to see any more devastation; they were convinced that the war was lost and that to fight on would be suicide. "What do you think, Herr Pastor?"

"I agree with you entirely," said Lobelius. "We must do everything we can to prevent the total destruction of our land."

There came another knock at the door, but this time it was not the signal agreed upon among the friends. They looked startled. Even now such a gathering could have fatal results for those taking part in it. Frau Kern went to the door and peeped cautiously through the little round spy-hole. "A soldier!" she whispered. Then they heard her cry out: it was her own son, from whom they had heard nothing since Christmas. After weeks spent partly walking, partly bicycling, he had come with a small band of soldiers from the Moselle. The bicycles had given out on the way, and some of his comrades had fallen victims to exhaustion. The worn-out young sergeant dropped into a chair, seized the nearest glass on the table, and emptied it at one gulp. His mother ran into the kitchen to bring him something to eat. The baker took a clean glass from the cupboard, filled it, and also filled up the others' glasses.

It was very quiet in the warm little parlor. All that could be heard was the rapid breathing of the young soldier. Then his father warily asked, "Will you be staying here now?"

72

"What do you take me for—a deserter?" the son replied. "Early tomorrow I'm going to get my men together again, and then we'll go on. Orders to proceed to Halle."

Herr Kern shook his head. "Do you still think you can win the war?" he asked.

The skin stretched over the cheekbones in the thin face with the dark stubble of a beard. "Orders are orders."

Frau Kern brought in a plate with roast potatoes and homemade sausage and put it in front of her son on the checkered tablecloth. All the tenderness and care of a mother were expressed in the gesture with which she smoothed this brightly colored cloth.

The miller and the baker smoked on in silence, and the pastor also lit his pipe. It is extraordinary, thought Carola, how one is accepted as one of them and trusted implicitly when one comes in the company of a proven friend. This comradeship of the few belonged to the things that still seemed to give a little grace and humanity to life in this dark time. They recognized one another as do members of a secret fraternity.

"I also got my orders today," said the miller. "The seven thousand hundredweight of corn in my mill must be delivered to the military authorities; that means Eberstein will have no bread until next autumn. I'm playing silly and doing nothing about it. If I can put off the delivery for a few more days, our corn will be safe."

"Each man must do as he thinks best," said the soldier.

From the radio came the BBC signal. "Just listen to this," said Herr Kern.

"No one need tell me anything," said the soldier. "I know how things are going with us. All the same . . . they are also liars."

The pastor nodded. "War and lying go hand in hand. But the English news bulletins have on the whole proved to be

73

dependable, which is something we cannot say about our own."

They listened with bated breath. They heard that the Allied advance was going forward according to plan. Position reports were given. It was more or less the same picture as two days ago. No news about the conquest of any big city; at any rate not on the American front, while the British had improved their front line at certain points. Again the warning was given not to pay any attention to the order issued by the German authorities to defend every town to the last man. They were told that any town that offered resistance would be razed to the ground.

"At least we can assume that there has still been no street fighting at home," said Carola, as they were walking back to the parsonage. "So the dreadful news that the Voice of the People brought us at noon must have been only a rumor."

On the way they met an acquaintance of the pastor's who belonged to the town council and had only just left a late meeting in the town hall. He told them that the Nazi mayor had taken flight with other local party leaders, and that Herr Barner, the bank manager, had been elected mayor in his place. He would stay all night in the town hall. In the morning they expected the American Army if they didn't turn off to the east, toward Leipzig. "The temporary mayor tried to reach you by telephone, Herr Pastor," the man said. "But there was no answer from the parsonage. He didn't say what he wanted from you. Well, let's hope that by tomorrow at this time everything will be over."

It was almost one o'clock when they reached home, but Lobelius went straight to the telephone, and Carola cast him a grateful glance when he handed the receiver to her. Once again she heard her husband's voice, giving her fresh strength. Franz assured her that he and Nurse Ottilie were going on all right, that the house was undamaged and the town still not occupied. Only the artillery fire sounded definitely nearer than yesterday. They were expecting an enemy attack any time now. "And then we'll be together again, darling. My love to everybody. Tell Lobelius how grateful I am to him for his hospitality. Best of luck! And keep a stiff upper lip, eh?"

"Yes, Franz," Carola replied. "Yes, of course . . ."

"The three minutes are up; I must cut you off now," called the operator from the exchange.

✦ Chapter Four ✦

That night there was no warning of enemy attack, and none the next morning either. The evening before they had discussed at the parsonage the reason for the delay. Had the Americans really suffered a setback or were the Allies perhaps deliberately holding back in order to allow the Russians to overrun central Germany? "That's very unlikely," Lobelius said, when Frau Lorenz expressed this opinion. "England and America couldn't allow Russia to penetrate into the heart of Europe. One can't believe they would be so unstatesmanlike; at any rate, not so long as the wise old man of the Thames still has anything to do with it."

Carola slept uneasily all night; the uncertainty of the situation with regard to the war, the impossibility of estimating how long she would be separated from Franz—all this prevented her from relaxing. She was up at five o'clock the next morning and went to the sheeppen to see if Schirin was giving any signs of lambing. To her astonishment she was followed a little later by Karin, who perhaps had a bad conscience because her mother had not seen much of her the day before. She helped her give the animals their feed and water and lay down fresh straw. After an examination of Schirin's udder had shown that the birth was not to be expected within the next few hours at any rate, the two women sat down on the straw in that strange condition, a mixture of drowsiness and suspense, in which all their days were now passed. The hens were softly cackling on the perches that Till had fixed up for them the day before along with a ladder. When Karin scattered a little corn, they hopped down and began pecking at their morning meal. One of them was already sitting on the new nest that had been made from an oatmeal carton.

"I shall be glad of every egg that we can contribute to the larder," said Carola. "But if this goes on much longer, we're not going to have enough feed. Don't you think Lobelius might get us some oats and hay from one of his farmers if I pay well for it?"

"Oh, Mutti, he so hates asking for anything," said Karin. "I don't even like to mention it."

Carola said no more. Until now she had valiantly stuck to her decision not to express any critical opinions.

The door squeaked on its hinges that had not been oiled for years, letting in Till and Bluebeard. "Morning!" Till cried; he was in his swimming trunks. "I'm going to leave my clothes here so that afterwards I don't have to go upstairs to change. Oh, before I forget. Yesterday Dorle saw the sheep. She definitely wants one of the lambs. 'Course it must be a ewe lamb. Afterwards we'll get her mother talked around."

"Don't count your chickens before they're hatched, Till. We don't know if Schirin will have twins; even if she does, they may be males."

Till slapped Schirin's shorn back. "Don't let's have any trouble from you, old girl! I want two at least from you, please, and no useless males, mind you! Well, so long!"

"He's not grieving over his hand grenade any more," said Karin.

"Let's hope he's given up *that* idea. He's an extraordinary mixture of the dreamer and the doer, and with such a happy disposition! Yet I'm worried when I think about the disappointments that lie in store for him; how will he get over his shattered illusions?"

"Oh, you know what he was like when he was little: if anything went wrong, he would just shake himself as Bluebeard does when he comes out of the water and then he would embark happily on some new adventure. Here they are calling up the Hitler Youth of his age group, just imagine. Fortunately he's not on the Eberstein lists. We've saved him from that at least."

"If only he doesn't hear about it!" Carola said worriedly. "Come on; we'll go back to bed for an hour or so. There's nothing more for us to do here. If I were you, I'd try to get a good sleep. You look dead tired."

"So do you," said Karin. "Is there anyone who doesn't? No, there's no question of getting a long sleep. Helmut and I must go into town early this morning. You can't imagine how interesting it is for me to be learning all about his work in the parish."

"Well, don't overdo it."

They went upstairs and lay down again. When Karin got up half an hour later, her mother's eyes were closed.

Karin went into the kitchen, put the kettle on the gas, and boiled up yesterday's coffee grounds again. Soon afterward Helmut appeared. They read the day's lesson together, drank the hot, thick brew, and ate some bread and turnip jam with it. Then they set out. The morning was gray and cold. It seemed to them that there was less artillery fire than yesterday. "They could by-pass us and from Gotha thrust on directly eastward to Leipzig, as someone suggested yesterday," said Karin. "That would mean a long delay. No wonder people are all on edge with the waiting. No one is really clear about what will happen. All they want is for the war to end."

"That's the main thing, isn't it? What will happen next? The third of the four horsemen of the Apocalypse, hunger. Who's going to feed the homeless hordes of refugees, and what shelter will they find in the bombed-out cities? It's going to be a hard time; we can count on that. But with all the misery, what opportunities to show mercy and brotherly love in our land, which has sinned so greatly against love. And patience! For now is the time when the victors, in the blind triumph of their victory, are likely to make mistakes. But that's not our concern, for we shall only be the sufferers, not the agents of suffering. What a power for peace will lie in our own powerlessness if we can only glimpse in it the sign of grace!"

"Oh, Helmut, in the history of nations it has always been the powerless ones who suffered oppression. We can only hope that the victors will have the sense not to discourage the forces of good in our land."

"I'm sure they will," said Lobelius confidently. He looked almost happy at the thought of the rebirth of his nation in the spirit of Christ, and Karin was sure that in order to bring it about he would willingly suffer any hardships. As for herself, she thought it was more likely that she would flare up against the overweening arrogance of the conquerors, and perhaps even against God himself for making the innocent suffer with the guilty. Oh, how much she still had to learn from Helmut!

When they reached the market place, the thirteen- and fourteen-year-old Hitler Youths had already assembled. In their khaki shirts, despite the daggers they wore in their belts, they looked anything but warlike. An N.C.O. was reading their names from a list. But he saw that of the thirty boys on the list, only seventeen were present. He had orders to take them to an SS division in the neighborhood, where they were to be armed with hand grenades. Women were standing around the square with woolen shawls over their arms and shoulders. They nodded to the pastor—even those whose children had been consecrated at the state ceremony instead of being confirmed. As if Lobelius's presence gave them courage, the mothers suddenly began to whisper among themselves; then the bravest of them stepped forward, strode into the middle of the market place, took her son by the hand, and declared, "Mine is staying at home. They took my other lad for the trenches in February, and my husband fell at Stalingrad. You're not going to have this one."

"Have you gone crazy?" snarled the N.C.O. "You'll pay for this, I can tell you." But now the maternal front had closed up against him, and complaints rained down upon him like machine-gun fire. "Hand grenades for the kids? Not likely! You better look out or you'll get a crack over the head with my rolling pin!"

"Why don't you send the Party bosses to fight the Yanks? You're not going to take *our* lads for cannon fodder!"

One mother after another seized her son and dragged him away with her; in the end there was only a small band of four boys left, one of them the son of Frau Borstel, the leader of the Women's Movement in the town. Everyone in Eberstein knew what *her* opinions were, and it was obvious that she hadn't dared to show herself among the rebellious women.

The N.C.O. stood there, not knowing what to do next; he took off his cap, scratched the back of his head, and looked in obvious dismay at the women and their offspring. Finally he marched off with the remaining four.

"If only women always stood together like this, men could never go to war!" Karin whispered triumphantly.

Lobelius shook his head. "Do you know the picture called Mad Gret, by Breughel? Here it's a woman who represents the evil demon. If you will come with me to the hospital, you'll see the sort of things women can do."

As they were going up the steps to the hospital of the Sisters of Mercy, Frau Wöllner was coming out. "She's been on night duty again," said Lobelius. "She earns a bit extra that way because she couldn't live on what she gets for playing the organ."

"Where does she come from actually, Helmut? Did you know her earlier or is she just a refugee like the others in your house?"

"I knew her and her husband in Berlin when I was a student there. Don't ask me to tell you any more, please. I can't give her secret away."

In the hospital he asked for the sister in charge, and after a few minutes a small plump nun with a white apron over her black habit came across the hall to them and took them to a door, which was locked on the outside. Lobelius introduced her to Karin. "This is Sister Scholastica. She will certainly have no objection to your visiting Lotte with me. Just stand quietly beside the door; then she won't notice you. How is she, Sister?"

"Still the same, Herr Pastor," Sister Scholastica whispered. "As far as her physical condition is concerned, she's turned the corner. Now we ought to deliver her to the University Clinic for Nervous Disorders at Jena. But you know what that would mean. Herr Dr. Wendel, the Father, and Reverend Mother are agreed that we must avoid that at all costs."

Eberstein had only a small Catholic community; the old priest, who also tended to the sisters' spiritual needs, lived in one of the wings of the hospital.

"If you can hold out for one, or at the most two weeks, I think there would be no more danger," said Lobelius. "Give the Reverend Father my best wishes." Then they went into the room, which the sister locked again from the outside.

In the narrow, half-dark room a girl lay in bed. She was all skin and bone, with bluish-yellow marks on her face, which was gray, like cheap writing paper. Her eyelids fluttered when she heard someone come into the room. Lobelius signed to Karin to stay in the shadow of the cupboard beside the door.

"It's me, Lotte," he said, sat on the edge of the bed, and

took the sick girl's hand in his own. "Soon everything will be all right. You needn't worry any more."

She turned her emaciated face toward the familiar voice. "Really?" she whispered. "Is it all over, Herr Pastor? Have they been beaten, the swine? Then those beasts of the Women's Guild will get their heads shaved and their clothes torn off their bodies—that would be justice, it would. Into the millpond with them, push them under till they're blue in the face and feel the water choking them, like I did . . ."

"Quiet, Lotte," said Lobelius, and Karin felt how he detached himself from her and gave himself entirely to the sick girl. "Think what Christ had to suffer. They spat at him and whipped him and jeered and mocked at him and dragged him through the streets also, and he was innocent."

"I'm innocent, I am," she hissed. "Is there a law against love? I loved Stanislas; he was so wretched and so lonely away here in a foreign land, a prisoner. Mustn't I prove my love to him?"

"No," said Lobelius. "That's not the way to prove love. True love knows how to wait and to deny itself, if it must. That goes for you and for him."

"I don't regret it," she said. "I regret nothing, and it was nobody's business what went on between us."

"Only yourselves, and your parents, on whom you have brought such sorrow. Come, Lotte, let us pray: forgive us our trespasses, as we forgive them that trespass against us."

"I don't want forgiveness; I want justice, that's all."

"Stop being so self-pitying," he said and held her twitching hands firmly in his. "We can leave justice to a higher authority."

The sick girl suddenly collapsed, as if she had been worn out by the fire burning in her brain. Her shorn head, on which a few tufts of hair had begun to grow again, and the disfigured face fell back on the pillow. A trickle of saliva ran out of her mouth.

Lobelius waited patiently. A fly buzzed on the window. From the hall came the soft rattle of a rosary. Sister Scholastica was patrolling outside like a faithful watchdog.

Time went by. Can one love one's neighbor when she is so repulsive? Karin wondered sadly. It was not the girl's appearance that appalled her, for she was not easily shocked by such things after working in her father's office. But the sheer hatred that poured out of the girl was so overpowering that it was as ugly as the things that had been done to her. One could clean and bind and heal bodily wounds; but such destruction of the human soul made Karin feel helpless.

Finally Lobelius placed the girl's hands together, and she made no resistance. "Go to sleep now," he said with authority. "And try to eat what the sisters bring you. You must grow strong and healthy again so that you can be of assistance to your parents when everything is over."

"Will he come back?" the girl whispered. "Do you think he's still living and will come back to me, Herr Pastor, so that we can get married? Because then the others won't be able to forbid it any longer."

"We shall pray that what is best for both of you may come to pass."

Outside, in the street, Karin walked silently along beside Helmut. There were a hundred questions she wanted to ask, but it was not easy to put them into words. At the next street corner a group of women stopped him again. "Old Bremer's been shot by a low-flying plane while he was out plowing, Herr Pastor."

"I'll go at once to Frau Bremer," said Lobelius.

Again it was grief clamoring for consolation. The weeping woman, an old farmer's wife, was still a figure of sturdy dignity, even in her anguish and terror. She had lost two sons in battle, and now her husband had been killed. Where did Helmut get the strength to help everyone, to give of himself entirely without asking how long his reserves would hold out?

Later they met the blacksmith, a hoary-headed Caliban with hairy arms. "Last night they blew Northeim to pieces, Herr Pastor," he said. "A fellow from the next village came over today; he saw it all from the hills. High explosive, fire bombs, land mines—the whole place blasted to smithereens, not a house left standing. And for why? Because they resisted the advance. Since day before yesterday they had a military commander there. Now if they come here and tell us we got to resist, what's to become of us, Herr Pastor? Who'll plow the fields if they snap up the last men for the home guards? And as for the prisoner-of-war workers, they'll make off with all the stuff we've got as soon as the Yanks come on the scene, and we can thank our lucky stars if they don't go a-murdering and a-looting, bloody-minded as they be."

"The Americans will see that law and order is upheld, Fleming," said Lobelius. "And the foreign workers will certainly willingly work a little longer on the farms where they have been well treated. Not out of sympathy for us, of course; but they can't be sent home until the whole of Germany is conquered."

"It's lucky for us that hereabouts most of them have been kindly treated. Though at the big house . . . they do say as the Herr Baron is pretty free with his riding whip!"

"Good day, Fleming," said Lobelius. "We have to be getting on."

"What was all that about Lotte?" Karin finally managed to ask when they were alone again. Lobelius told her. "Stanislas was one of the Poles who worked here on a farm. For the last two years he'd been helping Lotte's parents; he seems to have been a hard-working, decent chap. They treated him as one of the family and let him eat at the same table with them, although that was expressly forbidden by the Party. Nevertheless, many farmers do so—the Frankes for example. But it didn't do to talk about it or to have it known, else their foreign labor was taken away from them and they had to fend for themselves at harvest and plowing. Stani and Lotte had been going strong together for quite a while. The Women's Movement has been after such relationships like the devil on the lookout for a human soul. They call it "racial disgrace" when a girl is on friendly terms with a Pole or a Russian. Frau Borstel had been snooping around for some time. Then one evening she saw Lotte going into the hayloft with Stani. She called together a few other members of the Women's Movement, and the hunt was on. Two storm troopers hauled the Pole away to prison in the town, and next day the Gestapo took him off, to Buchenwald probably. The women hounded Lotte through the streets, dressed only in her underwear, with shorn head, bleeding, as far as the millpond, which was ice-cold. They would have let her drown, but the miller fished her out with a long pole, finally chased off the women, and took Lotte to the hospital. It's a miracle that she's still alive. These are your peace-loving women, Karin!"

"But the nuns who are looking after her now and who protected her from the Party—they are also women, aren't they?" Karin cried.

He smiled. "And what wonderful women! I only wanted to show you that warmongers exist in both male and female forms. We haven't come very far since the days of witch trials and the Inquisition!"

"Do you mean that such things have frequently happened?"

"I know of three places in Thuringia alone. But let's get home now. And this evening you can help me to compose my funeral speech for old Bremer and my sermon for Sunday. You have such a good style."

"You're the one with good ideas, and you know the Bible

inside out. You know more about everything than I do. But nothing makes me happier than to be able to help you."

The potatoes—well, they had forgotten them again. For that reason they felt rather guilty when they sat down to table, although everyone tactfully avoided speaking of the missing potatoes. With the cabbage they had thick barley—known derisively as "calves' teeth"—and that was punishment enough.

Only Till, although he too couldn't stand "calves' teeth," was talkative and full of news. "I'm not very hungry," he said. "This morning I helped Dorle to clean out the cow byre. The Pole had to go and help her father plant turnips. And afterwards Frau Franke gave me some wonderful sandwiches, simply bursting with sausage. Incidentally, Dorle spoke to her mother about the lamb, and Frau Franke said all right and would we care to swap it for food."

"Ask her what she's going to give us for it," said Karin, a true child of her time for whom barter was serious business.

"Potatoes first of all, I said. Then Frau Franke opened her eyes wide as saucers and said why doesn't the Herr Pastor say when he needs potatoes. Good, I said. Make it two hundredweight for the Herr Pastor and two hundredweight feed potatoes for us, and every day a quart of full-cream milk until the lamb is weaned and we can milk the ewe. Is that all right, Mutti?"

"It seems to me a bit outrageous to ask all that for a skinny little lamb," said Carola, who did not share her children's talent for barter. "And we still don't know if we'll *have* a lamb."

Till laughed. "That's true. Don't count your chickens, and so on . . ."

"You are a real treasure, Till!" Aunt Ulrike beamed at him. "Now you won't have to worry any more about the potatoes, Helmut dear."

"I never did, I'm afraid," said Lobelius with disarming candor. "Until now we've always had whatever we needed at the right time from one of our farmers. They don't let their pastor starve to death."

"Well, they must be told when the time for starving has come, or how should they know?" said Till. "Anyhow, Dorle and I will be bringing the potatoes this afternoon on the hand-cart. And I can work for the Frankes! Dorle's father is in a bad way with his arm and her mother has her hands full, and Wenzel, the Pole, can't see to everything at this time of the year when there's work to be done all over the place. Tomorrow he's going to show us how to knock muck. We'll be taking the horses into the fields on the other side of the river. The fields need the manure, alarm or no alarm; it's late enough to be doing it already. I told Dorle she must be nice to Bluebeard if she values my help. And Herr Franke will pay me in kind. Half a pound of butter every week doesn't sound bad, eh? And if you ever want feed for the animals, Mutti, you only have to say the word. Of course," he said, slapping his chest, "I shall be fed at the farm like a real farmhand."

"To listen to you, one would think we were here for the duration," his mother said; but it was easy to see how proud she was of her diligent son.

"A few weeks, at least, it'll last," was Till's opinion. "The war won't end as quickly as all that, especially when we start using our new secret weapon. Just feel my biceps, Aunt Ulrike! Dorle says they're the sort you need for knocking muck. Terrific, eh?"

"Like a young Siegfried!" Aunt Ulrike smiled delightedly.

"Till, the breadwinner—who would have thought it?" said Karin. "If you knock enough muck, perhaps on Sundays you could mount one of your steeds, young Siegfried, and join the Valkyries."

"You can bet your life I've arranged for that also."

The telephone interrupted the conversation. The pastor got up and answered it. He had a brief talk with someone. "I must go at once to the town hall," he said, as he put down the receiver. "The new mayor, Herr Barner, wants to talk to me. Are you coming, Karin?"

She nodded and stood up. On the way there she said, "Mother is sure to think I should take a nap. But we've got all the rest of our lives for sleeping as much as we want to."

Lobelius laughed. "I for one have no intention of becoming a Rip Van Winkle in peacetime. But I understand how anxious your mother must be about you, wondering if you can keep up the pace we're going at just now."

"Huh! I've got terrific strength, as Till would say. Now *you* are the one who needs rest much more than I do."

It must be torture for him to be running about all day with his bad leg; he always had a worse limp toward evening. But he shook his head at Karin's worried look. "I don't feel it, really. One gets used to things. And it's simply wonderful that I have you to help me now!"

She thought to herself that so far she hadn't been all that much help to him. It was Martha Born who lightened the burden of his tasks for him. In her unobtrusive way she kept all those things from him that might prevent him from doing his real work. Then, on the other hand, she could, in a respectful but determined way, be quite firm with him if it was a case of discussing church finances or interviewing people who would not be satisfied with just her own advice. And she still finds time to darn his socks, thought Karin, impressed by so much efficiency.

In the town hall the mayor's secretary led them straight to his office. Behind the writing desk there was a sharply defined, darker rectangle of wallpaper on the otherwise faded wall: a blank space, where only a few days ago the Führer's portrait had hung. *Sic transit gloria mundi!*

Herr Barner, a big heavy man, rose slowly from the chair behind his desk, held out his hand to Lobelius, and was introduced to Karin. He didn't seem at all surprised by her presence, for everyone in Eberstein knew about her. An unlit cigar hung in the corner of his mouth, and around his eyes were those dark rings that had become a universal uniform of sleeplessness and overwork. As soon as he began to speak, his thick-set face grew spirited and lively. Like a precious treasure, he laid his cigar on the edge of the ash tray, carefully saving it up for later consumption. After Lobelius and Karin had seated themselves, he made himself as comfortable as possible in his chair, which was a little too small for his big frame. "It lasts longer that way," he said, grimacing at his cigar. "Can you speak English, Herr Pastor?" he went on at once. Lobelius gave him a questioning look.

"The fact is, I wanted to ask you to come with me to meet the Americans, things being the way they are. . . . I can speak quite freely with Fräulein Lorenz here, I suppose? Good. Well then, we must hand over the town before it's destroyed. You've heard what happened to Northeim?"

The pastor nodded. "It must be ghastly, what they can do to a little town in just twenty minutes. And to its inhabitants also," he added. "As for English, unfortunately I'm not much of a hand at that. I'm a humanist, Herr Barner, and I don't think we'd get very far with the Yanks by using Latin and Greek."

"That's the worst of you theological chaps," grumbled the mayor. "The only languages you know are dead ones. I didn't ask your colleague of the other persuasion, not only because of his lack of linguistic ability. I'm sure you'll agree with me that we can't burden the old priest with all this. So you only know Latin and Greek, eh? Hm!"

"I'm very sorry. But wait a minute! Perhaps Fräulein Lorenz here can help us. Wasn't your first foreign language English, Karin?"

89

"Yes, it was!" she eagerly replied. "I can get along, anyhow. What do you want me to say, Herr Barner?"

"*You*, Fräulein Lorenz?" said the mayor, looking at the young creature in front of him and shaking his head. "Maybe you could brush up the pastor's English a bit. It's not child's play, you know, going to meet enemy tanks."

"I didn't expect it to be," replied Karin with all the dignity of her sixteen summers. "But it's not child's play either, drumming a bit of intelligible English into someone in so short a time. Besides, they might ask questions, and then where would you be?"

"M-m-m, yes," said the mayor. "But there's something else you must realize. If the Americans don't hurry themselves up, the Party bosses may come back again. Then those who prepared for the surrender of the town wouldn't get off any too lightly. So the greatest secrecy is necessary."

"We must just risk the danger of the return of the Party leaders," said Lobelius, looking across at Karin. She nodded vigorously at him, with a wide smile, as though she didn't care what happened to her as long as she could be with him.

"Well, then, can I count on the two of you?" asked Herr Barner. "Fine. Thank you. You must of course obtain your mother's permission, Fräulein Lorenz. I assume that we can depend on her also to keep quiet about it all."

"That goes without saying," replied Karin.

"Then I'll send a message to the parsonage as soon as I get word of the Americans approaching. Again many thanks for your cooperation, Herr Pastor, and you, too, Fräulein Lorenz. You're a brave young woman."

"He's misjudged me there," said Karin, as they went home. "I'm not brave; all I want is to be with you. And perhaps I'm attracted also by the spice of adventure."

"I don't really know whether I can hold myself responsible for you to your parents," said Lobelius, whose scruples were far from being entirely removed. "We should try and see if you can't coach me in a few useful English expressions. Oh, why did we learn French as a third language at my school instead of English, which would be so useful to me now?"

"You can put the idea right out of your head," said Karin. "The Yanks would think you were speaking Chinese. No, we've both made a promise, and that's that. As for my parents, I alone am responsible to them."

On Thursday evening the electric current was suddenly cut off, and that meant there was no radio news either. The railroad services had been suspended since Tuesday; there was no mail, no newspapers; now the local news sheets could not be printed either. The telephone was the only link between the little town and the outside world.

Thursday! thought Carola Lorenz. We've been here just four days, and already it seems like an eternity.

Public opinion in Eberstein again vacillated like the indicator on a sensitive instrument. If the Americans hadn't suffered defeat, they would have been here by now. Suddenly "Heil Hitler" began to be heard again. On Thursday afternoon Martha Born had returned from lunch to say that her uncle was back home, full of optimism and with correspondingly high-handed conduct. He had told Martha that she had better find another lodging place, as it could have unpleasant results for his family if he had a church worker in his house when the final victory was won, for then the church would be strictly controlled in Germany.

"Did he really say that?" asked Aunt Ulrike in horrified tones.

The pastor said, "You see what happens when the antichrist triumphs. Thank God there is not much danger any more of that happening."

A bed was set up for Martha in the parsonage's potato cellar;

she could stay there, too, whenever there were bombers over-head. Frau Lorenz seized this opportunity to bring down Till's camp bed and sleeping bag into the cellar, and despite Aunt Ulrike's resistance, a couch was hauled down from the attic for her and installed in a corner of the air-raid shelter. Only Carola, Lobelius, and Karin remained upstairs as before, until the throb of enemy engines became so threatening that they thought it was better to go into the cellar.

In the pastor's room a candle now burned instead of the electric light. By its light Carola read the *Tao Te Ching* to soften with the wisdom of the East the anguish she felt at the decline of the West.

Lobelius and Karin sat opposite her, sharing the same light from the fat church candle, deeply absorbed in the prepara-tion of the funeral speech for the old farmer who had taken the short step into eternity while still holding the handles of his plow. The interment was to be tomorrow, between air-raid warnings. When Carola looked over at them, she felt very strongly the oneness of life and death that Laotse speaks about, the meaning of the eternal circle, ceaselessly returning in it-self. There were two young people in love, and what were they doing? Composing a graveside oration, and even this pre-occupation with the great mystery of death seemed to be just another affirmation of their own hope-filled lives.

That evening again there came the moment for which Carola waited every day: when she heard her husband's voice on the telephone. Each time only a few words; nothing about the things that they had most at heart. But one day I shall say it, she thought; if I only get the chance, I'll say it. Some-thing the poet Rilke had said occurred to her then: "The love of one human being for another is perhaps the hardest thing, the most extreme, the final test and proof, the labor for which all other labors are only the preparation. That is why young people, who are beginners in everything, do not know what love is; they have to learn about it." Not only the young, thought Carola. Aren't we mere beginners in love all our lives? It's only that youth thinks it alone knows all about it. That's why it's so difficult for us older ones to help them or even to come to an understanding with them.

Bluebeard lay curled up on the red armchair. He was always the first to sense the approach of danger. He took no notice of the sirens, but as soon as the first insect-drone of planes began in the distance, still indistinguishable by human ears, he would wake up, grab his bone from under the cross-stitch pillow in order to take it down into the cellar with him, just as people would take a bag containing valuables or papers, and run excitedly from one to the other, trying quite unmistakably to make them understand that it was time to dive into the underworld again. The tenants of the house had had to get used to having him in the cellar. It was not the pastor, nor Krischan Möller in his capacity as air-raid warden who had made the decision; it was Martha Born, who had calmly declared that the perambulators at the bottom of the steps constituted a far greater danger than a well-behaved dog, and such a small one at that. Unexpectedly, the general had supported her, and the honorable old gentleman with his aura of long-forgotten heroic deeds still enjoyed a certain regard among the tenants. "The dog's not as disturbing as the everlasting noise of the children," he had pronounced in his penetrating parade-ground voice.

He was working away feverishly, although as he had once confessed to Lobelius, he had still not received any reply to the suggestions he had sent to the Führer's headquarters. Intrigue, that's what it was, always the same. But Lobelius suspected that his wife saw to it that the bulky letters were never posted. She looked after him lovingly and was encouraged and strengthened by what she called "the infallible logic" of her astrological calculations. It would all soon be over—that was what the stars foretold—and then they would spend the rest of their lives in the little dower house on the family estate in Mecklenburg.

That night, as soon as the heavens were quiet, Carola, Karin, and Lobelius fled from the stuffy cellar to get a breath of fresh air. Carola hurried to the sheeppen, because Schirin could be expected to give birth at any moment now. Karin and Helmut walked in the garden. The pond lay shimmering in the hazy moonlight. The fresh spring grass, so green by day, was now subdued, and the fanlike pattern of fields could only be guessed at. Thick mist was again rising from the river, the mist that had wrapped the town in its mantle of invisibility on so many nights. Sometimes a gust of ammonia came to them from the fields, a reminder of Till and Dorle's agricultural activity. The frogs in the pond were singing their marriage hymn unceasingly; usually it was the fortissimo of a full choir, then a quartet or a sextet, and suddenly a solo, *con amore*. Somewhere on a barn roof an owl was screeching. And once from the bushes along the river came a small melody of melting sweetness—a nightingale, who had made a mistake in the date. She sang just one small verse and then was silent. Bluebeard, wild with joy, dashed through the wet grass, down to the river and back again, around the pond, where the frogs could be heard plopping into the water. The disturbance quieted them for a few minutes, but soon their monotonous refrain swelled to its full intensity again, from time to time interrupted by the *bel canto* of a solo singer.

Karin and Lobelius sat on the bench behind the trailing branches of the willow, which fell down in front of them like a curtain. They didn't talk about theology, nor about their future tasks. But neither did they say anything about what was filling their thoughts more and more every day. Why can't we talk about it? Karin thought impatiently. Does Helmut think he oughtn't to press me to make a decision because the future is so dark and uncertain? How unsuspecting even the most intelligent man can be! When every day might be their last, shouldn't they love one another while there still was time? I'll soon be seventeen, she thought; as old as his grandmother was when she married. At times the thought alarmed her—how serious everything was now; so different from the rapture that winged her heels in last year's waltzes. The idea of giving herself entirely to another person sometimes made her head reel; it was like surrendering her whole identity, and until recently she had thought that the first and most important thing was to develop her own self. Now she was given up to him, something belonging to him, which he could form and change as he wished. No wonder that sometimes she felt a bit frightened about it all.

"All my life I shall think of this spring when I hear frogs croaking," she said, after a long silence, and laid her hand, wet with dew, upon his shoulder. For one breath-taking moment he let it lie there. Then he turned his head and kissed her finger tips, and as her mouth was turned toward him, he kissed her also on the lips, swiftly and passionately, in an overwhelming rush of feeling that welled up and was at once withdrawn.

"Oh, my darling," he said. "Life is going to be so hard."

"I know," she replied. "You don't think I'm frightened, do you?"

In the misty pallor of the April night shone the few white blossoms of the young plum tree, which might be destroyed by frost or singed by fire or blasted by a bomb. What would it matter, thought Karin; it has known at least one blossoming spring.

Again behind the hills the sinister roar of guns grew in intensity—a gloomy bass underscoring the sweet violins of spring. Did it sound closer now than in the last few days? Farther off —closer, closer—farther off. . . . How much longer would it last? They stopped to listen for a while. This time it came unmistakably from the south. "It's our city!" said Karin. "My father!"

Softly at first, but then louder came the noise of approaching bombers. Only now did they realize that there had been no full all clear during the day. Bluebeard was standing looking up at Karin and whimpering slightly. In less than no time the whole night sky was a throbbing dome of fear.

"We must go and find your mother," said Lobelius.

Carola was still in the sheeppen. As there was no light any more, Till had given her one of the Frankes' old farm lanterns he had borrowed, with a stump of candle in it. Now it was standing on a shelf illuminating the yellow straw, the two ewes, and Schirin's two newborn lambs. Carola looked up as Lobelius and Karin came in. On her face was an expression of happy relief. "Just look!" she said. "Two ewe lambs!" Only then did she notice Bluebeard's uneasiness. "What's the matter, little doggy? Are they coming again? Just a minute while I dry the lambs."

But Karin gripped her firmly by the arm. "Quick, down into the cellar! Schirin will see to everything now."

They blew out the candle and hurried into the house.

Dawn was breaking when the final squadron flew back home and everything was quiet again. Before they went to bed, Carola and Karin looked into the sheeppen to see how things were going.

"You haven't told me what the mayor wanted," said Carola. "Has he any news about the war?" Karin had not yet ventured to mention the mayor's proposal to her mother because she was afraid of her objections. But it would have to be discussed sooner or later.

"There's nothing new. He asked Helmut to go with him and meet the Americans and surrender the town to them, so that Eberstein won't be blown to bits at the last moment. But neither of them can speak English, and so I must go with them as interpreter. Of course, the whole thing is top-secret."

Carola looked at her daughter. She wetted her lips with the tip of her tongue, as if she were about to say something, but she only nodded and busied herself with the lambs. Franz wouldn't stand in Karin's way, she thought. It was a task in the cause of peace she would be performing, a dangerous task. But how could one protect one's children from danger in times like these? One must be satisfied if one could keep them from doing wrong.

"Thank you, Mutti," said Karin, and quickly brushed her mother's cheek with her lips. Then she went outside and found Helmut waiting for her. "Did you tell her?" he asked. "What did she say?"

"Nothing," Karin replied. "Mothers can sometimes be quite sensible."

He smiled. "Your mother is so most of the time, and I must say in the last few days we've demanded a lot of her. Here comes Till, our mighty landworker."

"You've slept like a log all night," his sister said. "Take Bluebeard with you. I hope Dorle's got used to him by now?"

"I told her she'd better! Of course, she doesn't know the first thing about dogs, but what can you expect of a girl! Just think; she calls Bluebeard's lovely beard a 'mucky schnozzle!'" Till nodded toward the sheeppen. "Additions to the family?"

"And how!" Karin said, upon which her brother swiftly disappeared in the direction of the shed.

"Let's just run up to the top of the church tower before we go to bed," said Lobelius. "Perhaps we can see the advance of enemy troops from there."

They crossed the churchyard, walking between the rows of gravestones, climbed the steep stairs to the top of the tower, and looked out of the tiny window. Far below them lay the little town with its town hall and market place, the broad ribbon of High Street, the two churches; all around were peaceful farms with their orchards, the fields, the wooded hills, and behind them a dark red horizon shrouded in clouds of smoke. They couldn't make out where the rose color of sunrise began and the fatal redness of burning houses ended. Here and there they glimpsed flashes of artillery fire. But on the high road to the south there were no tank movements to be seen.

When they had descended the many twisting stairs of the tower, they heard the organ being played in the church. "Frau Wöllner is practicing," said Lobelius.

They crept into the sacristy and listened to the music while outside the noise of war swelled and subsided again. There they sat near to each other, on a tiny island still exempt from the fury of destruction, surrounded by the tempestuous ocean of war. And now the woman at the organ began playing a Bach chorale, and it was as if God Himself were coming down on a cloud.

✦ *Chapter Five* ✦

"Well, well," said Till, as he went into the shed to say good-by to his mother for the rest of the day. "Twins, eh? Wonderful!"

"Two ewe lambs, Till. Tell Dorle that she can come and choose one. Aren't you going swimming today?"

"Nope. No time. The water's lovely just now, but the mist always clears about eleven at the latest, and then those low-flying planes start coming over. I'm off to work now; the sooner we get our potatoes in, the better."

Our potatoes, he said! And yesterday he had proclaimed, "I have forged my sword into a plowshare; one is as important to our country as the other."

"You mean you've exchanged your hand grenade for a dung fork," his sister had corrected him, but Aunt Ulrike, who had a weakness for Till, thought he expressed himself much more poetically.

Whether he was handling a plowshare or a dung fork, the Frankes, at any rate, seemed glad to have Till's help. And there was no doubt that he himself was contented. Nowadays when he came home, he no longer talked about the new secret weapon and glorious victory, but about Kathi the cow that would soon be calving, about new-hatched chicks and duck-lings, about planting, and above all about the two chestnut horses he was allowed to ride down to the horsepond in the evenings if he had finished his work in time. And today he was to drive alone with Dorle to one of the fields on the other side of the river to set potatoes. Carola tried not to think about what had happened to old Bremer. But she couldn't help saying, "Be careful, Till!"

He grinned at this motherly concern. "Oh, I'll be all right," he said, giving her a pat on the shoulder. "I'll look out; don't you worry. We always leave the horses and cart in the woods when we work up there. Dorle and I crawl under the south bridge as soon as we hear a low-flier coming over. S'long, Mutti. Let's go, Bluebeard!"

It was shortly before six when he arrived at the Frankes' farm. The farmer was already harnessing the horses, but why was he taking the trap, which he only used for country excursions? Till was surprised. Why hadn't the farmer waited for his arrival or called for Wenzel's help when his game arm made harnessing so difficult for him? "Good morning, Herr Franke," he said. "Are we going to load the sacks of seed potatoes in your Sunday-go-to-meeting trap?"

"Get yourself into the milking shed," growled the usually good-humored farmer. Till held his tongue, shrugged his shoulders, and went to the shed where Frau Franke and Dorle were busy milking. "The lambs have arrived!" he shouted from the door. "You may come and choose one, Dorle. Good morning, Frau Franke. If you want to get back to your kitchen, I can finish stripping them for you. Where's that Wenzel got to? Is he still dozing?"

"We've had some men billeted on us, and the Pole doesn't care for them. Neither do we. He's back in camp, but we have to stay on here. You two better see to it that we get through all the work."

Till shook his head in perplexity. Never before had he experienced such gloom at the Frankes'. He started milking, waiting for Dorle to enlighten him about it all. But she didn't say a word. There was no sound but the champing of the cows, the drumming of milk in the pails, and from time to time the rattle of a chain or the mewing of the farm cats that were sitting on a crossbeam awaiting their morning's ration of milk. Bluebeard was lying on the straw beside Till in the same pleasant state of expectancy.

"Dorle!" he said to her at last. "What's up? Has the cat got your tongue? Having people billeted on you isn't as bad as all that. You should have seen the amount of people who often spent the night at *our* house! If old Wenzel doesn't like it, we can get on well enough without him."

"I would run away too if I were in his shoes," said Dorle at last. "They're four storm troopers!"

"So what?" said Till. "They won't eat you."

"They eat our bacon and sausages that must last until autumn," Dorle said angrily. "Yesterday evening, while you were away, they suddenly appeared at the front door, three great bulls of men and a young boy. Their car broke down, they say. Mother had to light the fire again and cook and roast all kinds of stuff for them; you'd have thought we were back in peacetime, the way they gorged. They brought their own wine and brandy, and boozed and brawled till early this morning, so's we couldn't get a wink of sleep. Dad stayed downstairs because he was scared they'd set the house afire with their cigarettes. Dad says the young one drank next to nothing; he put his head on the table and went to sleep. They ordered the trap to be harnessed for six this morning, just as if we farmers were here only to take the great lords jaunting. Dad doesn't want to, but what can he do?"

"I'll take them," said Till. "Why, it's an honor to be able to do something for the Führer's élite. Surely you don't grudge them the bit of food they had after all they've done?"

"Just you ask Wenzel what they did in Warsaw. He went through it all before they sent him here."

"Wenzel shouldn't go around telling horror tales. And you

ought to be ashamed of yourself, listening to that kind of silly talk, instead of putting your trust in the Führer."

"We were dumb enough to believe all he said earlier. But since Dad nearly froze to death in Russia in '41 because they didn't have enough clothes to keep them warm, while the big shots went around in thick fur coats, and since my brother was killed in the trap of Stalingrad because the Führer didn't rescue them, we've begun to see the light." She got up from her milking stool and came across to him. "Do you think they're just horror tales, what Dad heard them saying last night with his own ears?" She whispered, as if afraid of being overheard. "Do you know what sort they are, these black death's-head knights? They go all over the country and capture the men who won't join the home guards or the soldiers who have left their regiments. They shoot them dead or string them up and no trial or anything. And they talked about Buchenwald. . . . Dad, he was quite sick when he came back upstairs."

"Oh, men always bounce and swagger like that when they're drunk. I don't believe a word of it."

"Then you're either dumb or dunderheaded."

"Ho-ho! Listen to who's talking!"

"Shut up, Mister Big!"

"You think I'd let a little village bumpkin like you tell me what to believe?"

"I'm a year older than you, don't forget, and I know what's what," she retorted heatedly. "But sensible folk can't talk with the likes of you." She went back to her milking stool. Wow! They had really quarreled now.

After milking, they sat themselves crossly at opposite ends of the long table in the kitchen and spooned down their porridge in dogged silence; neither of them enjoyed it. Frau Franke was shoving her pots and pans around on the fire, making a bad-tempered clatter. "Dad had to go off," she said.

"Aunt Frieda sent over for him from Bretterode, said she must speak to him right away."

"I'll go up and waken the gentlemen then," Till said. "It's seven already, and if they don't leave soon, we'll never get anything done on the potatoes today."

"Do that," said Frau Franke. "Two of them are sleeping in the room above; the other two in the hayloft."

Till went up and knocked, at first discreetly, then more loudly on the door of the spare room. Finally he took his courage in both hands and walked straight in. The room looked like a battlefield. Pieces of uniform, belts, and riding boots lay strewn among fragments of broken bottles all over the floor.

"Heil Hitler!" said Till, with upraised arm.

A swollen face rolled over toward him among the bedclothes. "Get out of here, you sod!" a hoarse voice shouted.

"Excuse me, I thought you wanted to be wakened early," said Till, "since you ordered the trap for six prompt. It's been ready this past hour, and we need the horses for the planting."

"We don't care about your planting. Shut your mouth. Scram!" What a vicious temper, thought Till. He clicked his heels and turned to go.

"Stop!" the voice roared behind him. "Fritz! Fritz!" A grumble came from the other bed. "Wake up, Fritz; we must get going."

A head with tousled blond hair emerged from the pillows. "Oh, my head!" groaned the man. "Daylight already!"

"You're telling me!" said the other. Then to Till: "Why didn't you wake us at the right time? Look sharp; hot water for shaving! Breakfast in half an hour! Then your father'll take us to Buchberg. Get it?"

"The farmer had to go away," said Till. He glanced quickly at the insignia on the tunic that lay on the floor beside the bed. "I shall take you, Herr Sturmführer." There was no point

103

in giving explanations. It didn't matter if they thought he was the son of the house.

The captain was already out of bed; he went to the window in his underclothes, opened it, and gave a whistle. "Come over and get shaved!" he yelled when an answering whistle came from the hayloft. Before Till closed the door behind him, he overheard a few words that were not intended for his ears. "We must see to Armin; the beggar knows too much." Then the other voice: "We'll take care of it."

What was the meaning of that, Till wondered. Were they really going around shooting people without court-martial and everything? Who was the Armin they were talking about?

When he entered the kitchen, he said, "They want hot water for shaving and breakfast in half an hour. Then they'll be off."

"Where to? And who's going to take them?"

"I will if there's no one else. They want to get to Buchberg. Is it far?"

"A good hour. Across the north bridge, then turn right and take the road up through the wood. From the top you'll see the village of Buchberg. Watch out and don't sweat the guts out of the horses on the way up."

Till nodded. No one needed to tell him how to handle horses. He said, "If we get away at eight, I can be back here not long after ten, and then off we go to start with the potato planting."

When he had taken the hot water up, he went to speak to Dorle, who had gone to the henhouse. "You haven't once asked about the lambs," he said, in a hurt voice. "Go on over and see them for yourself, and take Bluebeard with you. Otherwise, he'll run after me in the trap."

"All right, all right. Just be on your way with your SS friends, that's all. Watch they don't string you up on some tree for helping the farmers instead of lying in a trench with a hand grenade, waiting for the Yanks."

"Don't talk nonsense. They've got to report somewhere, and as their car's broken down, we must help them."

Dorle did not deign to answer him. She gathered the eggs out of the nests and then began to clean the perches and the board underneath—not an attractive occupation. She wrinkled up her freckled nose, and this made her look even more unfriendly. Pigheaded thing! thought Till. He, too, had not been pleased by the way the men were behaving—the appalling state of the room, their coarse language, the threatening tone in which they had spoken about Armin. But he'd rather have bitten off his tongue than admit this to Dorle. Probably they had had a lot to drink during the night. But the old Germanic warriors had also knocked back quantities of mead when they had done battle, and the Vikings too! You couldn't expect men like that to act as if they were in a kindergarten.

There was a smell of frying bacon in the kitchen. Eggs were swimming like great startled eyes in the pan; Frau Franke was making chipped potatoes in another. At last the men made their appearance; there were, besides the captain, two sergeants in tight-fitting tunics, each with a row of medals—well-built men with broad shoulders, self-confident as bullfighters. Their eyes were still a little puffed from the previous night's carousing, but under the pallor of the hangover their faces were healthy and tanned. The captain was a darker type with a rather yellow complexion, cold, intelligent eyes, a compressed mouth, and a nose like a hawk's beak. "Heil Hitler!" They addressed the housewife in a condescending way, as befits great lords when speaking to the lower orders. Then the fourth one came in; a young boy, eighteen at the most, thought Till. He still had no rank and not a single medal, but Till's eyes shown when he looked at him. This, at last, was the sort of storm trooper he had always imagined: a young

Nordic god in his black tunic, tall and slim, with a noble, finely shaped head and thoughtful gray eyes. Beside him, the two sergeants looked like slaughter-house men. He was the only one of the four who greeted Till, with a swift glance.

"Shove the spuds over, Armin," said the captain when they had sat down to table, and the young man got up, went over to the fire, and brought the pan that had been standing on the hot plate. He had the easy movements of a good rider or fencer. Something about him reminded Till of his beloved troop leader, Karl. What had the captain called him? Armin? Till suddenly felt hot all over. Was he the Armin who knew too much? At once he swore allegiance to him, as a squire to his knight.

He tried to overcome the anxiety of waiting by fetching kindling from outside and laying it on the hearth. Each time he came into the kitchen, he looked at the young man, and when their glances met, a surge of admiration and indefinable sorrow flowed through Till's heart.

The man whom the captain had called Fritz was cursing the ersatz coffee that Frau Franke had set before them. "That miserable slop! Look here, Missus! We're not used to this kind of thing. Let's have some real coffee, and look sharp about it."

"Real coffee? Where would I get it?" Frau Franke asked.

"Don't give me that story. All you farmers have coffee in the house, what with your underhand dealings, bartering this for that. Perhaps you'd like us to search the house, eh?"

"Leave her alone, Fritz; it's too late now. Whether the Yanks come or not, Missus, we'll be back. We have long memories, I'm telling you."

Frau Franke was frightened. Till could tell that just by looking at her. Her hands were shaking and her forehead was beaded with sweat. You had to be careful with the SS, even now. But Till knew that she would not willingly give them one single bean of her precious coffee. Dorle's obstinacy had been inherited from her mother.

He went out to see to the horses, patting their necks and giving them a little more oats. He had sent Bluebeard to the henhouse with Dorle and now heard him howling and scratching at the door. It was enough to drive you crazy—this fine, misty morning wasted! They sat there in the kitchen eating up everything like a swarm of locusts and smoking cigarettes while the fields remained unplanted.

It was not until half-past eight that they finally came out of the house. Till climbed up on the driver's seat and moved to make room for the young soldier, who, at a sign from the captain, climbed up beside him. The other three settled themselves as comfortably as possible in the trap. "Come on, get moving," cried Fritz. "We've no time to lose." You would think it was Till who had kept them waiting and not the other way around. His disillusionment with this kind of élite grew from one minute to the next. But when he saw Dorle's cross face peeping around the henhouse door, he affected a gay smile, as if he were going on a picnic. "Stay here, Bluebeard!" he shouted, as he set the horses in motion. Dorle hung on to the dog's collar; he was nearly throttling himself in his efforts to break loose and run after Till.

"Your father went away because he didn't want to drive us, lad!" Dorle heard one of the men shouting at Till. "Give him our regards, and tell him not to be surprised if one of these fine days he finds his farm on fire."

"Rabble of peasants!" another voice snarled. "Now put on some speed, young fellow!"

If they thought Till would make the horses trot over the cobbles of the city streets, they were much mistaken. Only when the bridge lay behind them and they came to the smooth main road, did he loosen the reins. The men were talking so much that for a while they paid no attention to the comfortable, leisurely trot of the heavy horses. Once one of them lifted his head and looked up at the impenetrable gray of the sky, in which they could hear squadrons of bombers flying.

"Do they never give alarms in this rotten hole?" he asked.

"Of course they do," said Till. "But since yesterday there has been no all clear. As a matter of fact, I should not be on the road with the trap like this."

"Leave that to us." And again they began talking among themselves. Till pricked up his ears, trying to catch something of what they were saying.

"If only we get the civilian clothes!" This must be the one they called Günther, a chap with prize-fighter shoulders and a Hitler-like forelock, only blond. "Maybe they've recruited your cousin for the home guards. In which case, we're done for."

Fritz laughed. "Not him! He's 'reserved.' He sits safely in the clerks' office at the town hall."

"Well, let's hope he's got the bikes and the fuel."

"Sure as death. And as for the papers, he has all the forms and rubber stamps and everything we need. It's all arranged."

"Well, let's see the map a minute. Now tomorrow we go to Leipzig. And until the Yanks arrive . . ."

"Careful!"

They now spoke more softly, and the sound of the horses' hoofs drowned the rest of their talk. Till was disturbed. Were these men on the run after having executed others? He cast a despairing glance at Armin, but he had just then turned around and was addressing the captain in the correct military way. "May I once more venture to inquire when and where I may set out for Jena, sir?"

"Shut up, Armin. Don't ask questions of the SS. Questions are unhealthy."

Again there was whispering from behind.

"What's your name?" asked Armin.

"Till Lorenz." The two youths looked at one another. Suddenly, it flashed upon Till that what the two of them would say aloud now was intended for the others to hear.

"Where I live it looks just as it does here," said Armin. "In Baden. Only there's more pinewood there and the foothills of the Black Forest are somewhat higher. You were born and went to school here, I suppose."

"No," replied Till. "We've been here only a few days. My father . . ." Armin cast him a warning glance. "We live in the parsonage."

"Oh, really?"

"Yes. The pastor is a friend of ours. The Frankes are his neighbors. I just help them out. So you are from Baden?"

"Yes. My father taught at the Freiburg High School. He was killed in battle in '43. We always lived out in the country, on a small estate belonging to my mother's parents. And every morning my father and I traveled into Freiburg on the little local train. Those were good days!"

"And then what?"

"Last spring, the final exam. Then a year of labor conscription. And this February I was called up for the SS."

"Called up? I thought they were all volunteers?"

"Not any more." Armin threw a quick look at the men behind. They were completely absorbed in their talk. He pulled out his handkerchief and wiped his nose. "Let me drive for a bit," he said. "It's a long time since I felt a pair of reins in my hands."

Till gave him the reins. He would have done anything the young man asked him. Armin took the reins in his slim, long-fingered hands, and as their fingers touched, Till felt something pressed into his hand. "Not bad horses," said Armin. "A bit heavy for a trap, but fine for farm work. Can you ride?"

Till nodded and slipped into the pocket of his leather shorts the letter that Armin had just given him. "We had riding lessons in the H.J. What about you?"

"I think I could ride a horse before I could run almost." And then Armin whispered, "The letter's for my mother. Will you see to it that she gets it somehow, when it's all over?"

"Will it soon . . . be over?" asked Till, his heart slogging like a hammer against his ribs.

"It's all over now," said Armin. Then, loud again: "The near horse has a buckle loose. You must see to it before you start back." And, in the faintest whisper: "I'm not going on with *them*."

Till felt he now ought to say something: say thank you for the precious gift of trust, something that Armin could take with him wherever he went. But he was too young and inexperienced to find the words that would express everything that filled his heart to bursting. And yet there was only this one irretrievable moment in which to seal a friendship that could last for this one moment only. At least I ought to warn him, thought Till in desperation. Or does he know? Oh, what can I do?

Armin slowly shook his head. It was as if he said: Don't worry about me.

The wood was now dense. The high, silvery beech trunks rose like columns out of the undergrowth that was already covering the forest floor with green. Among the trunks the last wisps of morning mist were still wavering. It was very lonely up here; no sound of planes, no artillery fire. A roebuck standing in the middle of the road was frightened by the approaching vehicle and fled in long leaps away through the trees.

"Stop!" cried the captain. "If we could bag that, we'd have a wonderful roast! Bring the guns."

Armin brought the horses to a halt and gave back the reins to Till. The three men got out. "A little drink wouldn't do us any harm," said Günther, the strapping one. "Wait a tick. There's still a bottle left in my knapsack. Hennessy, gentlemen! There's nothing like having good connections."

"Come on, Armin!" Fritz said; and to Till, "You wait here."

Till thought: If only Armin would stay here! But he had already jumped down from the driving seat, as limber and graceful as a ballet dancer. He nodded to Till, stroked the near horse's sweating neck, and tightened the loose buckle. "Put the blanket over them; they're overheated," he advised.

"Take care!" called Till imploringly. "The mare bites." He hoped good old Lola would forgive him for slandering her so.

Armin looked up at him. "Thank you, Till," he said. Fritz was waiting for him at the wood's edge.

Till got down and put the blanket over the horses. They were stamping and swinging their tails at the first horseflies. He went a little way along the road, listening to the noises from the wood. The voices died away and then could be heard no more. Why were they going so far into the wood? Were they really after the roebuck? Down below, he could see Buchberg: a large village with red and slate-blue roofs and a pointed church tower. They could have been there within ten minutes and he on his way back home. Smoke curled up out of the chimneys. A dog was barking. In the orchards the fruit trees were blossoming. The mist had almost completely disappeared. Everything lay in a kind of golden haze. It was like a village in a picture, a village in another land where there was no war. Peace? thought Till. He didn't know much about it, except that there were no bombing raids and you always had enough to eat. He had been seven when war broke out. He remembered some remarks overheard from his parents' conversations, things his sister had said. One memory was of a street corner in the city where two women had been standing gossiping. The February day had been so clear that one could see the barracks town on the slopes of the Ettersberg near Weimar in the east, and over the camp buildings rose a column of smoke. He knew that that was Buchenwald, where criminals were kept, the enemies of the German people. That was what he had been taught. And then he had heard one of the women whispering, "Adolf's black hangmen are burning corpses again up there today." And the other replied, "Shut up, Lisa. You'll find yourself there if you're not careful." "Not likely. Not now. The film's over." Over! Just now Armin had said the same word, and suddenly it meant something. Till remembered the conversations at the parsonage. It was not hard to guess that all of them there considered it to be "over," too, except for Aunt Ulrike and the old general. It was as if he had been reading endlessly something written in code and now at last had found the key. If Armin said it was over, then it was over. But how could the Führer allow thousands of people to die every day and their homes and cities to be destroyed, all for a lost cause? The Führer who, as he had been taught from childhood, thought of nothing but the good of his people?

Till was afraid. Anxiety about Armin gripped him by the throat. He felt as if the blood in his veins was suddenly running cold, for even to his unsuspecting nature, it was now obvious what was happening: the civilian clothes that Fritz's cousin had ready; the motorbikes; the faked papers they had hinted at. They must have shot people who no longer wanted to sacrifice themselves for a lost war; and now they themselves were making a getaway. What dreadful things did they have on their consciences that they must disappear before the enemy arrived? What did Armin know about them? If somebody knew too much, then he must be silenced. It was like a burning wheel turning in Till's head. His hands were damp with sweat. Something inside his stomach twisted and knotted. He was sick at the side of the road.

Afterwards, he went back to the horses, stroked their smooth necks, and combed their long forelocks with his fingers. Time crawled by.

Then two shots rang out from the depths of the wood, and immediately afterwards the roebuck dashed across the road again, unhurt. The scream of a jay, sharp and clear, shrilled out of the impenetrable thickets of the wood. Then stillness . . .

For a second Till stood transfixed. Then he blindly tore the blanket off the horses' backs, clambered up on the driver's seat, released the brake, and turned the trap. Away, if he could only get away! The horses were glad to trot homeward, especially as the road now went downhill; they set off at a spanking pace. Someone came running out of the wood and shouted something after Till. He gave a quick look back; it was Fritz, waving his arms. A bullet whistled over Till's ducked head. And then he was around the bend in the road.

Later he could not remember how he had spent the rest of the day; he only recalled that Dorle had kept eying him from a distance like a cat watching a dog. She didn't ask any questions. They were still not on speaking terms.

Twilight was already falling as he walked home along the riverbank. But instead of turning into the parsonage garden, he went over the little bridge and then along the other bank of the river that ran dimly among the willow plots. He wanted to get away, to see no one, to be asked no questions. From the pond came the endless croaking of the frogs, and above there was the endless drone of bombers. Across the drab gray of the western sky lay a slash of sulfur yellow, which slowly faded and finally disappeared.

If I could only creep into my sleeping bag without anyone seeing me, he thought. But how could he sleep when such a dreadful thing had happened? Armin was dead. They had shot him because he wouldn't run away with them and because he knew too much. Not for a moment did Till doubt that he was dead—fair Balder murdered by black-browed Loki, the enemy of the gods.

He walked slowly back to the bridge. A shadow dashed toward him. Bluebeard jumped up at him, barking loudly in an ecstasy of delight at seeing him again after their long separation.

"Till!" shouted someone. It was Karin's voice. "I went to the Frankes to see where you were. Frau Franke told me you'd been gone an hour. Where've you been?"

"Nowhere," said Till; his tongue felt thick and heavy as a lump of clay in his mouth. He went over the bridge to join his sister in the garden.

"Mother was worried," she said. He didn't reply. "What is it? Tell me!"

"It's nothing," said Till. His hand searched for his handkerchief in the pocket of his leather shorts, felt the envelope that was tucked away there, and his heart overflowed with grief.

"You don't go wandering around for hours in the dark for nothing. D'you think we don't know you drove the storm troopers in the trap today? Did they do anything to you, Till? Till, speak to me!"

He shook his head; he gave up trying to get his handkerchief and just stood there, his hands hanging helplessly by his sides. Karin gave him her handkerchief and waited patiently while he blew his nose and wiped his face. "Why . . . why didn't you tell me?" he burst out finally.

"Till," his sister said gently. "You know quite well that you wouldn't listen whenever we made an attempt to open your eyes to the truth." Karin sighed. She wished one of her parents—or even better, both of them—was there to help her in this difficult conversation, which she had always known must come one day. "It was even better that you should not know exactly what we thought."

"I know what you thought, all right," said Till bitterly. "That I was a stupid schoolkid that couldn't be told anything. Or perhaps even that I would give you away."

"Nonsense, none of us ever thought that, even though it did happen in other families. We would only have involved you in all kinds of conflicts if we had let you see too clearly what our opinions were. Didn't they ask you in school and at your H.J. meetings if perhaps your parents listened to the news from foreign radio stations, if they had doubts about the Führer and the final triumph of Germany's rightful cause?"

"Not as directly as all that, but in a way you are right," Till had to admit.

"You see. And wouldn't it have been terrible for you either to betray your family or to have to lie? There was no choice for us; we had to let you go your own way, just as one must not call and wake a sleepwalker who is balancing at the edge of a roof."

"But I believed it all so firmly!" Till groaned. Karin laid an arm around his shoulders, and once again he was the little brother who used to run to her when he'd scraped his knee or fallen and cut his remarkably tough skull; but this time it was his heart that was hurt.

"If you can, try to tell me what happened with the SS men," Karin said cautiously.

Till pulled the crumpled letter out of his pocket and smoothed it with Karin's clean hanky. "They shot him," he said. "I have to send this letter to his mother when the mail starts again."

Slowly, with many a pause, it all came out. Karin led him to the bench under the weeping willow. He sat stiffly upright, with his hands between his knees. "He is dead," he kept saying. "Armin is dead. They shot him because he knew too many things about them, because he didn't want to go with them and do what they were going to do. It was not the roebuck they went to hunt in the woods; they just said that so's they could take their guns with them. They shot Armin, and now he's lying dead up there somewhere. Promise me, Karin, that tomorrow morning we'll go up there with the pastor and find him and bury him, so I can tell his . . . where . . ." He couldn't go on. His voice was choked.

"Tomorrow morning?" Karin cried. "Why wait until morning, Till? Are you quite certain that he's really dead? He might still be alive and in need of help. Here we've been sitting talking and wasting time! Run to the Frankes at once and ask them if you can borrow the horses. I'll go in and get Helmut and the first-aid box. And we must let Mother know."

The wood was a woolly gray mass of darkness. The last quarter of the spring moon had still not risen. Heavy clouds were racing over the night sky. It was raining softly.

"Here," said Till. "It must have been here. It was only about a hundred yards after the bend in the road, just before it begins going downhill again to Buchberg." Now the night maneuvers he had taken part in with the H.J. stood him in good stead. He stopped the trap. They got down. "Into the wood on the right!" Till was holding Bluebeard firmly on the leash. Though he was not trained for it, they could depend on his barking if he found a body, alive or dead.

The two flashlights they had brought with them illuminated every step they took through the wood. Bluebeard was sniffing excitedly at last year's foliage. "Find him, Bluebeard, find him!" Till urged him on. "Oh, what an ass I was not to think that he might still be alive!"

"Don't talk so much, Till; that won't do any good now,"

his sister said. "Ow! I nearly fell over something. What's that down there?"

It was a bottle. An empty brandy bottle.

"Let's see!" cried Till, shining his torch on the label. "Hennessy! That must be the bottle the SS men had. I heard Günther say that name."

"If they drank a whole bottle in such a short time," said Lobelius, "then perhaps your friend Armin got away from them after all." Until then he had not had much hope. He knew that the SS were specialists in human slaughter, but he hadn't said anything about that.

Bluebeard was pulling on the leash, his hackles raised. Suddenly he barked sharply in a new, frightened tone. Among the low bushes lay a long shadow that the dog was trying to reach, darker than the darkness surrounding it.

"Shine a light!" said Karin and kneeled down. A young man's white face was illuminated by the ray of the flashlight; the eyes shut, the whole body motionless, lifeless.

"Dead," moaned Till. "I knew it."

"Let's make sure." Karin's fingers touched Armin's forehead, temples, neck. "No shot in the neck," she whispered. Then she took his hand, sought the pulse, and could feel nothing. Helmut and Till waited what seemed to them an endless time. Karin shook her head. She shoved her hand under Armin's back and drew it out again; the hand was wet and sticky. He was lying in a pool of blood. "Bring the light closer!" Then she found another wet patch in front, on the left side under the collarbone.

She tried to remember everything she had seen and learned in her father's practice. He was a women's doctor, but lately they had had some badly wounded men brought in after air raids. She laid her head on Armin's chest and listened. "Keep Bluebeard quiet, Till. I can't hear anything with him fussing around." Seconds passed. "Give me your hand, Helmut. Put it here. . . . He's still breathing, isn't he? If only I had a stethoscope! But I think . . . I'm sure I can hear the heart beating too. Very faintly . . ."

She raised her head and looked at Helmut, who was kneeling beside her on the ground. "He seems to be still alive," he said.

"Then we must get him to a doctor, to the hospital, as quickly as possible."

"But how shall we get him into the trap?"

"Hurry!" Till pleaded. "Please hurry."

"Wait. We must be careful. We don't want to start him bleeding again. He's lost enough blood already." She thought for a moment. In the beam of the flashlight her face looked stern and much older. "If only I knew more about these things!" she murmured sadly.

"Perhaps if we carried him in the horse blanket?" Lobelius proposed. "That's what we used to do at the front when there were no stretchers. Run and get one from the trap, Till." Till dashed away, followed by Bluebeard. Once he stumbled over a root and knocked his head against a beech trunk, but he jumped up again and ran on; he was back with the blanket within a few minutes.

Karin knew only too well how dangerous it is to move someone severely wounded, but there was nothing else to do. If the boy was not attended to by a doctor soon, he wouldn't have a chance.

"You take the legs, Till. Slowly, slowly! There. Helmut, take the shoulders. I'll push the blanket underneath. And now watch your steps."

"Are you sure he's still alive?" asked Till.

"Yes," said Karin. "I don't understand why they left him lying here without making sure that he was dead."

"They were drunk and in a hurry," said Lobelius. "The young man apparently fell over at once, or perhaps he deliberately threw himself down as quickly as possible after the shots. They must have thought that in any case he would bleed to death if he was not already dead. There was no one likely to come soon as far into the wood as this."

They lifted him into the trap. Till took the reins, and they started off down the road to Eberstein. When they had left the wood behind, it grew lighter. A few stars were blinking through the racing clouds. It had stopped raining. As on the previous night, the red glow of fires could be seen all around the horizon, a soft, almost tender red in the mist that had begun to rise again.

At the hospital they asked for Sister Scholastica. She appeared after a few moments; her coif was a little on one side, but she smiled at Lobelius as if it were the most natural thing on earth to be brought out of her cell in the middle of the night; she had left the chapel only half an hour before, when she had said her evening prayer.

Lobelius explained to her what had happened, and they helped her to place Armin on a stretcher and take him into the operating theater. He stirred once and groaned faintly. Sister Scholastica gave him an injection and asked Till to tell the night sister in the ward to ring for the doctor at once. Then she carefully examined the soldier's black tunic. "Help me to take it off, please," she said to Karin. "When the Americans come, I don't want any SS tunics in the place." She went through Armin's pockets and gave the pastor his paybook. Then she rolled back his sleeves, ran her finger over the smooth young skin, and gave a satisfied nod. He had still not been tattooed with the SS symbols.

"I'll put him in a private room," the nun said.

Lobelius asked, "Shall I take the tunic with me and throw it in the river?"

"I'll see to it myself, Herr Pastor," said Sister Scholastica. "Into the boiler furnace with it. The doctor will soon be here. I'll pass on your information to him."

"Thank you, Sister. I'll inquire tomorrow morning—I mean this morning—how things are going."

However, it was not Lobelius but Till who at five o'clock in the morning came to the door of the convent. The doorkeeper told him to go away. Who'd ever heard of visits at such an early hour? "I just want to know if he's still alive," he said in such a piteous voice that the stern guardian at the door felt she could not refuse him. She did not let him in, but telephoned to the ward and reported to him through her little sliding window what she had learned from the night sister. The wounded soldier had still not come out of the anesthetic. His heart and lungs were untouched. Only after the doctor's next visit could more detailed news be given. Till had to be satisfied with that.

After he had gone swimming, he went to work as usual. Wenzel too had reappeared, and Herr Franke had returned from his sister's the evening before. Not one word was spoken about the Blackshirts' visit. Only Dorle couldn't keep herself from asking about the young soldier who had had an accident in the wood and whom they had taken to the hospital in the trap. "He's better," said Till curtly; but privately he thought it was nice of her to have asked after Armin. Later perhaps he would tell her the truth.

It was a difficult day. The Frankes were worrying about whether the SS men would come back and set fire to their farm as they had threatened. People still had an almost superstitious fear of the SS. Wenzel hardly said a word all day; he looked as if he had seen a ghost—the phantom death's-head of Warsaw.

That Saturday morning the baron made his appearance at the parsonage, not in the uniform of a Brownshirt leader, but in civilian clothes, with riding boots, his silver-mounted riding crop in his hand, his monocle in his left eye. He kissed the hands of Fräulein Lobelius and Frau Lorenz, gave Karin a little bow, and greeted Martha as he passed her in the hall with an affable nod.

"Just had to come and have a word with the old aunts," he said. "Marvelous, the way they've been working in the garden. Most healthy occupation for old ladies. A pity your other tenants have dug themselves in so, Herr Pastor; in your place I wouldn't have it. These refugees! Give them an inch and they'll take a yard. . . ."

"I expect your own house is as full up as the parsonage, Herr von Reichau?" Karin asked innocently.

"Pardon me? Oh, we manage, you know. Now this is the reason for my visit, dear Lobelius. I'm expecting a real hard-punching sermon from you tomorrow." He slapped the pastor on the shoulder. "Resistance to the last man! Better an honorable defeat than a shameful surrender. No compromise, no giving-in, as our great Goethe said somewhere or other."

"Schiller." Karin gently corrected him. "*The Maid of Orleans.*"

"Indeed? Thank you! And then, my dear Lobelius, perhaps you can slip in a word that I don't want to see any white flags out in Eberstein. I should consider such an action as a betrayal of the fatherland. If it comes to them from the pulpit, you know, it makes a greater impression. You follow me?"

"Entirely, Herr Baron," said Lobelius. "But I don't see what all that has to do with my sermon. After all, during the last few years we've always been told that the pulpit is no place for politics."

Karin's eyes sparkled at him. Bravo, Helmut! Aunt Ulrike looked down at her hands in some embarrassment. Carola Lorenz could not suppress a faint smile, which she hid tactfully in her handkerchief.

The baron's monocle had jumped out of his eye, and without it he didn't look very intelligent. "Well," he said, slapping his boots with his riding stock. "Just as you like, my dear pastor. Far be it from me to exert any influence upon you. Only in your own interests. . . . Ladies, I wish you good day." A stiff bow. Two steps to the door. Half turn right, arm stiffly raised, and "Heil Hitler!"

"*Auf Wiedersehen*, Herr Baron," said Lobelius and conducted his visitor to the front door.

That was probably the last "Heil Hitler" that was ever heard in Eberstein. The local Party bosses, among them Martha's uncle, had left the town for the second time. And this time it was for good.

During the night, when planes flew eastward for hours, Carola sat in the cellar beside Till's sleeping bag for a while. Many thoughts passed through her head as she gazed at her sleeping son. She couldn't tell whether the shadows that sometimes moved over his face came from the flickering candlelight or from his own restless dreams. What sort of questions was he likely to ask her—soon, perhaps; perhaps much later—and how would she and Franz explain to him what he had only just begun to understand? Once he stirred, opened his eyes, and looked at her as if her face were a strange landscape in which he had lost his way. "Has Karin told you everything?" he asked at last. She replied, "Yes, Till. Now go to sleep again." He raised his eyebrows, pressed his lips together, turned his face to the wall, and fell asleep again at once.

In the pastor's corner Karin and Lobelius were sitting together talking in whispers about the sermon that he had to give in the morning. But on that Sunday, the first after Easter, it was impossible to hold a service because there still was a constant state of alert. For the same reason, they could not go to the neighboring parishes, where Lobelius wanted to baptize two children.

They had a short prayer meeting in the parsonage, attended

by the people in the house and by a few neighbors. After that the family had the day to themselves. Martha went to her aunt, who was badly in need of company and consolation.

Krischan Möller would not be done out of ringing the church bells at least, so for ten minutes the bells of St. Peter's rang out over the little town that lay between war and peace, between life and death, and no one was able to foretell what its fate might be within the next few days or hours.

Twice that Sunday Till tried to get into the hospital to see Armin. The sister at the door began waving him away as soon as she saw him coming up the steps. No visits—not today, at any rate. But at least she let him sit in the lobby, waiting for Lobelius who had to attend to some badly wounded home-guard men and two Hitler Youths who had been brought to the hospital early that morning. Then he had looked in briefly on Lotte and Armin.

"He's still weak from loss of blood," he told Till. "Everything possible has been done for him. You can do nothing now for your friend but possess your soul in patience. Be reasonable, Till, and go back to the Frankes. The cows need to be milked and foddered even on Sundays."

"If I can't see Armin, I may as well go to the cows," said Till. "But I'll come back this evening, Sister."

"I'd miss you if you didn't," replied the doorkeeper good-naturedly.

Sunday and Monday passed. A week had gone by since Easter Monday. What did time mean nowadays? It was something quite indefinable, something that had lost all firmness of outline. A week now could seem as long as a year, and whole years could be swallowed up in a minute.

If everyone in the parsonage hadn't had so much to do, the waiting would have been unbearable. Carola helped in the house and in the kitchen; she had to look after her animals, to wash and iron and mend for herself and for her children, those children who were daily growing farther and farther away from her, developing their own destinies.

Late on Monday night another call came through from the city. "Carola!" That voice was the core of her existence, that was what would remain when the children had gone their own ways. But today Franz Lorenz's voice sounded heavy-spirited. Nothing new had happened in the city either, but the atmosphere had changed. The grumblings of the distant storm were now more and more audible; the war, which had held off for days, like a cat playing with a mouse, was again fearfully close. One more good night, perhaps farewell.

✦ *Chapter Six* ✦

On Tuesday morning it didn't take much perception to see the signs of overstrained nerves in the parsonage.

The old ladies from East Prussia came upstairs and roundly declared that Frau Lorenz's lambs had been running over their radish bed and that Frau Lübzin's little Edgar had been blowing his tin trumpet for over an hour; its piercing tones could not longer be endured. When they had politely complained about the noise, Frau Lübzin had retorted that they had no right to deprive the poor little thing of his one bit of pleasure.

A little later Carola, coming out of the henhouse with three eggs in her basket, met Frau Merkel, who expressed her surprise at the Lorenzes' freely laying hens. Hers, she said, had laid hardly anything during the past week; perhaps it was because they were laying in the wrong nest.

"My dear Frau Merkel," said Carola, "my hens are Rhode Island Reds and lay large brown eggs; yours are Leghorns and lay small white ones; so please set your mind at rest about that question." She realized that her tone of voice was not particularly friendly; yet only yesterday she had been reading in Lao-tse: "He who quarrels not, with him no man can quarrel."

"Naturally," said Frau Merkel after glancing at the brown eggs, "poor folk must be content with small eggs."

Carola ran quickly upstairs, angry with Frau Merkel and

angry with herself; angry, too, with Lao-tse, who certainly could never have had to live at such close quarters with others.

Hardly had she got upstairs than a door was slammed in the hall, so hard that the whole place shook, and Frau Dünsing came out of her room and begged for quiet because her husband was not well. But then a second door whammed shut; this was followed by an argument between Frau Merkel and Frau Lübzin. It was about the use of the washhouse, one of the most sensitive spots in all overpopulated houses.

Fräulein Lobelius fluttered about like a flustered bird. Such dreadful language had never reached her maidenly ears before she came to live in Eberstein. It was fortunate that she did not understand most of it. "Fräulein Born!" she pleaded. "Dear Fräulein Born, could you not perhaps . . ."

Martha shut her books and smiled reassuringly at Fräulein Lobelius.

"Whose washday is it today?" she could be heard asking the contestants downstairs. "I thought we'd arranged it to everyone's satisfaction."

It appeared that it was neither Frau Merkel's nor Frau Lübzin's washday, but in fact Frau Wöllner's. But she had put no clothes to soak and had not even come back yet from night duty at the hospital. She really might have let them know, they declared, if she wasn't to use the washhouse when there were folks with little children who had far more washing than a single woman. In short, Frau Merkel had seized the opportunity·and put a tubful of children's clothes to soak. But unfortunately Frau Lübzin had had exactly the same idea and had stuffed the copper boiler full of dirty clothes and lighted the fire underneath. Did they or did they not all have the same rights and wasn't there any justice left in the world for a poor refugee woman who had lost house and home? And to think they were living in a Christian parsonage!

Frau Lübzin had to remove her dirty washing at once from

the copper boiler, screeched Frau Merkel, or she would take it out with her own two hands and bash her over the head with it. In any case, today was Frau Lübzin's day to scrub the hall; perhaps she'd conveniently forgotten that?

It was quite a while before Martha had smoothed things out so that they were at least able to come to an understanding. Would Frau Lübzin have finished her wash by midday? Good. Then Frau Merkel could use the boiler later, on condition that Frau Wöllner didn't claim her rights that day. And Frau Lübzin must then scrub the hall in the afternoon. "It's all so simple," said Martha. "But you must keep to the rules of the house; otherwise it would be impossible for so many people to live peacefully under the same roof. And we all want to do that, don't we? There you are!"

"How do you do it?" asked Karin, when Martha came upstairs again. "You never once lose your temper."

"If I were to lose my temper also, I couldn't calm them down. The women's nerves are on edge the whole time after all they've been through. In fact, they are both quite reasonable souls, but they need to be reminded of that from time to time."

That morning Lobelius had been called so early to visit a few new arrivals at the hospital that he had not wakened Karin but had left a note for her on the kitchen table asking her to meet him later at the town hall. When he had visited the wounded, he found Till and Bluebeard on the steps of the hospital waiting for him in the fresh morning air.

"How is he?" asked Till. "They still won't let me see him."

"Perhaps tomorrow or the day after you'll be able to," Lobelius assured him. "He has been asking the sisters how he got here, and they told him. He asked me to send his regards to you and Karin."

"Why to Karin? He doesn't know her."

"All the same, she led the rescue party."

"That's right. Incidentally, I've been wanting to ask you if it's true that you're going to marry her?"

"That's not an easy question to answer. You know it takes two to make a marriage."

"Hm. One would have to think it over very carefully, because after all it's for life, isn't it? Dorle happened to mention it to me. Don't think I've got anything against it. In fact, it would suit me fine, because then I could come and stay with you in the summer holidays and work at the Frankes'. Dorle and I have made it up again, and I'm awfully fond of the horses."

"The Frankes would certainly be pleased," said Lobelius. "But it's better not to talk about it, Till."

"It's just between us two men, Herr Pastor, of course."

Whereupon Till went off to his work and Lobelius made his way to the town hall.

Meanwhile, Karin was ironing a blouse in the kitchen while her mother was darning Till's socks. "To think we've been here now over a week!" said Carola. "Poor Father!"

"Nurse Ottilie's looking after him very well; don't you worry," replied Karin. "He'll hardly notice the difference. These last few years you've had no time for anything but hens, housework, and sheep."

"To hear you talk, you'd think I did all that just for the fun of it," her mother said. "But as a housewife, you have to do the most important jobs first, whether you like it or not. In a house without servants, you simply can't get into slovenly ways. You have to keep your family well fed and pots from boiling over and burning, to see to it that the house is neat and cozy and that there's a decent meal on the table when your husband comes home hungry from work."

Karin shook her head. "Even if a house isn't absolutely spick-and-span, I think it could be wonderfully cozy if you are happy and don't allow yourself to be worn out by the daily routine. For example, Helmut says it doesn't matter a bit to him if the potatoes are boiled away or the soup burned, as long as his wife has time for him and for their work together. What does a bit of dust in a corner matter if you enjoy each other and the higher things in life to the full? At any rate, that's precisely the sort of thing we mean by a real marriage."

Carola refrained from asking whether Karin considered her parents' marriage to be a real one or not. "That may be all right for a little while," she said. "At least as long as Helmut has, besides his wife, a good cleaning woman like Frau Möller and a secretary like Fräulein Born to help him cope with what you call 'the daily routine.' But try to imagine what it would be like if his wife were one day to have a baby. Such things happen in the most spiritual families, you know. With the arrival of diapers and a yelling infant, I think the higher things in life would have to take a back seat."

"Oh, Mother!" Karin cried reproachfully. "As far as marriage and love are concerned, we're worlds apart! I'd rather not talk about it." She put on the crisp white blouse with one of her mother's prewar suits. "Now I must go to the town hall," she said. "See you later." Even the oldest things seemed to take on an elegant air when she wore them.

Aunt Ulrike came into the kitchen just as Karin was leaving. "Lovely!" exclaimed the canoness, looking after her delightedly. "'May love's first happy hours blossom always like spring flowers!' It's the one consolation I have in these dismal days, to see the two of them so happy. I hope you don't mind my saying that? What would an old maid like me know about love? Only what I read about in books. Whereas you, Frau Lorenz, are certainly very familiar with this aspect of human relations, I'm sure."

"You do me too much honor," said Carola. "All the more

since my daughter has just told me that our opinions on the subject are worlds apart."

She'd landed herself in a nice situation now! There was a lot she could say about young love and its occasional bypaths, and even these bypaths would presumably have their attractions for Ulrike Lobelius. Poor thing! thought Carola. Imagine knowing love only from books! Carola would have liked to take her in her arms. But for the moment she could say nothing, since it would be indiscreet to discuss Karin's feelings. However, she succeeded in bringing the talk around to less risky themes, namely, what a relief it was not to have to worry about the potatoes; that yesterday Till had brought home half a pound of butter and a bag of flour; and that he was so good about seeing that the animals had enough feed. For the rest of the afternoon Aunt Ulrike sang Till's praises. Since Till's experiences with the SS men, she loved him all the more. No one could understand better than she did his deep disillusionment. When she heard that Till had taken down from the wall his picture of the Führer, she felt that in her old heart, too, a once worshiped image had started to fade.

That evening after supper the general came upstairs to find out what Lobelius had heard at the town hall. In the morning a captain had moved in there with his staff, declared himself to be the commandant of Eberstein, and told the mayor, Herr Barner, that the civilian authorities must from now on consider themselves subject to the commandant's orders.

"That means that Eberstein will be defended," the general said.

"Defended to the last man. That is the official statement," Lobelius confirmed. "It's scarcely believable. The command came from the Führer's headquarters; not only every town and city, but also every small village must hold out as long as possible, in order to gain time. But why? Last night they blew up the railway bridge here. Tonight the south bridge, over which the enemy will presumably enter the town, will be mined. In the town park the resistance men are digging trenches. Tomorrow morning at the very latest there should be warning of an enemy attack."

"What bungling amateurs!" the general cried bitterly. "For months now I've been bombarding the Führer's headquarters with strategic plans. Why don't they make use of us old professionals, who have learned the fundamentals of the craft of war? Instead of concentrating all their forces in one place, these fools are dispersing them and making useless sacrifices of towns and villages." He shook his head, and Karin thought, with a gasp of terror, that his face suddenly looked like the death-mask of Frederick the Great of Prussia.

"What was that you said before, Herr Pastor?" asked Till. "They're going to dynamite the south bridge? Are they out of their minds? How are we going to get to our fields if they do? Over the north bridge, I suppose, and then trail all around the town, because we have so much time to spare! I must tell that to Dorle."

"She can't do anything about it."

Till said, "I'm going over there again tonight. Kathi will be calving any time now, and we all have to take turns sitting up with her in the byre. Don't worry, Mother. The Frankes' cellar is right next to the cow barn, and it's deeper and safer than the one you have here. Good night, all! We'll meet again tomorrow evening."

"And what if there's warning of an enemy attack?" asked Carola.

"Then I'll be just as well off at the Frankes' as here."

Karin shook her head at her departing brother. "Only one week ago he was babbling about blowing up bridges, as if it were his favorite hobby," she said when he had left them. "And now he's furious because it interferes with the potato planting."

Carola wanted to know if Lobelius had heard anything about the situation in Erfurt while he was at the town hall.

"Nothing but unconfirmed rumors," he said. "At any rate, the town still seems to be unoccupied. It looks as if they'll come here first. Apparently a section of the American forces has left Gotha and is moving directly to the north." Then he turned to the general. "May I escort you downstairs now, Excellency?" He added, alarmed, "Perhaps you should lie down for a little while."

When he came up again, he went to the window and cautiously drew aside a corner of the blackout. "A real pea-souper," he said. "Perhaps they won't be able to find us in this mist." The fog was even thicker than it had been in the last few days.

"Why don't we gather everything that we'll need in the cellar in the case of enemy attack," Karin proposed. "Food for twenty-four hours, pillows, blankets, and so on, and above all, a big Thermos full of hot coffee."

"Go and collect all the Thermoses in the place," suggested Carola, "so that we can make sufficient coffee for everyone in the house."

"Yes. And then we'll lie down and try to get a couple of hours' sleep in the cellar because this droning sounds heavier than ever."

And indeed it didn't stop all night. The bomber squadrons roared ceaselessly over the blanket of fog toward the east, and the artillery fire hardly stopped for a moment. Things seemed to be getting really serious.

That night spent in the cellar was not a restful one, but all of them, including the children luckily, were now so weary that they could have slept through anything.

Wednesday, the eleventh of April, was dawning gray and cold through the narrow slit of the high cellar window when Carola stood up, stretched, and went to see to her animals, so that they would be provided for before the warning of enemy attack was sounded. To her alarm she found that Traude was restless and her udder thick and hard. A less suitable day for lambing could hardly have been chosen, thought Carola. Here the sheep was in labor, and over at the Frankes' it was the cow! But she betrayed none of her anxiety when Karin and Lobelius came in and helped her to put down fresh straw, bring clover from the shed, and tether Schirin in the meadow, where she would be safer with her lambs than in the thatched sheeppen. "What about Traude?" asked Karin. "Oh, we better leave her here. It's just possible that . . ." Carola got no further, for at that moment the five-minute-long alarm sounded through the stillness of the morning—the warning of enemy attack that they had been waiting for these last ten days. It was exactly seven minutes past six.

They took down to the cellar everything they had prepared the evening before. Karin and Lobelius stayed down there, while the rest of the household, wakened out of restless sleep by the howling of the siren, ran about trying to get ready for the next twenty-four hours. Lobelius sat next to Frau Wöllner and spoke softly to her. "As soon as it's all over, I shall try to get transport and a pass for you so that you can get to Buchenwald."

Karin sat between her mother and Martha Born, who meanwhile had wakened Fräulein Lobelius and brought her some breakfast. "The pastor and I promised the mayor to go to him at the town hall when there was warning of enemy attack," Karin whispered to her. "I don't like having to leave Aunt Ulrike and my mother, especially when Till isn't here. But there's nothing else for it. I am glad you will be here, Martha."

"And I'm glad to have your mother and Frau Wöllner here with me," said Martha. "If necessary, they can help me to keep the others calm. I'm most worried about the general.

He and his wife are wonderfully self-possessed, but if he has a heart attack, I really don't know what I should do."

"I hope everything will be all right. Wait! We still have a bottle of cognac in our box. It ought to be here, where you can get at it easily. I'll tell my mother."

Upstairs the doorbell rang. Lobelius signed to Karin; she swiftly pressed Martha's hand. As unobtrusively as possible the two of them went upstairs, followed by Carola. "Take the cognac down to the cellar, Mother," said Karin, as they were saying good-by at the door.

She held her tightly in her arms for a second. "Good luck. Everything will be all right. What a good thing Father doesn't know Eberstein is being defended!" She kissed her mother. "In a few hours it'll be all over."

The streets were totally dead as they went with the bailiff to the town hall. Only now and then they saw someone peeping out and waving to them through a half-open door or through the bars of a cellar window.

Outside the town-hall steps soldiers had set up a field telephone and a radio set. Orderlies kept running into the town hall and out again, to jump on motorbikes and roar away. A few home-guard men stood around waiting for orders. They had been called in during the night.

"The Yanks are close to the town on three sides," one of them whispered to Lobelius. "They have just signaled that our troops should withdraw and a white flag be hoisted on the town hall; otherwise in twenty minutes they'll begin their bombardment. Last night—" he looked cautiously about him and spoke with his hand in front of his mouth—"last night they put a mine under the south bridge, but they say the first tank is across the bridge and the thing hasn't gone off."

"Thank goodness!" said Lobelius. "God be with you, men."

"Thank you, Herr Pastor," they murmured, pulling at their caps. "We'll need it!"

The bailiff led Karin and Lobelius down some steps, deep into the public air-raid shelter. "The mayor asked me to say, would you mind waiting here until he calls for you. I'm going to let him know you're here. If the captain doesn't soon clear out with his soldiers, Herr Pastor, and the Americans begin their artillery bombardment, then we are done for."

In the deep, vaulted cellar women were sitting on mattresses and feather beds with all their movable belongings piled up around them. A few babies were sleeping on pillows and blankets. There was not one man to be seen. The older children were playing hide-and-seek behind the pillars; their laughter and shouting re-echoed from the groined arches, their shadows danced in the light of a flickering candle like ghosts flitting across the ancient gray walls.

"Will you be staying down here with us, Herr Pastor?" one of the women asked, and they all looked at him hopefully. He went and sat down beside them. "I have some business with the mayor," he said. "But whenever you need me, I shall be here. In this place you'll be as safe as anywhere."

At once they began to tell him of their personal worries and needs; it was a relief for them just to be able to talk to him. Worries about husbands and sons, about their houses and fields; irritation and argument; despondency and a kind of childlike trust that God would not let anything happen to them if they prayed hard; the small world of ordinary folk whose personal fates had no part in the grim game of higher politics. And Helmut can listen to it all again and again, thought Karin, always with the same friendly patience, as if he were hearing it for the first time.

After a while Herr Barner came and took them to the former underground offices of the Air Raid Precaution Station, where now the commandant had set up his headquarters.

"Of course we have our own lighting system down here," said the mayor, "but now, when it's most needed, it doesn't work." He led them even deeper, through labyrinthine passages, down many steps, which he lighted for them with his flashlight. Finally they entered a vast hall whose confines were shrouded in darkness, because there were only two thick church candles shedding a dim light over tables and benches, cupboards full of tools, fire hoses and extinguishers, hatchets and shovels, and a huge box of sand. On the walls hung detailed aerial maps. There were two operations rooms cut off from the main hall by glass panels. In one of them they saw the commandant, an elderly captain, his head bent over maps as he stood at his desk. An electrician was cursing somewhere as he tried in vain to get the electric light working. In the background an open door led to a first-aid post.

The town councilors were sitting morosely around one of the long tables. They nodded silently to Lobelius and Karin and made room for them on the benches. Behind the glass partition they could hear the commandant talking to his adjutant, a young lieutenant to whom he was giving defense instructions. Regular soldiers, strengthened by home guards, were to occupy the trenches in the park to hold up the advance of the American tanks.

Whoomp! The detonation shook the cellar walls, more noticeable here below as a vibration than as a sound. It was like the subterranean rumbling of an earthquake. Almost at the same time an orderly came running down the stairs and announced that the enemy artillery had fired the first two shots into the town.

In the operations room next to the commandant's the telephone shrilled. The mayor took the call. "Regimental staff headquarters, sir!" he cried. "Please try to persuade them to spare Eberstein." Without answering, the captain took the receiver from him.

"*Jawohl*, Herr Major," he could be heard saying. "Eberstein will hold out."

From the telephone came the crackling sound of a voice.

The captain answered, "According to orders, I have not countenanced demands to surrender the town. The mining of the south bridge did not succeed. The first American tanks passed over without resistance. They are to be stopped in the park. Sabotage? Impossible to investigate now, Herr Major. No, no heavy weapons. Fifteen machine guns. Just over two hundred men, all told. *Jawohl*, Herr Major, Eberstein will hold out."

The adjutant came back to announce that only the road to Karlsberg still remained open in case of retreat. "Retreat?" snapped the captain. "You've no idea what the big brass expects of us." He gave the information by telephone; it seemed to make no impression at the other end of the wire. Once again he said, "*Jawohl*, Herr Major."

Whoomp! Yet another explosion. Herr Barner, who was standing beside the captain, put his hand on the officer's shoulder in a quite unmilitary fashion. "It's sheer madness, Captain, to try to defend Eberstein with two hundred men. We'll be wiped out in half an hour!"

The captain shrugged his hand away. "You heard what the general staff think, didn't you? Well, then!"

"But you can't allow a town of four thousand inhabitants to be blown to pieces for nothing!"

"Sir!" shouted the captain, suddenly at the end of his tether. "Do you know what I should do with you?"

"Shoot me," said Herr Barner as calmly as ever. "But do you really think that would make a difference? I know you have to carry out your orders. As for me, I'm here to look after the welfare of my town."

"If you wish, speak to the major yourself," snapped the captain.

"Helmut!" Karin whispered, and placed her hand in his under the table. They had heard everything. That "*Jawohl*,

Herr Major!" was like a death sentence. Karin's whole being revolted against this final idiotic display of power. White-faced, wide-eyed, but very upright, she sat among the men and felt Helmut press her hand. They all turned their heads toward the operations rooms where their fate was being decided. They were afraid: afraid for their town, for family, for house and farm, and for their own lives. If the town hall should get a direct hit, they would be buried alive in its deep bomb-proof cellar.

Nearby, Barner on the telephone was giving a brief factual résumé of the situation. But the staff headquarters somewhere out there already knew all about it. Delay was what they needed. When Barner's voice stopped, there was a sharp, decisive noise from the receiver, and shrugging his shoulders, the mayor gave it back to the captain. While the latter was once more receiving instructions about the defense of Eberstein, the mayor walked over to the table. They looked at him. Only now did Karin realize that he had kept his hat on all the time. He took it off, wiped the sweat from his forehead, put his hat back on, shoved his unlighted cigar stump from one corner of his mouth to the other, and said, "That's the end. Now we'll be blown to bits."

As if in confirmation, two more explosions followed quickly on one another.

No one said a word. Orderlies kept running in with dispatches. Wounded were brought into the first-aid station; their groans could be heard plainly. Then another voice, presumably the doctor's, made itself heard, calling to the electrician that he couldn't work by this miserable candlelight. There was silence for a few minutes. Then the light suddenly came on. And again the doctor's voice: "Isn't there anyone in this pigsty who can give me a hand?"

Karin exchanged a quick glance with Lobelius, stood up, took off her coat, and went across to the doctor, who was bending over the wet reddish-brown pulp that oozed from a ragged trouser leg. He looked up, said, "Scissors!" and when Karin handed them to him, he cut away what was left of the trouser leg. "Nurse?" he asked, and cast a swift look at the girl standing beside him in a light cotton dress, wearing no cap, no nurse's badge.

"My father's a doctor," said Karin. "I've often helped him."

He shrugged his shoulders. "Come on, then. Swab. Syringe."

Though Karin was worried, it was a relief to have something to do. She was glad that she could find things fairly quickly in the well-equipped first-aid cabinet.

They worked silently, without stopping. More wounded were brought in. There was a sweetish smell of blood and a sour smell of sweat. Meanwhile, Lobelius had joined them. He talked to the wounded. There were a few Eberstein men among them. For the others he wrote the names and addresses of their next-of-kin in his notebook. He took the instruments from Karin when the doctor had finished with them and placed them in a pan on the spirit stove.

Orderlies kept running down the cellar steps, staggering with weariness and strain, their faces caked with dust and sweat. One of them told the captain that the Americans had once more radioed to say that as soon as the white flag was hoisted on the town hall, they would stop shooting. The workers in the first-aid station didn't even look up from their work. Scissors, scalpel, swabs passed from hand to hand. Blood-stained bits of uniform were tossed into the rubbish bin. The captain spoke on the telephone once more. "*Jawohl*, Herr General!" he said now.

Karin, her head bent over a severed artery, tied a ligature and thought of her father and mother and Till. It was her fault that they were in Eberstein. Dear God, dear God, she prayed silently. . . . There wasn't time for any more. She must keep her wits about her in order not to make a mistake.

"Swab!" She handed over the forceps with the muslin compress, held the needle ready for injection. Helmut cleared away the bloody dressings, pressed a hand clenched with pain, said a few words. From time to time he looked at Karin, at the soft down on her cheek, the expression of intense concentration that made her face look older, the shadow cast on her clear skin by her lowered eyelashes, and also the shadow of sorrow that cut him to the quick. She seemed to have forgotten everything but what was to be done. Only once did she look up quickly, sketched a smile, formed the word "coffee" with her lips, and pointed to the doctor. Helmut brought the Thermos, held it first to the doctor's mouth, then to Karin's, gulped a mouthful himself, and then took it over to the men.

The telephone conversation was still going on. "No, there are no tank barricades, Herr General. . . . Ammunition low. . . . Only the road to Karlsberg, Herr General. . . . *Jawohl*, Herr General. . . . *Jawohl*, Herr General!"

Always the same tune. But then suddenly a new word. It sounded like . . . withdrawal. Had they heard correctly? The heads around the long table were all raised at the same time. None of them had dared to hope for any change. The mayor pushed his hat back on his head, wiped his forehead again, and chewed more desperately than ever on his old cigar stump, listening intently. He was holding the Thermos in his hand, and the steaming coffee ran slowly out over the table and onto the floor.

A short, sharply pitched crackling came from the telephone. "Withdrawal along the Karlsberg road? *Jawohl*, Herr General!"

All of a sudden everything moved unimaginably quickly. The captain and his adjutant left their operations room. "Withdrawal, Doctor!" he shouted as he passed the open door of the first-aid station. The doctor simply lifted his face for a second, shook his head. "Next one—we're through the worst by now, Fräulein. . . ?"

"Karin Lorenz. And this is Pastor Lobelius."

"Dr. Münter," he replied. "You're doing a fine job, Karin. Let's keep going."

But the mayor was standing beside them now. "Sorry, Doctor, I need Fräulein Lorenz. I'll send you one of the men over there. Our butcher. He can stand the sight of blood, at least."

"Hell and high water! Oh, well! Good-by, Karin. Next shift, please!" His unshaven, blood-spattered face flashed a smile at her. "Lots of luck!"

"Come on, Herr Pastor, Fräulein Lorenz!" the mayor urged them. "It's our turn now."

They went up out of the cellar and emerged into the brightness of a clear spring day. The chestnuts in the market place stretched out green fingers to the sun, just as at home in the Lorenzes' garden. April sunshine poured like a shower of gold over the little group of people who had just come into the light of day out of a world of shadows, out of a grave. Spots of green light danced on the walls of the ancient timber-framed houses. There was a smell of burning. Clouds of smoke stood above the roofs, but not in the direction of the parsonage. Karin and Lobelius exchanged a long look. It was as if they had returned from the dead.

A soldier ran across the square, and at the same moment a salvo of shots, sharp as whipcracks, sounded dangerously close. Karin felt as if she were awakening from a wild dream. Aren't we mad, now we've got this new lease on life, to gamble it away going to meet an army that certainly doesn't care whether we have a few dead more or less? But then, looking up, she saw a white flag flying from the town-hall tower; saw the bailiff who had brought them from the parsonage a few hours ago (it seemed more like days) standing at the foot of the town-hall steps, holding up a big sheet by the two top corners. Herr Barner, who had chewed his cigar into mush, threw it away with a sweeping gesture. "Forward!" he ordered them, and they set off. Karin's hand was tucked securely in Helmut's, like a hermit crab in its shell. They walked behind the man with the sheet, Karin in the middle, on her left the mayor, on her right Helmut, a strange little procession. Nobody seemed surprised when Karin pulled out her white handkerchief and held it high over her head—just in case the Americans didn't notice the sheet.

She counted her steps mechanically—a hundred and eleven —as they walked over the deserted square. Then came a sound like a mowing machine on a summer's day, a rumbling noise that gradually drew nearer. And there they were: the first American tanks. Almost at the same moment a troop of infantry came around the street corner, rifles at the ready, on their faces the masklike rigidity of soldiers in action.

Karin looked at Helmut. It was a moment that neither of them would ever forget. "There they are, Helmut!" said Karin, her voice choking. "Everything will be all right now!"

Then the four people with the sheet and the Americans— an officer and a dozen men—halted facing each other. The tanks moved calmly on into the town. The foot soldiers looked astonishingly clean and well-groomed, despite the dust; so different from the ragged German troops. To Karin's amazement, they all seemed to be eating! Imagine eating when they were about to conquer a town! All of them, including the officer, were working their jaws up and down.

She was so astonished by this that Helmut had to give her a little push before she remembered why she was there. Like a child giving a recitation, she spoke slowly, in her best school English, frowning in concentration. "This is the newly elected mayor of Eberstein, and this is the Protestant pastor. These gentlemen wish to surrender the town to you. What must we do to prevent further shooting?"

The officer replied arrogantly, "White flags on every house. Any house in which we find soldiers or weapons will be destroyed."

Karin translated. Barner and Lobelius nodded in agreement. She asked next, trying hard to speak in as impersonal tones as the young American officer, "How much time will you allow us?"

He looked at his wrist watch. "Half an hour. If by that time every house is showing a white flag, the town will be taken without further fighting. At three o'clock all men must assemble in front of the town hall and surrender whatever weapons they possess. Repeat."

Karin repeated it, first in English, then in German.

Silently they walked back. The mayor put his arm around Karin's shoulders for a moment. "You're a girl in a million. My most grateful thanks for all you've done. Now I have to go back to the town hall. I leave the rest to you." Lobelius, Karin, and the bailiff separated and went on their individual errands through the town. They ran everywhere, shouting urgently, "Put out white flags!" Already these were hanging outside many houses; it was obvious that the inhabitants had had them prepared. Sheets, towels, diapers. . . . A window opened on the first floor of the baron's house, a finger was shaken disapprovingly at Karin, but—in a moment—a small white towel was hung from the casement.

People were streaming out of the cellars. Women stood at front doors with babies in their arms and wept. "It's all over," Karin shouted to them as she dashed past. "Nothing will happen to you if you have no soldiers or weapons hidden in your house. At three o'clock all weapons must be surrendered in the market place."

Bedding and clothes were being thrown into the street from burning houses. Furniture stood on the pavement. The neighbors were helping to put out the flames. As in earlier days, they had formed a long chain to pass buckets of water from the fountain in the market square.

Somewhere the cry arose: "The foreign workers are plundering the shops in Railway Street!"

At the churchyard Helmut and Karin met again. They kissed each other in the open street. There stood the old parsonage, undamaged, and the church, too, was still standing. Their eyes shifted to the tower. There'd been a hit there, fairly high up toward the top. Krischan Möller was sitting astride the steep roof pouring water on a still-smoking hole. Stina just then handed him a bucket of water through a window in the tower, and both of them waved. The old seaman sat on the tower as once he had sat in the crow's nest of a freighter.

"The Voice of the People has certainly something to talk about now!" said Lobelius gravely, after kissing Karin again. She blushed a little; but then she laughed.

"So what!" She beamed. "Now let's go inside and see the others!"

In the parsonage they found everyone gathered in the hall talking loudly and excitedly, all of them finally united in the relief of knowing the danger was over. Aunt Ulrike fell weeping on her nephew's neck. Karin brushed her mother's cheek with hers. "It's all over, Mutti! Oh, how glad I am! I came past the Frankes'; everything is all right there. If we only knew that Father too was safe and sound!"

The tenants dispersed after Lobelius had answered their questions, going back to their own rooms. The opportunity to enjoy a meal in peace and comfort at last was so irresistible that for the moment they forgot all other worries. Aunt Ulrike determinedly wiped away her tears and hurried to the kitchen. Martha had already lit a fire there, had put on water for the soup, and was busy peeling potatoes and scraping a few shriveled carrots left over from last year.

"Don't you think that today for dessert we could allow ourselves a pancake, Fräulein Lobelius?" she asked. "Till brought such lovely white flour, there's enough milk, and Frau Lorenz has said that as it's a special day, I may take three of her eggs. Three eggs for six people! What luxury!"

The sixth person was Frau Wöllner, whom Carola had invited. To celebrate the end of the war, she now fetched a bottle of wine from her treasure chest, and when they had all eaten their fill, they began to tell their stories.

Lobelius and Karin were brief. After all these agitating hours, they didn't want to upset Aunt Ulrike with a detailed description of their experiences.

"But what was it like here?" asked Karin.

They were told nothing further had happened in the parsonage cellar, but precisely because they didn't know what was going on outside, the atmosphere had grown more and more tense. When the firing began, they listened breathlessly for the next bomb to fall. The general sat for the first time in his corner with nothing to do; he had no maps, no notepaper; but still he held himself in the stiff, upright position of a Royal Prussian officer of bygone days. His wife was holding his hand, and she, too, was doing nothing; what was the use of horoscopes when the end was there!

"Fire bombs!" the general pronounced once, sniffing at the cellar window like a hunting dog. The two old ladies from East Prussia raised their heads inquiringly.

"Fire bombs, he said!" shrieked Aunt Roswitha into Aunt Mechthild's ear trumpet.

"Let's all sing a hymn!" Aunt Ulrike had proposed suddenly and produced her hymn book from the crocheted bag, which had come down to her from her mother. She intoned:

"Abide with me; fast falls the eventide;
The darkness deepens; Lord with me abide . . ."

She had always been an enthusiastic choir member, and in whatever disturbing situation she might find herself, a good hymn seemed to her the best kind of consolation. This one was in the hymn-book section devoted to the hour of death, and perhaps some people would not have found it encouraging. But they all sang with her; even Krischan joined in with his nautical bass. One verse followed after the other, and as long as they kept on singing, at least they couldn't sit cowering in wait for fire bombs.

But when the hymn was over, Carola declared that she absolutely must go up and see to her sheep. "Imagine my anxiety, Karin dear," said Aunt Ulrike. "There was no holding your mother. No, up she must go to the sheeppen, with its wooden walls and thatched roof. . . . My dear, I already seemed to see her going up in flames, and all on account of an irrational creature! When an hour had gone by and she had still not returned, Frau Wöllner went up to see what she was doing. And then she, too, didn't come back. I can't tell you what I felt like: I was nearly out of my mind with worry! I feel quite ill, even now, when I think of it."

"But everything was all right, after all," said Carola. "You worked yourself up quite unnecessarily, my dear Fräulein Lobelius."

Carola came to Traude just in the nick of time. The poor beast was lying there, wheezing and panting pitifully. Two skinny little lambs had been born, and it looked as if there might be another. During the next hour Carola had so much to do that she had no time to think of anything else. The third lamb lay awkwardly in the womb, and it was quite a job to bring it into the light of day alive and without damage to the mother. When it had finally been born, Carola realized that there was still a fourth to come.

"This is really overdoing it, Traude, old girl," she murmured exhaustedly, and with her bloody hands wiped the sweat from her forehead.

"Good gracious!" said a voice from the door. "What a commotion!" It was Frau Wöllner. "How many are there? One, two, three . . . but that's not possible!"

"Four," said Carola. "Oh, yes, it sometimes happens with milk-ewes, but it's not desirable really, because then the lambs are small and weak. I must try to get them to feed. Will you help me? If they're strong enough to suck, then I shan't have to worry about them."

As a sheep has only two teats, the lambs had to feed two by two, and they were unbelievably clumsy. The women had their work cut out to make them understand what they had to do. Their matchstick legs kept giving way beneath them all the time. Carola and Frau Wöllner had to hold them up and lift their heads for them. But finally the lambs caught on, and soon all four of them, by turns, were sucking vigorously. When they were full, they collapsed in the straw and only managed a tinny bleating when their mother turned them over to lick them dry.

When all that was done, the two women heaved sighs of relief and sat down together on a bundle of straw. "You look a nice mess," said Frau Wöllner; she wet her handkerchief in the drinking bucket and gave it to Carola. "One would think you'd just emerged from battle."

"That's what it was," said Carola, wiping her face with the wet cloth. "And now please tell me where we have met before?"

"I don't think we have actually met, but perhaps you have heard me play sometimes? I am a concert pianist, and even after I was married, I went on playing under my maiden name, Maria Bergmann."

"Maria Bergmann! Of course I heard you! But it must have been quite a long time ago now. In Berlin, perhaps about the end of the twenties. Then later on, one evening in the Gewandhaus in Leipzig. That time you played the Beethoven *No. 4 Concerto in G Major*, didn't you? Max Wöllner was conducting . . ."

"He's my husband."

"Strange that I didn't connect your name with his. But my dear Frau Wöllner, tell me—no, you mustn't tell me anything if you don't want to."

"He is a Jew," said Maria Wöllner. "They suggested to me that I should divorce him. When I refused, I was not allowed to give any more public concerts."

"And now?" asked Carola gently.

"All this time I've been wanting to talk to you about it, but I had to be so careful, especially as I didn't want to make trouble for Helmut. Now of course I know that we should have attempted to emigrate much earlier than we did. But neither of us were exactly celebrities, and there was no reason why foreign countries should clamor for our presence. We still had money and our lovely home in the Grunewald; I gave lessons in secret, and there were friends, so many good friends who stuck by us through thick and thin. And then we loved Germany. Our roots were here, and we knew that the—the *others* were not the real Germany. Then came those awful days in November 1938 . . . nothing happened to Max; friends hid him, but I saw that we must get away. In the summer of 1939 Max was able to go to Paris, to his brother's, who had been practicing there as a doctor ever since '36. He found work at once, nothing very grand, because there were so many refugees, but it was better than nothing. I was to wind everything up in Berlin and follow him. That was another mistake, not to have gone away when he did, but it is easy to be wise afterwards. The war broke out, and I couldn't pass the frontier. I tried every way, but without success. Through Swedish friends we at least heard from one another until France was occupied. It would take too long to go into all the details, and there is much that I don't even know myself; but when the Nazis occupied France, he was arrested and sent to a German concentration camp. And much later, toward the end of '42, there was a letter from a discharged Buchenwald prisoner, or it may even have come from one of the SS men there—after all, there were a few human beings among them. It was a letter without any sender's address or signature, but at least I learned from it that Max was in Buchenwald and that until then he had not been sent to one of the extermination camps. I heard nothing more after that. Helmut brought me here from Berlin. I don't need to tell you what sort of man he is. I had been bombed out and was staying at some friends' house. When they were bombed, I stayed with other friends. I was glad to come with Helmut, particularly as I wanted to be near Buchenwald. Also, the Gestapo had twice been to see me, and asked me—*me!*—where my husband was. When I said I didn't know, they again insisted on a divorce. It was good for me to get away. Now I'm just waiting until I can get a pass from the Americans and some sort of transport to Buchenwald so that I can look for Max."

Heavens, thought Carola Lorenz, what a heart the woman has! Still to have hope, after nearly six years of separation and everything that must lie between. "You must find him," she said, and against all reason she believed what she said. "You *must* find him."

"Yes," said Frau Wöllner, "I will find him."

"And now we'll go down again," said Carola. "Otherwise poor Fräulein Lobelius will be worried to death."

After luncheon they all went to bed to enjoy at last a few hours of the luxury of unbroken sleep, which they had been deprived of for so long. But the peace was not altogether undisturbed, for an American patrol appeared, searching all the houses for soldiers and weapons. After this, Karin and Lobelius decided to go to the Frankes' farm to find out how Till had spent the historic day. But their plan came to nothing because, as they were leaving the house by the back door and the garden, the bailiff appeared at the front door and announced that the mayor requested the presence of Fräulein Lorenz at the town hall when the men assembled at three o'clock to hand in their weapons.

There was not a very large crowd of men and youths assembled in front of the town hall at three o'clock. They handed in a few hunting guns, pistols, and H.J. knives. The home guard, who had retreated with the army, had not yet returned.

Two American N.C.O.'s were receiving the weapons, checking identity papers, and selecting a dozen men who were to present themselves the next morning in order to form a temporary watch committee. The mayor interrupted at this point. He told Karin to ask if these men, who were to be a kind of police force, would be armed. The lieutenant whom Karin addressed said that no German was allowed to carry arms. Then, on her own initiative, she asked if the Americans themselves would be responsible for law and order during the coming night. The lieutenant obviously didn't want to commit himself to anything. Next morning, he said, the commandant would be prepared to receive the mayor, who might then ask him any questions he wanted. A curfew had already been ordered for the whole community, and regulations in German had been posted throughout the town. Until further notice people would be allowed to use the streets only between the hours of eight and nine in the morning and five and six in the afternoon. Karin asked if these regulations also applied to the foreign workers. The lieutenant merely shrugged his shoulders and disappeared into the town hall.

"If only nothing happens during the night," the mayor said. "I'll stay at the town hall in case there's any trouble."

Karin and Lobelius went back home feeling depressed. On the way they met the miller standing in front of one of the posters; he walked on with them. He was worried about his corn. With cunning and courage he had managed to keep it out of the hands of the Nazi forces; was it now to be sacrificed to the blind rage of the foreign workers?

After some hesitation he came out with his request. "Could you perhaps keep me company at the mill tonight, Herr Pastor?" he asked. "We'll barricade ourselves in. If there is an attack on the mill, your presence would be its best protection. You've got a good reputation in the workers' camp. Perhaps you could make them see reason if you were to talk quietly with them."

"I'll be glad to do all I can for you," Lobelius said at once. "Shall we say about eight o'clock? If an American patrol gets me, I hope my identification card will be acknowledged."

"I was thinking that tonight we'd at last be able to read together quietly for an hour or so," said Karin, when they had said good-by to the miller. "And you so badly need a good night's rest! How long do you think you're going to be able to burn the candle at both ends like this?"

He laughed. "Don't be too severe. *One* stern lord and master is quite enough for me. No, I can't miss such a good opportunity of trying out on a small scale my theory of nonviolent resistance. And now let's look in at the hospital so that we can give Till the latest news about his friend. God be praised; he seems to be really out of danger now."

After the evening meal Till at last made his reappearance in the family circle, submitted with composure to the embraces of his mother and Aunt Ulrike, settled himself with Bluebeard in the red armchair, and declared that he was certainly tired and was glad he could finally count on a good night's sleep in a proper bed.

"You really do look exhausted," said his mother, who had already brought his sleeping bag up from the cellar. "Did you have to keep watch over Kathi all night long?"

"Only till twelve," he replied. "Dorle and I were playing checkers to while away the time, and Frau Franke was darning or something. Old Kathi was behaving queer; she kept standing up and lying down and from time to time gave a bellow as if something was hurting her, but not a trace of a calf. Herr Franke and Wenzel relieved us about midnight, and we went down to the cellar for some shut-eye. But when Frau Franke was sound asleep, Dorle and I suddenly felt like a little stroll, and Bluebeard, too, hadn't had any exercise all day."

"What a glorious idea, to go walking in the fog in pitch darkness!" his sister said.

"Do you think we should have taken our stroll during the day with the constant alarm on?"

"You can't deny that there was also an alarm during the night."

"That's why the fog is such a good thing, don't you see? Besides, there was something I had to do down by the bridge."

"Oh?"

"Yes, Dorle and I had agreed that on no account should our bridge be blown up. They had already started to mine it, dodging about with their flashlights, when we got there. Like ghosts they looked in that thick pea-soup fog; uncanny, I tell you."

"Ghosts in pea soup!" said Karin. "An oriental storyteller has nothing on you!"

Aunt Ulrike shuddered. " 'Erl-king's daughter in darkness drear . . .' " she quoted. "It sends shivers down my spine."

"It wasn't anybody's daughters; it was soldiers," said Till. "Not from these parts, I'm sure, because the commandant wouldn't be so dumb as to send Eberstein men to blow up their own bridge. Dorle and I lay in the little wood and waited. Bluebeard behaved marvelously, didn't bark once. It was quite a while before the soldiers went back into town, and then I was able to take my time and have a good look at the thing by the bridge."

"Till!" cried his mother.

"No reason to yell. I know how to go about that sort of stuff. I had tools and a flashlight with me. It doesn't need much skill to render a mine harmless when you know where it is. Old Karl back home showed us all that and explained it hundreds of times. Dorle held the light for me and Bluebeard kept watch in case somebody surprised us, and when I'd finished, we went home and had a couple of hours' sleep. Frau Franke hadn't even noticed we'd been away. Unfortunately, the calf is a bull, black as a sweep."

"Oh, Karin, get me a glass of brandy; I feel quite faint," groaned his poor mother.

"What's the matter?" asked Till. "Did you have such an awful time here?"

"Traude has quadruplets," said Karin, coming back with the brandy bottle.

"Quadruplets!" exclaimed Till. "Why, that never happened before. Have you heard anything more about Armin, sir?" he asked the pastor.

"He's much better," said Lobelius. "But you can't go running to the hospital at all hours now, Till. There's a curfew, and you must keep to the regulations: we're allowed out only from eight to nine in the mornings and five to six at night."

Carola took a swallow from her glass, and Aunt Ulrike also had a drop poured out for her. People with weak nerves needed a restorative that day.

"What a pair of children I've brought into the world!" said

Carola, when she had recovered a little. "Here's my daughter who goes marching to meet advancing enemy tanks . . ."

"Really, Karin? Tell me about it!"

"Some other time, Till," Karin said.

". . . and my son playing about with land mines! . . ."

"And our model of a mother sitting under the thatched roof of a wooden shed while fire bombs were falling!" Karin said, rounding out the family report. "Helmut, to fit into the picture, has promised to keep watch in the mill tonight. You'd better get used to that sort of thing, Mutti."

✦ Chapter Seven ✦

At half-past seven the next morning, when Lobelius was coming back from the mill, he met Carola on the steps of the parsonage. "Good news!" he cried with that radiance that sometimes made his face beautiful. "May I go with you to the sheeppen?"

"About my husband?" cried Carola. "Please tell me quickly."

"He's all right. Erfurt has not yet been occupied. Last night when the miller was lying down for half an hour, I suddenly had the idea of trying to get through on long distance. It was nearly a miracle—but I *did*. From occupied Eberstein I spoke without interruption for a few moments to Dr. Lorenz in the unoccupied city. He sends all his love to you and the children."

"I got up once or twice during the night to try to get through, but long distance didn't answer. No wonder, though, it was you and not me who was blessed with this little miracle! Thank you! So we have been occupied before the city. Strange! Is Erfurt being bombarded?"

"Only on the southern outskirts, Dr. Lorenz said. It was long past midnight when I called him. He said there had been fighting in the Steigerwald toward evening. Today they are definitely expecting the enemy attack."

He sat on the straw while she looked after the animals and drew a can of milk from Schirin. One of the newborn lambs had clambered onto Lobelius's lap, was sniffing inquisitively at his face and trying to suck milk from the lobe of one of his ears. He sat without moving, as if he were afraid of hurting the skinny little creature.

"Shove it away, if it's bothering you," Carola said, laughing. "They don't break all that easily."

"Really?" he said. "How warm and alive it feels!" Now one of the hens had fluttered up onto his arm because he had picked up a few grains from the floor and was holding them out to the lamb, who didn't know what to do with them. "When I was a little boy, I always wished the birds would peck grain from my hand. My father's parish was in one of the poor districts of Halle, very far removed from anything that could be called 'Nature.'. . . Ouch!" As there was no more corn in his hand, the cheeky hen had begun pecking his fingers.

Carola laughed. She was so happy, she could have hugged him, though she didn't dare to think of what might still be going to happen in Erfurt. "Now I know who you remind me of," she said. "Saint Francis of Assisi—a Protestant one, of course."

"Oh, he was a great Protestant, the *poverello!* Here, how do you do that? I mean, when you pull on the teat, how do you get milk to come out?"

"I don't pull it, I stroke it. You see? Like this! Schirin's lambs must now learn to drink out of the pail, so I'm taking a little more milk from her each day and letting them get at her when her udder's almost empty. Dorle will be coming to choose hers soon, and it must know how to drink alone."

When she had taken enough milk, she let the lambs go to their mother, and at once they began to butt their hard little heads against Schirin's belly. Carola sat down beside Lobelius. "It's so like you, Helmut," she said, calling him for the first time by his Christian name. "In the middle of the night, unarmed, in a mill that might be overrun any moment by hordes of drunken men, you think of a woman who is longing to hear a word from her husband! We were worried about you. Late yesterday evening the Voice of the People came across with the news that the Poles and the Russians had completely ransacked two wine shops. And even the wisest words are thrown away on drunkards."

"The mill was well barricaded with two hefty iron girders in front of the door. We sat there quite peacefully together, the miller and I, and went the rounds every hour to make sure nothing was on fire. We took turns in sleeping too. Everything was quiet. I, too, was anxious to know how the doctor was getting on. I owe so much to him, and to you. The evenings spent at your lovely house meant more to me than I can ever tell you: that atmosphere of books and music and of intellectual freedom, the conversations, your little circle of friends, the conviction that there was still, and always would be, something like that in Germany. Karin would never have been as she is without the influence of such a home."

What a pity she's not here to listen to this, thought Carola. But it was good to know that Helmut Lobelius had sensed something of the spirit of her home and of what she and Franz, during the long years of national depravity, had endeavored to save for the future. Material things had never played a very important part with Franz and herself, neither in the first lean years of their marriage nor later when things were going better for them. They both came from old but never very wealthy academic families, closely associated with creative art, science, religion. These traditions were of the greatest importance to them. They were always thankful that, after the necessities of life had been paid for, there was enough left over for books, the theater, and concerts; hospitality in a small circle of friends; for the education of their children; and, above all, for helping others whenever they needed it. And people had been in need so often during the last twelve years! Yet all that would have been impossible if they had not, to the best of their abilities, provided for the morrow. And now here was this lovable young country pastor with his small stipend and his touching indifference to the necessities of daily life, who literally believed that tomorrow would take care of itself, and he also believed that someone like Karin, a young girl, hungry for life, could share with him forever this lilies-of-the-field existence!

"We both like you very much, Helmut," she said, rousing herself from her preoccupied thoughts. "Please believe me when I say that we would be proud to have a son like you."

Lobelius blushed. "Thank you, Frau Lorenz! You couldn't have told me a nicer thing. Yet I know that you would not be quite so happy to have me for a son-in-law."

Carola raised a warning hand. "You are right, but that has nothing to do with our feeling for you. It's . . . no, we won't say anything more about it. You and Karin alone must come to a decision. That is your right and your duty, and I know that you will not take it too lightly."

"No," he answered. He stood up and put the lamb down carefully beside its mother. "No, I don't take it lightly. Believe me, I am honestly trying to do only what will make Karin really and permanently happy."

"I believe you, Helmut," Carola Lorenz replied. As she looked at him standing there with a few straws in his tousled hair, wearing an old suit with darned cuffs, she could only feel amazed at the inherent dignity that seemed to flow from him.

When they came out into the stable yard, the neighborhood women were standing around the pump filling their buckets, for neither the electric light nor the electrically driven waterworks were functioning yet, and few farms in Eberstein still had old-fashioned wells or pumps in them.

Karin too was standing there with a couple of buckets. "How was it last night?" she called across to Helmut.

"All quiet at the mill," Lobelius answered. "But some of the farms and some parts of the center of town were looted."

The foreign workers were in fact roaming around the town without observing the curfew, and the Americans did not check them unless they actually caught them in the act of plundering. The excited women complained that no one was protecting them against the thieving mob. The temporary police were helpless without weapons.

"If the people had been left where they belong, they wouldn't have become a thieving mob," said Lobelius.

"But you told us, Herr Pastor, that the Americans would see that peace and order were maintained."

"Give them time. They've only just arrived. The mayor will try to persuade the Americans to place their own sentries at night outside the camp gates. . . . Come, Karin. We are due at the town hall at nine!"

As they were walking through the town, they saw a Russian, covered with blood, lying in the gutter in a side street. The pastor bent over him to help him to his feet. A wave of alcoholic fumes assailed his nostrils and a fist punched him in the stomach. For a moment he was winded. Karin dragged him away. "The Yanks must intervene," she said disconsolately. "Otherwise, there's going to be murder."

Herr Barner was already waiting for them at the town hall; he had set up his office in a neighboring room. "It looks bad," he admitted. "The men who marched into Eberstein yesterday are moving on again today. They haven't even got their own interpreter yet. Come on with me to the commandant's office. Perhaps we can at least get them to issue a temporary ordinance."

A young major sat smoking at the mayor's writing desk. He did not respond to the newcomers' greetings, nor did he offer them chairs. There was a war on still, and they mustn't forget it. Barner, through Karin, explained to the major that the foreign workers were destroying irreplaceable stocks of food. At three farms they had already poured gasoline over grain, seed potatoes, and animal foodstuffs and set them on fire. In view of the threat of famine, such actions must be avoided.

The major shrugged his shoulders. "We didn't bring them here. You'll have to learn how to get along with them."

Couldn't the Americans put a guard at the gates of the camp, Herr Barner asked? He was willing to spend the night at the camp himself.

"The men have been prisoners long enough," answered the major. "If you want to spend the night at the camp, that's your business. Anything else?"

"What about church affairs?" asked Lobelius. "How are they to be arranged?" The severe young major unbent a little. The two spiritual leaders of the community, the Protestant and the Catholic, would be given passes permitting them to move freely about the town. They would have to come to an arrangement with the army chaplains about church services. Did they require a guard on their houses?

Lobelius declined the offer with thanks. He believed he was speaking for the Catholic priest also in refusing any special treatment. Besides, it was at their houses that guards were least needed. But if the major could issue a pass to Fräulein Lorenz, his interpreter, the mayor would be grateful.

The American nodded and lit himself a fresh cigarette. "Sergeant, it grieves me to have to interrupt your dream of bliss. Perhaps you would have the goodness to issue a pass to the interpreter."

The sergeant, who was sitting at the end of what had once been the mayor's desk, grinned like a guilty schoolboy. He had been gazing the whole time at the dark-haired girl with the turquoise eyes. Karin had been too occupied to notice it. Now for the first time she looked at the young man, and suddenly she realized that he was not *eating;* he was chewing in the presence of a superior officer, and not even bothering to keep his mouth shut. Of course the infantry troops to whom she had surrendered the town yesterday hadn't been eating either. This man was chewing gum! So had the troops! For the first time she observed this characteristic of the American way of life and found it remarkably unaesthetic.

The sergeant unscrewed the cap of his fountain pen and busied himself asking her age, name, and whether she was a member of the Party; he wrote it all down on an impressive-looking sheet of paper. It was Karin's first encounter with yet another facet of the American way of life that was to become very familiar: the questionnaire.

When all this was done, the pastor ventured to ask for a pass for Frau Wöllner, who had to get to Buchenwald as soon as possible in order to look for her husband. The major seemed to regret that he was unable to grant this request. They were still in the immediate battle area, he explained. It was not within his power to issue passes for travel outside the town. But the Herr Pastor might tell his acquaintance that the American Army had occupied Buchenwald camp and had freed the prisoners, at least those who were still alive.

Those that were still alive. Karin and Lobelius exchanged a swift glance. It sounded sinister.

To the astonishment of Herr Barner, the major declared at the conclusion of the interview that he would now send two of his men to the foreign workers' camp in order to bring him a report about the situation there. He had no objection if the pastor and the mayor would like to go with them. So they all went to the camp, but found few people there, as most of them were again wandering through the town, looting and plundering. The mayor tried to talk with one of the camp leaders, and the pastor too had a short talk with him. But the man was too drunk to be capable of rational discourse. He behaved quite respectfully but refused to make any kind of promises.

Out of one of the camp huts came a Polish woman and asked Karin to look at her sick child. The camp doctor had disappeared at the approach of the Americans, and Dr. Wendel already had more to do in the hospital and the town than could be attended to by a single man.

"You . . . understand?" the woman asked and stared distrustfully at the young girl. Only her anxiety about her child allowed her to overcome the hatred that blazed from her dark, passionate eyes.

Karin went with her into the camp hut and looked at the horrible infection on the leg of a little girl. Then she cleaned it carefully and promised to go back next morning with ointment and bandages.

The Americans had already ridden back into town in their jeep, so Lobelius and Karin returned on foot. It was midday now; the streets were empty except for men and women from the camp who were trying to get into locked shops, breaking a window here and there, collecting the food they were entitled to get from the farmers for whom they had worked, and finally going back to the camp to cook it for their lunch. But before leaving, they went shouting through all the streets that they were coming back in the afternoon to set fire to Eberstein and tear everything to pieces. Behind their shut windows the Eberstein folk listened anxiously to these threats and armed themselves for any eventuality with pitchforks and cudgels.

At the town hall there was great agitation. Some of the Americans had already left, and new ones had arrived. Lobelius and Karin had to go with the mayor from one officer to another and in each place had to make the same declarations they had made that morning. So the day passed.

When Karin and Lobelius had not returned to the parsonage by two o'clock, the three women sat down alone to table. Then the canoness went into her room to rest her sensitive nerves. Carola took a book into the garden, and Martha busied herself with Aunt Ulrike's darning basket. But the afternoon quiet was rudely interrupted by Till who had heard the threats of the foreign workers and felt it was necessary to "take steps," as he put it.

"And what kind of steps are you thinking about?" Carola asked.

"First of all the bridge. It must be pulled down," Till declared. "Herr Möller is also of my opinion, and Frau Möller is already rounding up the neighbors to lend a hand . . ."

"But that seems to me rather hasty and unwise, Till."

"Then you don't have a proper picture of the situation. The bridge leads over the river, doesn't it? Well, then. The road on the other side forks, and the left fork goes straight to the main road, and on the main road lies the foreign workers' camp. See?"

"But until now none of them has tried to do any looting here in the parsonage or in the neighborhood. If they're really planning an expedition on a big scale, they'll plunder the town where the shops are, or the larger farms."

"But the road over the meadows and across our little bridge is quicker for them. And if they once get into our garden, then they'll slaughter our lambs and hens. Just you wait and see."

"I would not undertake anything without the consent of Herr Lobelius," Carola advised him. But now Aunt Ulrike joined them, having heard the animated discussion through the window of her bedroom. The canoness was wearing her black Sunday dress and bonnet and was holding her hymn book between gray-string-gloved hands. "I am going into the church," she proclaimed, pale but decided. "If I have to be murdered, I would rather it happened in the house of God."

"I really don't think there's any danger of being murdered," said Carola, trying to reassure her, but Aunt Ulrike was determined to go into the church. Martha now came downstairs, not because she felt anxious for herself, but because she was worried about the old lady. Frau Wöllner was at the hospital all day, where her help was urgently needed with all the wounded who had been brought there during the last few days. The other tenants, except the Dünsings, had assembled in the hall and were listening to Krischan's instructions about the dismantling of the wooden bridge.

"The old ones first!" the seaman was saying. "I know a hiding place in the garden where no one'll ever find you, ladies. A real lifesaver."

"I'm going in the church," Fräulein Lobelius repeated. "I want to die in the house of God."

"Now then, you just go with me," Krischan persuaded her. "If it comes to dying, you'll still have time enough to switch to the church."

Carola and Martha took Aunt Ulrike by the arms and followed Krischan's little band that was composed of the two old ladies from East Prussia, the elderly Frau Lübzin, and the two children. Carola had looked in briefly at the Dünsings, but the general's wife had shaken her head. Her husband was lying motionless on his bed with his eyes closed. "We'll stay here," his wife said. "We have nothing more to lose."

Krischan led the old folks to a corner between some long-disused outbuildings, where there was a bench underneath some elderberry trees and a brier hedge. Until then none of the tenants had discovered this little nook, and they agreed that intruders would not find it very easily. Frau Möller brought another two chairs, cushions and blankets out of the cellar, and then the old folks could be safely left to themselves.

On the bridge there was already much coming and going when Carola and Martha got back. Boards and beams were being detached and dragged to the bank. Krischan was in charge of the whole operation, and Till was his most energetic second-in-command. Dorle too had set to work with a will, though her parents had preferred to remain behind at their farm with the animals. Carola still thought it was unnecessary to pull down the bridge, but there would have been no point in trying to persuade the excited helpers to desist. All were working as hard as they could. Till and Dorle jumped from beam to beam after the boards had been removed, and then balanced over the swirling depths of the river, holding long, heavy wooden laths. Bluebeard enjoyed the excitement more than anyone. In everyone's way, like a clown at the circus, he tirelessly participated in everything that Till was doing, running backward and forward along the still remaining beams. He took boards between his teeth in order to help carry them, had a refreshing, though unintended, bath in the river, and then shook himself gaily, scattering water over everyone. Stinking but happy, he raced through the meadows, chased the frogs into the pond, and dashed snorting back to Till, who assured him that he was the most helpful dog of the century.

Now came the sound of distant voices. It was like the noise made by off-stage forces in a grand opera. And then suddenly the cry: "The Russians are coming!"

It was good that the bridge was down and no one could get across! Till and Dorle were determined to drag the last beams to the riverbank and hide them among the bushes, but now Carola asserted herself. "Run home, Dorle, so that your parents won't worry about you. And, Till, you go with Fräulein Born into the house until the commotion's over. I'll see to Aunt Ulrike."

165

The shouts drew nearer. By now everyone had fled into the houses; only the old ladies were sitting outside in their hiding place, where the noise sounded far off. Carola sat down with them until after a while the row gradually subsided. When everything was quiet again, she led the canoness back into the house, and the others followed them.

Evening was already falling when Karin and Lobelius came home, tired and hungry after their long day. Aunt Ulrike quickly brewed up the last spoonful of tea for them, and then she told of the frightful dangers the tenants of the parsonage had had to go through during the afternoon. Only Till's firm and prompt action had preserved them from death, she said. If he had not had the idea of dismantling the bridge . . .

"Our bridge? Our good old bridge?" Lobelius asked.

"It was unavoidable," said Till. "Otherwise, they would certainly have come over the meadows and straight into the parsonage garden. I'm sorry, Herr Pastor, but Krischan Möller says that with my help he can put it up again within two hours. But I think we ought to wait until things have calmed down a little. Didn't you see any of the rumpus in town?"

"Yes, there was a certain amount of rioting," Karin reported, "but the temporary police fought valiantly with the camp people, and in some of the farms the women defended themselves with scythes and flails, and after a while everything was over. We had so much to do that we hadn't time to bother about all that, especially as they said there was no danger in the region of the parsonage."

"It was the baron who got the worst of it," said Lobelius. "They stole a fat porker out of his sty and slaughtered it before his very eyes; then a few Poles who had worked for him and who said he had treated them badly gave him a thorough hiding. Perhaps he deserved it, but I'm sorry for him all the same."

"You haven't heard the most important news," said Till.

"This morning I was allowed to go in and see Armin for the first time. He was so pleased, but Sister Susanna threw me out again after a few minutes. I'd like to know why they're called Sisters of Mercy! But when I went back in the afternoon, Sister Scholastica was there; she's not so hardhearted and let me stay a quarter of an hour with him, and now I may go and see him every day. . . . Listen! Who can that be ringing at the door so late?"

"Go on down and see, Till," his mother begged him, suppressing an irrational little hope that rose in her heart.

Till brought a stranger upstairs with him, who had come to ask for lodging for the night. His pastor had told him that they would certainly put him up at the parsonage in Eberstein. He had been working in an Erfurt seed merchant's business and was now on his way by bicycle to join his family in a village to the north of Eberstein.

"What's it like in Erfurt?" Carola inquired. "Is fighting still going on? Do you know anything about my husband, Dr. Lorenz?"

No, he was sorry, he knew nothing. Dr. Lorenz was known to him only by name. Where did the doctor live? On the western borders of the city? As far as he knew, nothing much had happened there. In the last few days they had had heavy raids on the factory districts and the center of the city. Then the artillery bombardment had begun. Around the old university and behind the Kaufmänner Church fires were still burning. Today at midday the city had been occupied by American troops. In the general confusion he had left without a passport but wouldn't care to make such a journey a second time. The roads were thronged with refugees. Marauding bands of foreign workers were seizing cars and trucks, for they all wanted to get back home as quickly as possible. If he hadn't known his way through side streets and field paths so well, he'd never have got through. "I'm sorry, Frau Lorenz,

167

that I can give you no news of your husband. If I had known that you were here, I'd have looked him up on my way."

Carola and her children concealed their disappointment. They sat with the man a little longer before making up a bed for him on the sofa. The miller had said that tonight Lobelius didn't need to stay in the mill; everything was quiet in the town. The mayor had gone with two American MP's to the camp, and they would stay the night there. Perhaps the threats of the foreign workers during the afternoon had had a beneficial effect after all in persuading the commandant to take these measures at the last moment.

The next morning it was raining; a gentle, mild spring rain that made the fresh green leaves and grasses flourish everywhere. Karin looked out longingly at the wood. She liked nothing better than to go walking in such a softly falling shower; to feel how the earth and the plants were absorbing the welcome moisture; to sniff the strong fragrance of the wet ground beneath the trees and the dripping bushes; to catch the acid scent of last year's fallen leaves and scan the fine calligraphy of twigs and foliage against the silvery gray of the sky . . .

But the bridge was pulled down, and even if it had still been there, she and Lobelius would have had no time to cross it and wander alone under the trees, free for once from the burden of responsibilities.

This morning Lobelius had to stay at home. A few women had arrived with their children whom they now suddenly wanted to have baptized. In the past six years or so they had not been in such a hurry. Martha Born thought that the pastor himself should give them a serious talking-to.

"The pharmacist has promised to let us have bandages, ointments, baby foods, and medicine for the people in the camp," Lobelius told Karin before his interview with the women. "Perhaps you can go and get the things, and this afternoon we'll take them to the camp. There'll be plenty to do there."

So Karin fetched a large basket of medical stores from the pharmacist and also requested a few other things, which he gladly gave her. When she returned home, she got out her swimming suit and for the first time since she had come to Eberstein swam up the river a little way and back again and then stood for a few minutes in the warm rain—alone, thoughtful, but suddenly refreshed and ready to shake off all doubts, just as she shook the drops of water from her wet body. Doubts? Had that word risen to the surface of her mind from the depths of the river? As if there could possibly be any doubts . . .

In the afternoon she and Helmut went to the foreign workers' camp. The long rows of huts, behind the high barbed-wire fence, looked forlorn. The few narrow strips of cultivated ground that lay here and there and on which a few pallid and sparse shoots of green were appearing made the picture even more depressing. Women were standing with their washtubs by the water taps at the end of each block. A few men were lounging about, smoking American cigarettes and talking excitedly with one another; most of them seemed to have left again for the town. Some lay dead drunk on their two-tiered bunks. The children playing in the streets of the camp looked as pale as the green shoots in the scanty gardens. Obviously these people would hate the Germans as long as they lived. Karin could understand that. But such hatred would only produce further wrongs; it would eat away men's souls like a poisoned wound devastating the countenance of humanity that God had once made "in His own image."

Karin was already expected in the married quarters. The women who had been living here for years had gradually given up trying to create an atmosphere of home in these inhuman surroundings. They had all learned a little German from the foremen in the factory or from the farmers they had been working for. "Work no more!" one of them shouted at Karin. "Germans do it alone now. We town go night, get stuff, take things from shop. Children no medicine. Look children!"

Karin took the cloth off the top of her basket and said, "The pharmacist has given us this for you." The women watched carefully and in silence as she unpacked her basket: there were eyedrops, vitamin tablets, aspirin, bandages, ointments, pills. First of all she treated the small patient she had seen yesterday. The mother placed the child on the long central table of the hut, where hundreds of flies were crawling over the remains of food. Karin cleaned the infection, covered it with ointment, and tied a paper bandage around the leg. The child let her do everything without uttering a sound, but when Karin smiled at her, she quickly turned her dark eyes away. "I'll leave you a few bandages," Karin told the mother. "You can easily change them yourself. If you keep the wound clean, it will be healed soon."

A child with influenza was given Vitamin C tablets. "One every four hours," Karin explained to the mother, a blond, broad-hipped Pole. One woman unrolled a stinking rag from a festered finger. "No soap," she said, shrugging her shoulders. Of course, even the Germans for long enough now had been getting only stony little slabs of soap that looked like cement and gave not the slightest lather. Only doctors were issued better quality soap. Karin took a packet of camomile tea out of her basket and explained to the woman how to bathe her finger with it. Probably it ought to have been lanced. There were so many things that ought to have been done! But she had no time to waste on idle thoughts. A child was ill with fever. Karin felt its pulse, looked down its throat. It might be scarlet fever or diphtheria. She went hot and cold at the thought; there were at least a dozen other children in the hut. "Keep them away from this one," she told the women. "I shall try to get an American doctor sent up here."

Then Helmut came back; he had been to see a sick man whom he had met before. "Please come as soon as you can. There's a badly wounded man over here."

Karin attended first to two other women and gave them aspirin for their rheumatics. Then she went with Helmut to the men's barracks. He led her to a Russian who was lying on his straw sack with his face to the wall, groaning and cursing in his own language, with blood-soaked bandages around his head and left arm. The more pungent stink of alcohol cut through the dank odor of old straw. Karin thought she recognized the man whom they had seen yesterday lying in the gutter.

"Men with white armbands, they beat him," said one of three men who were standing around the bed. "We catch, we hit kaput."

"Turn over a little," said Karin to the wounded man. "Otherwise, I can't examine you."

"You go devil, rotten Nazi wife!" he growled, like a wounded bear. He really did look like a big, angry bear with his furry chest and arms, in which the muscles were like steel hawsers. Despite his momentary misery and filth, one could see that he was a strong, magnificent figure of a man. He could have crunched up delicate little Karin in one of his great fists. But neither she nor Lobelius seemed to think of that.

"Listen!" she said. "Do you want to die now, when you'll soon be able to go back home? You've got a high temperature. You can get blood poisoning. Do you understand? Now let me attend to your wounds or else I'm going away and you can die for all I care."

"Karin!" Lobelius softly warned her.

The three men shook horrified heads. "Ivan Petrovitch!" one of them pleaded. "Not to die!"

Karin beckoned them closer. "Don't just stand there. I need your help. Turn the man over."

They obeyed at once. The three of them rolled the patient over so that his head and arm were within reach and, as they were doing so, uttered strange sounds like nurses trying to soothe a frightened child. It was a difficult job to get the man into a position where Karin could unwind the bandages with which his wounds had been bound. But first she had to give him something.

"Baldrian tablets," she said to Lobelius. "They'll calm him down and I'll be able to examine him more easily." Lobelius took the tablets out of the basket and handed them to Karin.

The men watched all this silently. The wounded man gulped down two tablets and a glass of water, and then he became quiet with surprising suddenness and did not resist when Karin unwound the ragged cloths from his head and arm. A gaping cut ran from the top down the back of his head. The arm had bled profusely but did not look too bad. She carefully probed and cleaned the wounds as well as she could. Ragged threads, hairs, and dirt were sticking to the edges of the wounds, and she began to sweat with anxiety.

"They must be stitched," she said, looking at Lobelius. "I've got neither needles nor clips, and even if I had them, I don't know if I could trust myself with them. The Americans simply *must* send a doctor out here. I can't do anything else but put on fresh bandages."

"Woman stay!" begged the patient, clinging to her sleeve when he realized that she was about to go.

"I send doctor!" she told him and the men, who nodded silently. She gave a few tablets for relieving pain to one of them. "One for now, and another for the night," she explained, "in case the doctor doesn't come. And you have to keep him quiet, understand?"

"Keep quiet!" They nodded eagerly and went to watch her and Lobelius walking back along the road.

"That doctor who ran away should really be locked up!" said Karin. "Now we must go to the commandant at once. Don't look so worried, Helmut. I've seen worse than that after the air raids."

Meanwhile, a new commandant had arrived at the town hall, this time a colonel, who refused to see any of the German inhabitants without a previous appointment. Only when he realized that it was the pastor who wished to speak to him did he consent to see him.

"Pastor Helmut Lobelius?" he asked, looking at the lean man with the black eye patch. "That's who you are? And who is the girl?"

"My interpreter."

"O.K. Please translate, Fräulein. Well, we have a surprise for you, Reverend. The Party leaders apparently forgot one or two things when they burned their documents. Our men found this list here when they were house-searching, signed by a certain Lans, local Party leader. The names of five Eberstein townsfolk stand on this list, people who were to be liquidated at the last moment. You can be grateful to us that in the end we were quicker in getting here than they expected."

Lobelius took the paper that the colonel drew out of a briefcase. His own name, that of the Catholic priest, and three others were on it; all men who had nothing to reproach themselves with but who had been classed as opponents of the Nazi Party. Only yesterday Helmut had said that perhaps a true Christian should have become a martyr, thought Karin. He never suspected how close he had come to martyrdom. And then she remembered her father. It was quite possible that his name also appeared on such a list.

She would have liked to sit down; her knees had turned to water. But no one thought of offering her a chair. The room began to spin before her eyes; the colonel with the bright medal ribbons on his chest turned for a few seconds into a wheel of color that kept revolving faster and faster. Then she pulled herself together.

"Just too bad," said the colonel. "But as you are still alive, you could have no better recommendation, Reverend. We need people like you now."

Karin had to clear her throat twice before she could speak; then she translated what the colonel had said, and after that described to him the situation at the camp. He promised to send a doctor that very day.

"Don't mention to Martha that her uncle signed that list," said Lobelius as they were going home.

"Of course not. She has worries enough already. Her aunt seems to have broken down completely; Martha was going to see her today. But we won't be able to hide the affair of the list from Aunt Ulrike. It is better that she should hear of it from us than from the Voice of the People, who will certainly get wind of it sooner or later."

"Poor Aunt Ulrike! She's had enough shocks in the last few days. But this will definitely put an end to what is left of her enthusiasm for the Führer."

The canoness broke down completely when she heard that her darling nephew was to have been executed like a criminal. She wept silently and without moving, the tears pouring over her wrinkled face, and she did not even raise a hand to wipe them away. For years she and the old ladies with whom she had lived in the foundation had listened in a kind of enchantment to the modern St. George who promised to save Germany and the world from the dragon of Communism and who was so fatally misunderstood by the rulers of the Western world. The canonesses had little connection with the outside world; no hints of doubt had penetrated their secluded life. The Führer's fascinating oratory had bewitched even more

174

world-wise people than these old ladies. But now the enchantment was shattered once and for all.

Carola gently laid an arm about Aunt Ulrike's shoulders. She herself felt wretched enough whenever she thought about Franz. Karin looked at her mother and knew exactly what she was thinking. She said, "Don't worry any more, Mutti; after all, Helmut did speak to Father the night before last. Yesterday afternoon the town was occupied. I'm sure everything is all right."

"Yes," said Carola with a brave smile, though she felt as if she was going to choke. A lot could happen in twelve hours!

"If they've done anything to Father . . ." said Till, but Karin signed to him to be quiet.

"Can't you get your motorbike from the baron, Helmut," said Carola finally. "Then Karin could get us travel permits, and I would go on the pillion with you to Erfurt."

"Over my dead body!" cried Till. "A pillion is no place for old ladies, Mother. Didn't you hear that man yesterday talking about the state of the roads? No, if anyone's going, it's me."

"We could go by secondary roads," said Lobelius. "Anyway, I'll try to get the bike back from the baron."

Till had changed in the last few days. It was as if the shock had not only wounded him but had also given him a push forward on the long journey from childhood to manhood, thought Carola. If Armin had died, then something in Till would have snapped, something that we, with all our love, could perhaps never have healed. But Armin is alive, and we must hope that Franz is alive too. Till will find his feet again and in conversations with his friend will discover many things about which he would probably never think of asking us.

"If I go away for one or two days, you must visit Armin, Karin," said Till. "Today he sent you his regards and he asked when you were coming to see him. Of course you can only stay a short time."

"I'll be glad to visit him," said Karin. "But you'd better put that motorbike trip right out of your head. I'm older and more sensible than you, and younger and more able to cope with hardships than Mother. No one can deny the fact that I am the only suitable person to ride on the pillion."

The dispute would have gone on raging, but suddenly the general's wife appeared in the doorway and said, "Would you have the kindness to come and see my husband, Herr Pastor? He's in a bad way. Would you please call the doctor, Frau Lorenz? It's urgent . . ."

That night His Excellency, General of the Infantry Friedrich Wilhelm von Dünsing, died in his eightieth year.

✦ Chapter Eight ✦

"I'm going to visit Armin today," said Karin on Saturday morning when they had come back from the town hall. "It's a week now since we brought him out of the wood."

"Good! In the meantime, I'll look in on Lotte and a few others," said Helmut. "Then this afternoon and evening we'll have time to compose a speech for the general's funeral and my sermon for tomorrow. It could well be that it will be the most important sermon I'll have to preach in all my life."

"I am so proud that you are letting me help you with it. Give my regards to Lotte. How is she getting along?"

"She has been better ever since she no longer had anything to worry about. In a day or two she'll be going back to her parents, where there is work enough for her; that will do her good. But first of all I must once more have a good talk with her. I'm afraid she regards the fact that Frau Borstel's youngest son was killed with the H.J. as a just punishment for the wrongs the woman has done to her."

"How terrible!" said Karin. Since her first visit, she had not gone to see Lotte again. "I can clean an infected wound and look upon it without too much disgust, but this sort of hatred makes me ill. I have the feeling I can't breathe in Lotte's presence, as if I were being poisoned by this lust for revenge that comes from her like a repulsive smell. It can only cause more unhappiness—as if there were not enough in the world already."

"And yet one must treat that kind of wound with love and patience too," said Lobelius. "It's true that a certain harshness is also necessary sometimes, and now I want to give Lotte a dose of that bitter medicine."

Armin lay in the narrow hospital bed, still looking rather white and frail. "Hullo, Karin!" he said happily. "For you must be my friend Till's sister. It's nice of you to come and visit me!"

Karin had come with what might be called maternal parish-visitor feelings, the mental attitude she adopted when she accompanied Helmut on his rounds. And now this boy was calling her familiarly by her first name and talking to her in the free and easy way that young people have with each other! She felt rather amazed; she had gotten so used to being treated with formality everywhere she went with Helmut. No one ever called her anything but Fräulein Lorenz; only in the parsonage was she Karin. It was enough to make her forget that she had been a schoolgirl still only four months ago.

"How are you?" she said. "I have strict orders from Till to stay only a very short while. I believe he himself comes to see you twice every day?"

"He certainly does. He's a first-rate fellow, but don't let him frighten you off. I may now receive visits as often and for as long as I like. First of all, I must thank you. What would have become of me without you and Till and the Herr Pastor?"

"We are so happy that everything has turned out all right," she said. "Look, here's a cake that my mother has baked for you. And here's a bottle of sheep's milk: I hope you'll enjoy it."

"Many thanks. And thank your mother for me."

"If there's anything else you want, please tell me."

"It would be lovely to have something to read. I had *Wilhelm Meister* and the *Iliad* in my knapsack, but who knows where that is now."

178

"We didn't find it. But of course we have Goethe and Homer at the parsonage."

"If possible, I'd like Homer in Greek. And I'm going to be greedy and ask if I may also have Virgil, in Latin."

"I'll see what we have. Then Till can bring you the books."

"I'd rather you brought them yourself."

How young he suddenly looks, thought Karin. Like a schoolboy begging for a piece of chocolate. "When did you leave school and how old are you?" she asked.

"Eighteen. Final exam in January '44, one year labor conscription, and then I had the misfortune to be called up for the SS. They seemed to think I was the ideal racial type; on my identity papers I'm described as 'Allemanic-Dinaric.' What about you?"

"I'll soon be seventeen," said Karin. She thought that sounded better than just saying she was sixteen. "And what would you have done if there hadn't been any war?"

"Classics, history, literature, history of art."

"Is that all?"

He didn't notice that she was making gentle fun of his ambitious program. "I'm not sure yet," he said soberly. "There are such countless possibilities; one shouldn't make up one's mind too quickly. One thing I am clear about, and that is, later I'd like to teach, just as my father did. He taught classics and history at the Freiburg High School; that's where I get my interest in the Greeks."

"Oh, then I've got the very thing for you. I brought with me Spunda's book on Greece, which we all read together at home last year in the long winter evenings. It was sort of a consolation prize for me because my parents couldn't take me on the trip to Greece that they had promised me after graduating. That sort of thing's out now."

"What do you mean, out?" he cried "Nothing is out—everything's just beginning again. Of course it'll be tough going at first. But Germany was poor after the Napoleonic Wars, and just think what a flourishing spiritual life there was at that period, during Goethe's old age!"

"That poverty will probably be nothing to what we have to expect now. And there are other reasons, too, why travel will not be possible for us."

"That'll be forgotten eventually. As soon as Germans can show their faces outside Germany again, I'm off to the land of gods and heroes, even if I have to bike it or walk it. My father, too, was poor when he was a student, but he wandered twice all over Greece. Later he went there with my mother and, shortly before the war, with some of his students, with very little money and always keeping off the usual tourist routes. And they saw a hundred times more than the people who go there on Mediterranean cruises, spending a thousand marks or more on luxury liners."

"I don't doubt it. But even if one has a little money, one must also have time . . . time!"

"Oh, there's all the time in the world. The way I'm feeling now, it's as if I'd got a new lease on life, and you may be sure I'll make use of it. We're young, Karin, and soon there will be peace; just remember that all the splendid things are still there, waiting for us, and one day we'll see them if only we care enough."

"Do you think so?" said Karin, and looked past him through the window at the convent garden, where a poplar tree was thrusting its fresh green like a fountain into the sky and a nun was reading her breviary as she paced along the wall.

"I *know*," he said. "Oh, I expect the Yanks will lock me up for a bit, but it can't last all that long."

"Why should they lock you up? You've done nothing wrong."

"First of all, I'll have to prove that because I was in the SS. Just since February—I can't tell you what I saw in that

short length of time. And the last four weeks spent at Buchenwald, though only as a clerk in the office to begin with . . ."

"Don't talk about it or your temperature will go up again.
We shall explain to the Americans why you are here. Did you
ever come across the name of Wöllner at Buchenwald?"

He thought for a moment, then shook his head. "Wöllner?
I don't remember it. Among forty thousand prisoners—think
of it, *forty thousand!* . . . I was glad that after a probation-
ary period they found me unsuited to the work and transferred
me to a unit in Jena—though perhaps even that was just a
pretense to get me out of the way."

"You shouldn't talk about it now."

"O.K. At the moment I'm chiefly concerned about how I
can get news to my mother. The postal services and the telephone will certainly not be working for quite a while yet."

"We must find someone who is going to Baden. Perhaps a
demobilized soldier or someone evacuated to central Germany
who wants to get back home. We could entrust a letter to
such a person."

"That would be fine. But don't send the one Till has; it's
out of date. He should burn it."

"You can do that yourself. As soon as you can get up, we'll
put a deck chair for you under the willow tree in the parsonage garden. You can lie there and dream about Greece—with
white lambs bounding, hens cackling, and frogs croaking all
around you. What do you say to that?"

"It sounds like something out of an old-fashioned novel.
Tomorrow they'll let me walk a little in the hall; and from
there to the parsonage garden is just a step."

When Lobelius came to fetch Karin, he found them both
in animated conversation. From Greece they had passed on
to Sicily and Egypt. "Are you coming to take my visitor away
already, Herr Pastor?" Armin asked. "The days are so long

when you lie here alone and no longer feel really ill. Come again soon, Karin!"

The streets were empty as they went home. When you had just come away from a long talk about foreign lands, the little town behind its medieval walls had a cramped, shut-in feeling. Greece, Egypt, how out of reach they were . . . Karin thought.

On Saturday evening Lobelius and Karin were sitting alone in the kitchen working on the funeral speech and the sermon for the next day. This was pure joy to Karin; she could have given up more than Egypt and Greece for this. Only these shared adventures of the spirit, these talks about the profoundest problems, took up much less of a pastor's life than she had thought.

On Sunday morning they buried General von Dünsing in the churchyard. It was not possible to transport the body to the vault on the Dünsing family estate in Mecklenburg, and no one knew when it might be possible in the future.

The commandant had granted churchgoers permission to go out between ten and twelve, so that Sunday the whole of Eberstein streamed into the churches. St. Peter's in Eberstein was one of the beautiful old Thuringian country churches. A brightly painted gallery went from the organ loft along the sides of the nave. In the lofty choir there still stood the baroque altar, flanked by dark carved choir stalls. Only two candles burned on the altar. Church candles had been used in recent days for the lighting of other rooms, and as things were now, they had to be used sparingly. But through the stained-glass windows the April sun was shining, bathing everything in many-colored light. Carola was looking forward to the first sermon she was to hear Helmut Lobelius preach. What would this young pastor have to say on such a unique occasion? She cast a glance at her daughter's radiant, uplifted face, at Till, whose forehead was creased in the effort of concentration,

and at the three others who sat with her in the parsonage pew
—the canoness, the general's widow, and Martha Born. Frau
Wöllner at the organ began a prelude by Pachelbel who had
himself once been an organist in Thuringia. Then the first
hymn rang out:

> "Lead, kindly light, amid the encircling gloom,
> Lead thou me on . . ."

After the hymn all heads were raised toward the pulpit. And
again Carola thought: If only he finds the right words! Even
the hardest hearts had been moved in these days; it all de-
pended whether the right kind of seed now fell upon the
tilled soil of their souls. And as she looked up at the man her
daughter loved, she was once more moved by the natural dignity of his presence.

The lesson for the second Sunday after Easter read: "I am
the good shepherd: the good shepherd giveth his life for the
sheep. But he that is an hireling, and not the shepherd, whose
own the sheep are not, seeth the wolf coming, and leaveth
the sheep, and fleeth; and the wolf catcheth them, and scat-
tereth the sheep."

As the text for his sermon Lobelius had chosen: "The flower
fadeth and the grass withereth away, but the word of God
remaineth for ever."

Carola thought she had never known such a deathly hush
in a crowded church. There was no sound but that of the
voice from the pulpit, an unemphatic, almost a soft voice; and
yet every word could be heard in the farthest recesses, and the
voice, quite without rhetorical subterfuges, immediately had
them all in its spell. "Once again," Lobelius said, "we have
experienced the way in which the flower fades, the grass
withers, and the splendor of the earth vanishes away, even
those among us who for a few years had forgotten the everlasting nature of that eternal wisdom. What we have before

us now will be hard to bear. It must be accepted in the spirit of penance and humility; not before earthly judges, who are themselves sinful men, but before the highest Judge, for we are all guilty. We have sinned by omission, by silence, by indifference, and by fear of temporal powers. We all, therefore, have to bear our share of what the victors call the collective guilt of the German people. But in God's eyes there is no such thing as collective guilt. Before Him there is only the guilt of the individual, for He looks into the hearts, and nothing can be hidden from Him. Things of unimaginable horror have been taking place in Germany. They were hushed up with all the means at the disposal of the absolute power. Only today can we begin to grasp their extent. Fear of those in power and of their hirelings has made most of us blind and deaf and dumb. It is not for us to wonder how other peoples would have behaved under the same compulsion. We have to think of ourselves. And now we shall be forced to see and hear these things, as the poet Dante on his way through the Inferno had to see and hear, though he would rather have hidden his head; for hell shall open its gates in front of us all, and the survivors among the innocently condemned will bear witness. But louder than the voices of the living we shall hear the voices of the millions who were murdered—above all the voices of our Jewish brothers. They shall arise from their mass tombs and their lime pits and from the cigar boxes in which a handful of ashes were delivered to their relatives. The men and women and children who went to the gas chambers shall cry out against us, as Abel's blood cried out against his brother Cain. And it is we who bear the mark of Cain. The Master Race, which claimed in sinful pride that it was better than other races, shall become the race of shame. Our children, who are innocent, will have to suffer under that shame; and they will ask, why did you deceive us? But shame and disgrace can be atoned for; they are perishable things, for they are of this earth. Ten years, twenty years, and once more we shall have earned our place in the community of nations. What we must never allow to die is our own memory of what happened, so that it may not happen again. We shall promise ourselves that today, and we shall pass on to our children the memory of these twelve years, so that they may not be forgotten; for to forget would be a sin against the Spirit, the kind of sin of which the Bible says that it cannot be forgiven either in this life or the next. A new Germany must arise from the ruins and ashes, and it is the responsibility of all of us to see that it will be a land of which we need not be ashamed. Our guilt is written in the book of life. God has taken it into His own hands, and nothing that men proclaim can happen without His will. His word remaineth, though the flower fadeth and the grass withereth away. It remains when grass and flowers grow again over graves and when new homes arise out of the ruins. It is in His chastisement and in His forgiveness; in His judgment and in the rainbow of reconciliation that one day shall stand again over Germany. It remains for ever and ever. Amen."

After the liturgy and the final hymn the people of Eberstein crept home in the same silence in which they had listened to the sermon. At noon the streets were empty again. Even the foreign workers, some of whom had attended the service, kept themselves quiet for the remainder of the Sunday.

At the gate to the churchyard Lobelius left the others, saying quietly, "I'm going now to the baron's to see if I can get my motorbike back."

On his return he had the old bone-shaker, a 1938 model. So that no one might be tempted to steal the precious vehicle, it was placed in the downstairs hall. All the inhabitants of the house stood around it admiringly, but the only one who could really give a proper opinion about it was Till. He examined it from all angles and in particular tested the pillion seat.

"Totally unsuitable for ladies," he declared. "So be a sport, Karin, and see if you can get a travel permit for me tomorrow. The Frankes will give me a day off; I've spoken to them about it already. We'll get there and back in a day, Herr Pastor, won't we?"

"Easily," said Lobelius. "But as we've not been able yet to obtain a pass for Frau Wöllner, I have little hope of getting one for you, Till. If I get one for myself, it will only be because I have to get in touch with the clerical board. They're very accommodating when it's a question of church business."

"But I don't like to think of your traveling alone, Helmut," Aunt Ulrike pleaded anxiously.

"You need have no worries about me, Aunt Ulrike. What could happen to me, anyhow? First of all, naturally, I'll go to see your husband, Frau Lorenz. Then to the clerical board, and finally I have to do various things for the baron in town. We'll go early tomorrow morning to the town hall and see what we can do, Karin."

That Sunday afternoon a farmer from the neighboring village sent a big old-fashioned coach to fetch the pastor, who had received permission from the commandant to attend to his two other parishes. Karin went with him, and it turned out to be a real country Sunday afternoon, with a service in each of the churches, a burial, three baptisms, and a wedding. They had coffee and cakes in the house of mourning and supper with a brass band and dancing at the wedding.

Early the next morning they went to the commandant's headquarters. Karin was still secretly hoping that she would obtain a pass for herself. But her hopes were dashed. Ready as the colonel was to issue a pass for Lobelius, he was deaf to all other applications. He couldn't even do anything for Frau Wöllner. "I'll gladly help her as soon as possible," he said, just as his predecessor, the major, had said. "The concentration camp at Buchenwald is strictly closed to visitors for the time being, until our investigations have reached some provisional conclusion. Then you must apply to my successor. We won't be here much longer."

At ten o'clock they were back in the parsonage, and Lobelius wanted to start at once in order to lose no time. Martha quickly made up a few sandwiches for him, as Aunt Ulrike was too upset to be able to think of practical things. He had to give her his promise to be back before dark, and he gave the promise with an easy conscience: thirty kilometers there and thirty kilometers back were really no great task for a motorbike. Carola and the children gave him many messages and good wishes for the doctor, and about half-past ten he set off with a loud rattling and banging. He wobbled a bit at first. Lobelius hadn't ridden the bike for two years and presumably had never been a good rider. But in the place of driving skill he relied upon his own determination and trust in God. In a wink he was around the corner of the churchyard, vanishing in a cloud of gasoline fumes and accompanied by the blessings of all.

With Helmut gone, Karin found the parsonage changed. Walls that ought to have been whitewashed long ago now stared at her gloomily. The old plush armchairs with their fringe and cross-stitch cushions suddenly seemed to offend her beauty-loving eyes. The noises made by the many people in the house, the constant bickering of the two women downstairs, the worn stairs that Frau Möller was just then scrubbing all irritated her today and drove her out of the house.

She went to the hospital to give Armin the books she had promised him and sat beside his bed for a while, but her thoughts were elsewhere, and Armin too seemed to have retreated into himself and to be far removed from the happy optimism he had displayed on her first visit. "Forgive me," he said, as they parted. "There are often days like this when one feels haunted by ghosts. I'll be better company when you come back again. The books will help."

At the town hall Karin asked the mayor if she could help him with anything. But for the moment there was nothing for her to do. The new occupation troops were expected that evening, and Herr Barner expressed the hope that perhaps the new commandant would provide a more effective protection against marauders. The previous night some of them had set fire to a barn. Only with great difficulty had the cattle in the neighboring byre been rescued. But the mayor sent Karin away with one good piece of news: the commandant had given permission for the townspeople to go out from seven in the morning until seven at night. This was a great concession, especially for the farmers who had still not gotten very far with their spring planting. On her way home Karin passed by the Frankes' to let them know the news. Dorle had just fetched her lamb and with Till's help was giving her the first meal of cow's milk, which the little thing resented violently. But plump little Dorle was a determined and energetic person. If there was to be a struggle, the lamb had small hopes of being the victor. As soon as the lamb was really hungry, she would certainly lap up the cow's milk; Dorle gave her a gentle slap on her curly hindquarters and shoved her into an empty stall. "And now to drill the turnips, Till!" she ordered.

At the parsonage Frau Wöllner had taken her few bits of furniture out into the yard; she said she wanted to give her room a thorough cleanout, so that everything would be nice when her husband came home. Karin offered to help her. They beat the couch that served Frau Wöllner as a bed and a shabby old armchair. They scrubbed the wooden floor and hung the threadbare carpet in the sun, dusted everything, and finally moved all the things inside again. The furniture that Lobelius had begged for his refugees from parish members was bits of old junk that had been lying around in attics and lofts and sheds. Now it stood crammed together in the narrow rooms. But in Frau Wöllner's case the jumble of objects had taken on, inexplicably, a touch of artistic style. The couch was covered by a hand-woven cloth in several shades of brown. The curtains at the window were also hand-woven. "From the Loheland Studios!" said Frau Wöllner. "A few trifles saved from the great shipwreck." She placed a lovely wooden candlestick beside the picture of her husband on the rickety chest of drawers. In the cooking corner stood a few gray-blue peasant pots, and on the tablecloth, of the same material as the window curtains, a vase of a luminous blue with a few branches of willow.

"Many thanks for your help, Karin," said Maria Wöllner in her warm voice. "Now let's just go and gather a few larch boughs down there by the wall. Max was always so fond of them in the spring, with their charming little coral buds. Well, what did the commandant say about my travel permit?"

"Still the same thing. But you may be sure we won't forget about it. Today I feel how long even one day's waiting can seem! And it isn't half over yet!"

"Waiting is something you have to learn," said Frau Wöllner. "May I come up this afternoon and play for a little on the pastor's piano? He put it at my disposal, to practice on as much as I like. But things are already so crowded for you upstairs, I don't like to trouble you. There is a piano in the convent too, which I am allowed to use, and every day after work I play for an hour or more. Sister Scholastica sometimes sends in a few patients to listen. Today, I think, it would be good for us all to listen to some music."

The long day was drawing to a close when Maria Wöllner came upstairs. At first she played Schubert, then a Beethoven sonata. Carola Lorenz, Fräulein Lobelius, Martha, and Karin sat quietly listening, calmed and consoled by the indestructible beauty of great music. That's it, thought Karin suddenly, the "glassy essence" of which Shakespeare speaks. Here we have it in its purest state, purer even than poetry and painting. But if this can be produced by the human spirit, how are those other things possible? Why does God allow them to happen when *this* is how He meant us to be? Oh, why was she always asking questions? She had entered the church group with passionate zeal because she was looking for the complete opposite of the totalitarian state—the Spirit as defense against the idolizing of nation and race; the eternal Word against the slogans of propaganda; a timeless value in a time that was out of joint. And yet she was tortured by a hundred unanswered questions. Only in Helmut's company did she feel calm and safe. But she had gradually realized that that was not enough. You could not live forever on the spiritual strength of another human being. You had to learn to stand on your own feet, to make and be responsible for your own decisions. No one could take that away from you.

When Frau Wöllner left to go on night duty at the hospital, Martha also said good night and went down to Frau Dünsing's room, which she was now sharing since the general's death. Aunt Ulrike, Frau Lorenz, and Karin stayed up. It was now dark outside, and each of them was listening to the sounds of the road, hoping to hear the welcome rattling of Helmut's motorbike in the quiet of the night. The windows were wide open: at last, after five years of darkness, no more blackout! Across the square, by the churchyard wall, honey-colored candlelight gleamed in the Möllers' cottage. Carola and Aunt Ulrike were reading or at least trying to read. Karin kept walking backward and forward in the room. Her eyes sought for something that would give them a point of rest. There were Dürer's praying hands, but today even they remained silent. If they had anything to say, it seemed to her that it was the word "resignation." In a kind of sudden panic she got the feeling that the whole room was filled with this word. The pictures of Helmut's forefathers seemed to be saying it also, in a kindly way, but nevertheless urgently, speaking to her with quiet persistence out of their old-fashioned frames. Finally she stopped in front of the portrait of the married couple above the sofa and gazed at it a long time, as one looks at a puzzle picture in which, besides the recognizable shapes, there is another, a hidden, shape to be discovered, which gives meaning to the whole thing.

Aunt Ulrike had been watching her for quite a while. "My parents," she said now. "The Reverend Johannes Martin Lobelius and his wife Susanna Christine."

Karin nodded wearily; she had heard all that before. But now the hidden shape suddenly manifested itself. "Not the same woman as Christine, the pretty young girl in the drawing in our bedroom?" she asked incredulously, and as Aunt Ulrike nodded: "So *that's* what she looked like as an old woman!"

"She's not *old* in that picture," Aunt Ulrike countered vigorously. "A little more than forty, I think. No, wait a moment; that photograph was taken on their silver wedding day, when she was forty-two."

"Forty-two!" said Karin, and looked swiftly across at her mother, who on her last birthday in January had been forty-four.

"She was a wonderful wife and mother, a shining example to her daughters and the parish," the canoness said proudly.

"Was she?" said Karin in a voice she herself felt to be strange. "But she was not a happy woman." And quickly, as if running away from something, she left the room.

Aunt Ulrike looked after her, shaking her head. "We're all nervous," Carola said soothingly. "Yet there's really no need to be. We know that your nephew's conception of time is somewhat different from that of Greenwich Observatory."

"You're right," said Aunt Ulrike. "I've gotten used to waiting for him. But today is something rather special. It's not as if he didn't know we were all on tenterhooks about him. No, there's no explanation for his prolonged absence but that he's lying murdered in a ditch, crying in vain for help. Or there may have been an accident."

Carola didn't even smile at the thought of a murdered man crying for help. "But my dear Fräulein Lobelius," she said, "now you're not to start imagining all kinds of dreadful possibilities. He had to go to the clerical board and to see my husband and who knows how long the baron's commissions would take him? My husband will certainly have persuaded him to stay the night if it was too late for him to think of coming back."

But the old lady couldn't be talked out of her gloomy forebodings. Midnight came before Carola was at last able to persuade her to drink a cup of valerian tea and go to bed.

Till and Bluebeard were peacefully sleeping behind the partition when Carola entered her bedroom, but Karin was still awake, and she sat down on her bed. The candle was burning and Karin's face looked pale and stern in the soft light; its childlike outlines had suddenly vanished.

"That woman," she said after a long silence; then stopped and started again. "Forty-two, Aunt Ulrike says. I always thought you were old, but compared with that care-worn, faded creature. . . . To think that Christel should have become *that!* Please, will you hand me the drawing? Thank you. Here she's so pretty, so radiant. How is it possible that in twenty-five years of marriage she could have turned into that wretched bit of misery? Please, Mutti, explain it to me. You must know about marriage and what it does to a woman."

A few days ago, thought Carola, she was saying I understood nothing at all. Karin sat up in bed, laid her head on her mother's shoulder, and spoke again. "He must have been an extraordinary man, this Johannes Martin Lobelius," she said, striving to speak calmly and in matter-of-fact tones. "A great preacher, an outstanding shepherd of his flock, almost a saint, Helmut claims. Why then does his wife look so . . . so miserable, and oh, so bitter, as if there were no beauty left in the world?"

"I think saints are not the easiest kind of husbands to live with," said Carola. "But you mustn't only think of *her*. Do you believe she made *him* happy?"

"No! Someone who looks like that could never make others happy. It must have been a frightful disappointment for him that she was too small for him, that she didn't have the strength to submit her life to his and yet remain the personality that he needed to help him in his heavy task. One has only to look at her to know that she failed."

"She probably didn't know what she was taking on. He, so much older than she, should have known."

"You think she was too young to decide about her own life, young and in love and unsuspecting, don't you? Of course the girls in those days were quite inexperienced. They knew nothing about life before they married. It's quite different nowadays."

"The basic things remain the same at all times, I think," said Carola. "When I was seventeen, I believed that one could die of unrequited love, that it meant the end of life. And remember that if I had married then, I'd never have met your father, and perhaps at the age of forty-two I would have looked as this woman did."

"Not you!" said Karin. And despite the fact that she had been trying to control herself, the tears ran down her face. "There's something else," she said with difficulty, "but I don't know if I can explain it to you. I've been disappointed in you and Father for some time. Before that, it was so nice at our house; none of my friends had such a lovely home; not just for Till and me, but between you and Father there was something so good. And then it was no longer so. . . . Oh, I oughtn't to talk about all that."

"Yes, tell me," said Carola. "Tell me whatever you have on your heart."

"Well, everything changed, don't you see? I told you the other day that you didn't seem to have time for the most important things any more. Even . . . even the love between you and Father, which used to fill the house with warmth, seemed gone. They've grown old, I thought, and I was shocked; the daily routine has devoured them. How can I expect them to understand what it means to be young, to be aflame inside like wildfire, to have to learn by suffering what love is? They have forgotten how it was. They've been married twenty years, and all that's over and done with for them."

"Well?" Carola softly asked.

"Everything over and done with, I thought. It will never be like that with me, never, never, even if I live to be a hundred. But tonight when I saw that picture properly for the first time, and when you said that perhaps you wouldn't have met Father if you had married at seventeen, as if it would have been the greatest misfortune on earth, then I understood how different things are between you two than between Johannes Martin Lobelius and his wife. And to think that every evening last week I heard your voice when you were speaking to Father on the telephone and never thought anything about it, because I was so much occupied by my own affairs! For your voice was—it was the voice of a young girl talking to the only man in the world for her." Karin wiped her eyes with a corner of the sheet. "If only we had news from Father!" she said. "Believe me, I'm just as worried about him as I am about Helmut."

"We're not going to worry any more but try to sleep.

You'll see; tomorrow Helmut will return safe and sound, bringing us good news from Father."

"Yes!" Karin sighed, exhausted with weeping. "Good night, Mutti, good night."

Carola kissed her daughter's tear-stained face that felt like a dew-wet fruit.

Helmut did not come back the next morning. Karin went again to the hospital in order to give Armin the Greek text of the *Iliad*, which she had only just found. He was trying to take a few steps around the hall, and Karin, relieving the sister, accompanied him. He leaned on her arm, and they went together along the hall with its many white doors. "Funny how soon your legs turn into cotton wool," said Armin. "But it's going better today than yesterday. Soon I'll be able to come over to your garden. We must talk about the books. There are so many things we must talk about."

When Karin got back home, Aunt Ulrike was completely overwhelmed by worry. She was sitting at the window, looking out over the road in front of the church and from time to time wiping her eyes. "My hay fever has started again," she said to excuse herself. "I've never known it to come so early before."

Martha Born tried to cheer her up. "We know what the Herr Pastor is like," she said. "Quite possibly on the way back he's encountered someone who needed the motorbike more than he did—some poor wretch of a foreign worker who couldn't wait any longer to start off home. And as a motorbike cannot be split down the middle like Saint Martin's cloak, I shouldn't be at all surprised if he has given it away. Or maybe the baron didn't leave him enough gas in the tank, or the motor gave out. Machinery is not his strong point. There are so many unalarming explanations for his lateness that there is no need to think the worst has happened."

"I envy you," said Karin. "You have an astonishing trust in fate."

Martha looked at her with her enigmatic smile. "You can call it fate," she replied.

The women silently agreed to do without a hot lunch that day. Martha sat down at her desk in the hall. Carola signed to Karin. She had the feeling that nothing would please Aunt Ulrike better than to be left alone.

They tethered the sheep in the garden, as far away as possible from the tenants' vegetable plots. The lambs capered about happily, white and woolly, like lambs on an Easter card. Carola sat down on the bench under the willow, where she could keep an eye on her flock. She had brought some mending with her as well as a book. Frau Wöllner came out of the house and sat down beside her. American planes flew slowly over the garden; it was still surprising to feel that one didn't have to run away from them.

Karin put on her bathing suit and went down to the river. For a moment she stood beside the dismantled bridge and gazed over at the wood, where now the fresh green of beech leaves stood out jubilantly against the dark background of a bank of fir trees; then she jumped into the water. She swam as far as the Frankes' farm, heard the voices of Till and Dorle who just then were harnessing the horses to the cart and arguing all the time about the care of lambs, accompanied by Bluebeard's expectant barks. The cows, replete, were lying contentedly in the lush grass of the meadow. Karin did not get out of the water but let herself float back to the parsonage garden, where she clambered over some rocks slippery with weed and lay down under a bush on the riverbank. The afternoon sun was hot for the time of the year, and she was sleepy on this, the first day in Eberstein when she had had time to feel sleepy.

The willow wands printed a constantly changing pattern

on the dark blue of the sky. It was a sleep-inducing quiet. Even the frogs were silent in the heat. There were smells of water, grass, and wet stones. The sunlight glinted on the sparkling water of the small river. Karin wouldn't have been surprised to hear the laughter of the old heathen god Pan suddenly sounding from the hills. She closed her eyes, and when she opened them again, she had difficulty in remembering where she was. Then she put her arms around Helmut's neck; he was kneeling in the grass beside her. "You tramp," she said, still dazed with sleep. "So you've gotten back! Have you been to see Aunt Ulrike?"

"I've come straight from the Frankes'."

"From Frankes'? And where's your bike?"

"Gone. That's why I've come from the Frankes'. Till and Dorle picked me up on the main road. They were on the way to their turnip field with the cart, and I happened to come along, on shanks' pony."

"Tell me exactly what happened."

"Yesterday I'd almost reached Dittelstedt, about halfway to the city. Then an American patrol suddenly roared up beside me, demanded my papers, and took possession of my bike, because Germans may still not use motor vehicles without special permission. And the clever young sergeant had forgotten to enter this permission in my papers. I must make a claim to the military authorities in Erfurt, and then perhaps I'll get my bike back."

"You poor thing! And how did you get to the city then?"

"I didn't, unfortunately. It's awful to have to disappoint your mother. But I can't attempt fifteen kilometers on foot any more. I had no choice but to stay in Dittelstedt. I've known the teacher there a long time. He tried everything to get me transport into town, but there wasn't even a pushbike available. His family put me up for the night, and early this morning a farmer gave me a lift as far as Werda."

"If only I'd been there," said Karin. "I would have been able to explain to the MP's that it was just an oversight your not having the special permission. But now to Aunt Ulrike. She's already given up all hope of seeing you again in the land of the living."

The joy at the return of the prodigal son was great. As there was no calf, and certainly not a fatted one, they had to make do with coffee instead. Lobelius was made to take his ease in the red armchair, which happened to be free because Bluebeard and Till were still at work. It was good to rest his legs. Between Werda, where the farmer from Dittelstedt had dropped him, and the spot on the main road where Till and Dorle had picked him up, he'd had to walk for a good two hours.

The coffee was hot and strong; Karin brought bread and butter from the kitchen, for she thought they all needed a little sustenance. "Butter!" cried Lobelius. "You extravagant young thing!"

"Sheep's butter," Frau Lorenz explained. "We can spare it. And now tell us your story."

"I'm most awfully sorry. . . ." Lobelius began, but Carola waved away his apology; Karin had told her all about it. "The people of Dittelstedt naturally know more about what is going on in the world than we backwoods' dwellers," Lobelius went on. "At any rate, I found out that in the city things are exactly as they are here and that only in very exceptional cases are travel permits given. Moreover, the teacher knew that an anti-Fascist society was to be founded, called Antifa, in which it is hoped to assemble all those who are ready to fight against the remaining traces of Hitlerism and work for the setting up of a new order. We talked about it for a long time, but neither of us feel very happy about it. It looks too much like a Communist affair, and that would be jumping out of the frying pan into the fire. The important thing at the moment is to found a Christian Democratic central party. I shall speak to the mayor about it tomorrow morning, for we must do something soon; otherwise the radicals of both the left and the right will hold all the cards, as happened in the Weimar Republic. Everyone in Germany who is seriously concerned about democracy must now take an active part in politics. At any rate, it is my intention to do so."

"But for goodness' sake!" cried Karin. "Where are you going to find time for that?"

"Oh, I'll find time all right," Lobelius answered confidently. "There's always time for things that *have* to be done."

Then Martha Born was standing beside him with her notebook. "I have put down four women and the schoolmaster, Eduard Schöller, for an appointment tomorrow morning at eight," she said.

"Schöller?" Lobelius asked, surprised. "He was one of the bitterest opponents of the church in Eberstein."

"I suspect that's exactly why he wants to talk to you. May I suggest that, now that there are no more air raids, we should institute a regular consultation time? Oh, yes, then the mayor's messenger was here asking that you and Fräulein Lorenz come to the town hall to talk over various things with the new commandant. Finally there are a few papers for you to sign, Herr Pastor."

"I think we should go at once," said Lobelius, after signing the papers. "It is written: 'Be ye obedient to authority.'" He smiled up at Martha, she blushed, and it was uncertain whether by authority he meant her or the gentlemen at the town hall.

"But you ought to take a rest, Helmut, dear!" his Aunt Ulrike complained.

"I've got the whole night to rest in," he answered, and gave her a kiss. "First of all, I must change my shoes. The ones I've got on have holes in both soles."

"Your best pair!"

"It doesn't matter. Some time in the future we'll be able to buy a new pair."

"I really think Till's Sunday shoes would fit you," Carola said. "The boy has such elephant's feet that they're already too small for him."

Lobelius beamed. "And yet our heavenly Father doth provide for them! Didn't I always say so, Aunt Ulrike? Thank you, thank you, Frau Lorenz! Come on, Karin."

✦ *Chapter Nine* ✦

The new commandant was a colonel, a plump, pleasant-looking man who turned out to be what German soldiers called "a self-acting boiler." When, through Karin, the mayor made known his worries about the foreign workers, who were becoming a more and more serious threat to the restoration of peace and order, the little man exploded like a bomb. Probably he had already become acquainted in other towns and villages with this problem, which the Americans did not want to discuss.

"If these constant complaints do not stop, I shall billet the Russians and the Poles with private families in the town, and let the Ebersteiners see how they like that!" he shouted; he went on in this vein for a while, and Herr Barner, the pastor, and Karin stood there like schoolchildren being scolded, without saying another word. It wouldn't have helped anyway. When the colonel had finished blowing his top, he gradually calmed down, as there was no resistance, which would have added fresh fuel to his rage. "What are you standing there for?" he finally asked in a somewhat milder tone. "Do you think I have all day to waste on you?"

A lieutenant who was sitting at a small table by the window and who through all this had been calmly leafing through official documents, saw that the Germans were going away and signaled to them to stay. "Just a moment, please!" Then to his colonel: "We must discuss with them the questioning of the Buchenwald people, sir."

"That's right! Why didn't you say so before, Mackenzie!"

The lieutenant beckoned Karin to his table and signaled to Barner and Lobelius to sit down for the time being. "The first of the prisoners released from Buchenwald arrived here yesterday," he said to Karin. "We have accommodated them partly in the hospital, partly in the hotel. A Russian intelligence officer has announced that he will come tomorrow to ask them a few questions. We think it would be proper for the minister and the mayor to be present at this questioning, for the German population must be told about what has been going on in these camps. The Russian speaks English and German. A small division like ours usually has no interpreter, and I didn't have time to get one here. What we want to know is, would you be prepared to take the job on, Fräulein—" he looked down at his papers—"Fräulein Lorenz?"

"If there is no one else to do it, I can try," said Karin.

"Thank you. Now I need to enter a few more details on your paper. You belonged to the German Girls' Movement, which is a Party organization?"

"Yes."

"Can you tell me why?"

"Because otherwise it would have been difficult for me at school. We were all in it."

"But you have declared that your father, who is a doctor, was not a Party member."

"My father had a Jewish grandmother, and so was one quarter non-Aryan. That is how he avoided Party membership. The eighth non-Aryan blood that we children had was not enough to keep us out of the H.J. and the B.D.M."

The lieutenant shook his head. "What utter nonsense," he said. "A quarter, an eighth—higher mathematics obviously. But now I should like to know more about your activities in the Girls' Movement."

"I took over the visitation of the sick in a suburban district. In the last two years there were very few social workers left there; and in the hospitals they could only place those who were seriously ill or badly wounded in air raids. The rest had to be treated and cared for at home."

There were a few more questions. Then: "O.K.," the lieutenant said. "Have you anything else to ask, sir?" he inquired of the colonel.

"Let me point out to you, Fräulein, that you may refuse to interpret for us. You will hear a lot of very painful things. But if you undertake the job, then we must insist that you translate everything literally, leave nothing out and put nothing in."

Karin considered for a moment. She was a little afraid of the colonel; but that was no excuse: she must say something. "*If* there is anything I don't want to translate, may I say so?"

The colonel went red again and was just about to start bellowing at her when he changed his mind. Karin had put her question very modestly, and he realized that it had been the result of an inner compulsion. At the same time the young creature was so sweet and delicate that any man would have felt himself to be a monster if he had shouted at her. "O.K., O.K., O.K.!" he growled, and ended the audience with a wave of his hand.

The lieutenant accompanied them to the door. "Nine o'clock tomorrow morning, gentlemen," he said. "And, Fräulein, please don't get the colonel peeved. He's a swell guy, but when he loses his temper, he hits the ceiling. And in the presence of the Russian, I'd like to avoid that."

"I understand," said Karin. Nothing was further from her desires than to put the colonel in a bad temper.

"The Russian! What's he doing in all this?" she said later to Helmut. "I had the impression that the Americans were not altogether jumping with joy at the prospect of their ally's visit."

"Probably the released prisoners are Communists. He'll be particularly concerned about those," was Lobelius's opinion.

The next morning when they entered the council chamber of the town hall, five men were already sitting on the benches that ran along the walls. They all wore the red sign of a political prisoner on the chest of their far too large suits. They looked emaciated, and each one had a few front teeth missing. As they later declared, the civilian clothes of every prisoner were carefully preserved, an astonishing bureaucratic measure in the midst of so much senseless destruction.

Lobelius introduced himself to the men and sat down beside them. The officers had not yet arrived. Barner and Karin stood waiting by the window, but Lobelius soon was deep in talk with the men. They told him they were among the first twelve released from Buchenwald. But among the twelve, seven were in too wretched a condition to be questioned. The great majority of those remaining at the camp could not be transported and would be looked after in the camp by the American Red Cross.

"Did you know a man named Wöllner up there?" Lobelius asked. "He was a Jew."

None of them remembered having heard the name. The camp had had the population of a middle-sized town, after all. Most of the Jews, they said, had long ago been taken away to the extermination camps. In the last few days before the American occupation a contingent of three thousand remaining Jews had been sent away. But there was a possibility that the leaders of the prisoners, called the illegal camp authorities, might have been able to conceal the fact that he was a Jew, given him another number, other papers, another name.

The colonel came in with three American officers and the Russian. They took their places on the slightly elevated magistrate's bench. The lieutenant beckoned Karin to sit beside him at a smaller table underneath the podium. He was there in the capacity of recorder. Barner and Lobelius sat beside the men on the benches.

The Russian officer had the rank of captain. His round, smooth-shaven face had an almost childlike expression; his head was close-cropped. Only the brilliant eyes in the otherwise inexpressive Slav countenance betrayed intelligence and intense interest.

He first asked in German about the organization of the camp, about the rations, the nature of the work required, or rather forced, from the prisoners, and about the punishment system. Karin translated for the Americans from German into English, and when one of the Americans asked questions, she had to translate these into German for the men.

Then there were questions about the sick bay, where medical experiments were carried out and those incapable of work were liquidated with the stab of a hypodermic. But even in the much-feared sick bay there were sometimes opportunities for the underground camp leaders to remove a prisoner from the clutches of the SS. There were, in fact, prisoners among the nursing personnel, who worked together with the "illegals" or underground, which were composed exclusively of political prisoners. In this way a person who was in danger of being shot or sent to an extermination camp sometimes could be smuggled into the t.b. ward, which the camp doctors would not enter for fear of infection. The underground had connections also in the office, where papers could be exchanged or the number belonging to a dead prisoner could be transferred to a living one who was in danger. Of course, this was carried out by all participants at the risk of their lives, but the closer the American Army approached, the more daring became the activities of the underground. Finally, even a few SS members in the lower ranks were helping them in order to provide themselves later with an alibi, or because they really belonged to those who had not been volunteers and didn't like the situation they found themselves in.

The men spoke with a calm matter-of-factness, as if they were contributing a report on a journey of anthropological discovery to some savage race. Lobelius from time to time cast a glance at Karin, whose voice gradually became softer and softer. But not once did she ask the Americans to be allowed not to translate something. She had made up her mind. If men had endured such things, then she could also endure them by listening and repeating them.

Once the lieutenant asked her to speak a little louder. "It won't last much longer," he whispered to her, and she managed a pallid smile because she saw that he meant to be kind.

If only the Russian hadn't kept coming back to the punishment system and the treatment of sick patients! Finally they came to a report of the last days. On the orders of the Gestapo in Weimar a number of political prisoners were to be shot before the camp was evacuated. But now the strength of the underground was so great that they were able to conceal all those who were in danger.

I wonder if Max Wöllner was among them? thought Karin. She had him on her mind all the time. Under no circumstances must his wife hear of this interview.

The closer the Americans approached, the more uneasy became the camp commandant. Finally he issued an appeal and gave those prisoners still remaining in the camp his word of honor that nothing would happen to them if they would allow themselves to be transported without opposition. A small group accepted this proposal, despite the warning glances of the others.

Their bodies were found later in the forest. The others stayed on at the risk of being blown up with the camp by the SS before they pulled out. The Americans' artillery fire, drawing closer every day, gave them courage.

On the afternoon of the eleventh of April the SS men suddenly left the camp and locked the gates. The political prisoners took over the telephone exchange. A call came from the police headquarters in Weimar demanding to know if all prisoners had been either transported or killed. They carefully gave evasive answers. In all the confusion of these last days the secret police in Weimar didn't seem to know that the SS had already decamped. So they repeated that the guards were to leave immediately. The commander of the Nora airfield had received orders to exterminate the remaining prisoners in the camp with poison gas, they said, believing that they were talking to one of the SS. For the prisoners it was now only a question of time: who would get there first, the Americans or the poison-gas air squadrons? As it later turned out, the commander of the airfield refused to carry out the order. One hour later the Americans entered Buchenwald.

The spokesman of the group being questioned, a tall, broad-shouldered man with a Rhineland dialect, was obviously a well-schooled member of the German Communist Party. It was to him that the Russian addressed most of his questions; then the latter turned to the colonel. "I should like to ascertain something more about the medical experiments carried out on the prisoners," he said in English.

"Go ahead," said the colonel, but one could see that he'd had enough already. The Russian, on the other hand, seemed to register, like an efficient machine and without any trace of human sympathy, everything he heard, and now obviously he wished to hear it in even greater detail. Surprisingly the Rhinelander cut in with: "Excuse me, sir. I should be glad to speak to you of these things in private. But in the presence of a girl I would rather not say anything more on this subject." He looked at his companions, and they all nodded agreement.

"Not say . . . anything . . . more . . ." Karin translated,

and then collapsed slowly sideways from her chair into the arms of the recording lieutenant. "A glass of brandy!" he called. The Russian calmly drew a flask of vodka from his jacket pocket and handed it over.

Five minutes later Karin was on her feet again. The mere smell of the strong spirit helped to bring her around; then a little sip, which ran down her throat like fire. It tasted horrible, but it helped. She was ashamed at not having been able to hold out and declared herself ready to go on, but how thankful she felt to hear the colonel say that the interview was over. Meanwhile, the Russian had beckoned the Rhinelander to his side, was firing questions at him and jotting down the answers in his notebook.

"Thank you," the colonel said to Karin. "Lieutenant Mackenzie, will you see to things, please?"

He meant the interpreter's salary, and nothing could have surprised Karin more. Tea, coffee, chocolate, a big tin of cookies, and a few packets of cigarettes appeared out of the blue, and the lieutenant displayed them before Karin as if he had been a Santa Claus. "I'm sorry you had to listen to all that," he said. "The comrade couldn't get enough of it, though."

"We have to know about it sometime," said Karin, still feeling giddy and sick.

When Lobelius saw the riches she had been offered, his first thought was to share them with the men who had suffered so much. After a few words with Karin the prisoners were invited to the parsonage for that evening. When the Rhinelander had finished conversing with the Russian, he said, "We wanted to speak to you anyhow, Herr Pastor. Would it also be possible to arrange for us to meet the Catholic priest at your house?"

As Karin and Lobelius came down the town-hall steps, a jeep was waiting for them with Lieutenant Mackenzie at the wheel. "I'm taking you home," he said.

* * *

During the rest of the afternoon Karin lay on a blanket on the grass beside Armin's deck chair. Till had brought his friend over from the hospital in a wheel chair and then had gone back to work.

The sun was warm, the birds were singing in the willow, and a soft wind stirred the branches and carried the scent of flowering fruit trees with it.

"You look miserable today," said Armin. "What's the matter with you?"

Karin told him in a few words what she had experienced that morning. He knew all about it; there was no need for her to go into details.

"For heaven's sake!" he said. "Poor little Karin! You, of all people, having to be interpreter for that!"

"I'm sure that the men were particularly restrained in their descriptions. My presence apparently disturbed or inhibited them. And to think that you were there in the thick of it and could do nothing to help!"

"Don't let's talk about me. Do you know what the men were called?"

"No names were mentioned. One of them spoke with a Cologne dialect—a tall, strong fellow."

"That must have been Tünnes. That's what the comrades called him. In the files he was down as Anton Häuser, Communist. It was a strange thing, how all the decent elements in the camp held together, whether they were Communists, democrats, ex-officers, or Jews. Protestant and Catholic ministers and priests belonged to the camp's underground and despite all ideological differences worked together with the Communists. It is impossible to say how many of their comrades these men saved from death. At the same time they were very hard on antisocial elements among the prisoners and on SS stool pigeons. You can only understand the social structure of this strange community if you have lived in one of the camps. It was possible because the SS themselves didn't trust each other. Each one wanted to serve his own ends as much as possible: they were like a pack of wolves that would just as soon have eaten each other up. That accounted for the extraordinarily intricate system on which the underground worked. I should like to have a talk with Tünnes."

"I asked him about Max Wöllner, but neither he nor the others knew the name. The five of them are coming this evening. I hope Frau Wöllner will be at the hospital then because as the men would have nothing to tell her about her husband, it would be a sad disappointment for her."

Again she looked so despondent that Armin stroked her hand with a tender little movement. "I've heard her playing once or twice," he said. "It's a wonder how out of so much grief, so much sheer beauty can emerge, for the men who created the music suffered too. It seems that perfect things are always born from pain and sorrow. If only we could do something to help her!"

"I'm afraid it's hopeless."

"Don't say that. Everything is possible."

"Even after so many years?"

"Yes," he said. "Think how long Penelope had to wait for her Odysseus. He, too, went through one danger after another for ten long years."

The living room at the parsonage had never been so full of people as that evening. Chairs had to be brought in from the bedrooms and the hall, but finally everyone had a seat. The red armchair was reserved for Father Haller, who was the last to arrive because he had had to listen to confessions. He was an old man, strict and sharp-witted and by no means an accommodating shepherd of souls, but his flock knew that they could depend on him. They had experienced that more than once during the last twelve years.

Till and Bluebeard had had to find themselves another place;

they lay on the old sheepskin rug under the pastor's writing desk, where they could see and hear everything.

The strong coffee scented the air and the smoke of American cigarettes filled the room with a bluish haze. That afternoon Karin had presented Armin with a packet, a princely gift, which had touched him deeply. In those days cigarettes were the most longed-for commodity in Germany; next in importance came coffee and then chocolate. The box of cookies made the rounds. (Karin had secretly filled one of Frau Wöllner's bowls with some.) But despite all these aids to conviviality, conversation was at first rather stilted. Aunt Ulrike begged the guests to help themselves; again and again she found herself gazing in amazement at the five men. What would her friends in the foundation say when she told them that she had sat at table with prisoners from Buchenwald, whom they had always regarded as dangerous criminals? And what would these dear, pious old ladies think about the experiences that Ulrike Lobelius had had in the great world outside and that had cost her so many bitter tears?

Frau Lorenz sat next to the man from Cologne, Tünnes, and the first thing she asked him was about Max Wöllner. His head shakings did not put her off, and she went deeper into the question. "His wife heard definitely that since the end of '41 he has been in Buchenwald. She lives with us here, and I have seen his picture in her room. He was a musician, of medium height, thin, a long face, blue eyes, not a typical Jew in his appearance."

"Max? A musician?" the man said. "We did have a Max in our block once who conducted the little orchestra. Don't you remember, Lippert?"

"Didn't he go to Auschwitz with that contingent in March '44?"

"Wait a minute, now I remember; he was smuggled into the t.b. ward by the comrades. I can't say what happened to him in the end."

"His wife simply must get a travel permit to go to Buchenwald," said Carola. "It seems there may still be hope that her husband is alive."

"Considering the confusion of the last few months, there are good grounds for hope," said Tünnes. "Listen! The day after tomorrow the Americans will be sending a truck with members of the Nazi Women's Organization to Buchenwald, so that they may see what went on there and not be able to assert later that the Americans invented it all. I promised to serve as a guide. If your friend would care to travel in such company, I can easily arrange for her to go without her needing to have a permit. But she'll have to have strong nerves."

"I'll speak to her about it first thing tomorrow morning," said Frau Lorenz. "Please, would you take me too? It would be too much for Frau Wöllner to go there all alone."

"If you think you can stand it," said the Rhinelander. "All I can do is to warn you. And now, Herr Pastor, we should like to discuss the real purpose of our visit here." Lobelius nodded, and Tünnes began to draw a picture of what the new Germany would be like in the future, according to the plans he and his Communist comrades had drawn up during the long years of imprisonment. They were convinced that the Allies would listen to their proposals.

"I'm afraid you may be disappointed," said Lobelius. "There will be an occupation government which we shall have to defer to, even the victims of the Nazi regime. We can't hope for help from outside; the new order must start from within."

"That is so." The Catholic priest concurred. "It must come from the Christian spirit that has been suppressed for the last twelve years. I hope that it still has enough authority among the Western nations to play a part in the peace that is to come."

"Instead of the spirit of Christianity, I would rather say the spirit of humanity and social order," one of the men said.

The Rhinelander took the lead again. "We'll soon have free elections in Germany, and we are sure they will show a strong Communist majority."

Lobelius said, "I don't know on what grounds you base such an assumption. I think we in Germany have had quite enough of *one* totalitarian system. The great majority of the Germans will certainly not be prepared to throw away so lightly such hard-won freedom. We are reckoning on England and America giving their support to a Christian Democratic party in Germany, as they themselves are democracies with a Christian basis."

"Just let me finish what I have to say, Herr Pastor," said Anton Häuser, the man called Tünnes. "We have no intention of using any kind of compulsion. The German Communists don't aim at another dictatorship. On the contrary, they want to build up a true People's Democracy that will stand for peace and freedom and the friendship of all nations."

"For us Christians the prospect of a People's Democracy on lines laid down by Moscow is not an attractive one," said Father Haller.

"You're laboring under a misconception there, Reverend Father. That is why we value so much this opportunity of talking to you about it. In our People's Democracy the Christian churches will be incorporated as long as they do not work against the state. Moreover the early Christians themselves were communists, and in Russia today there are countless Christians who live unmolested under the Bolshevik regime."

"That contradicts everything we have heard about conditions in Russia," said Carola Lorenz.

"Propaganda!" cried Lippert. "In any case, German communism would take its own form."

"As if Moscow would tolerate any departure from the Party line!" Father Haller threw in.

"We won't quarrel about the form the new Germany will

take; there's no time for that," Häuser continued. "The first and most urgent thing is that there should now not be a lot of small parties, as in the Weimar Republic, but one great movement that will unite all men of good will, independent of earlier Party membership, in a single anti-Fascist league. This Antifa would have as its aim nothing less than a complete breaking with the past and all its faults, and it is important for the clergy of all denominations to support it, in order to guide their congregations along the right path."

Lobelius was silent, because he wanted Father Haller to have his say. The men sitting round the table might be of good faith, but Lobelius was convinced that without knowing it they were tools in the hands of superior powers that would use them unscrupulously to forward their own ends.

Father Haller looked at each of the five men in turn and shook his head. "My friends," he said, "you have suffered for your convictions. I have great respect for you and I am not without hope that the sufferings you endured under a godless regime will finally convince you that there can be no peace and no freedom for humanity without God and his church. I assume that you will respect my own convictions as I do yours, even though I must say no to Antifa."

"The same goes for me," stated Lobelius. But the men were not so easily discouraged.

"Precisely because we do not undervalue the influence of the church," said one of them, "we place great value on your cooperation. Antifa is only a temporary measure. We must wait and see how the political situation in Germany develops, and also how the occupation zones are distributed."

Lobelius pricked up his ears. But Häuser had already begun to speak again. "There is no need for you to feel that you have to make a decision right away. Think over what I have said. It may well be that there are developments at hand which will not be without importance for you."

Karin exchanged a glance with Lobelius. They were both thinking of the conversation that Häuser had had with the Russian officer.

"Did you perhaps know my friend Armin Lederle who worked in the office at Buchenwald?" came Till's voice from under the writing desk.

"Lederle, yes indeed we knew him," said Häuser. "But he was there only for a short while. A decent young chap, always ready to help us if it was possible. Toward the end a couple of our most ferocious SS officers took him away, nobody knows where. I'm afraid he must have lost his life."

"He is alive!" cried Till. "If you have time, I can take you to see him."

At that moment the door bell rang; Bluebeard barked and ran down the stairs behind Till. A man's voice was heard, an astonished cry from Till, then heavy footsteps on the stairs. Carola's heart nearly stopped beating in a sudden access of hope. But it was a stranger who came into the room with Till: a blond, square-built young fellow with a shy smile on his bright, beardless face.

"Don't you remember Jan, Mother, Karin?" cried Till.

"*Mevrouw!*" the young man said.

And then suddenly Carola and Karin saw the light. Of course, Jan was one of the "Jongs" from the Dutch labor camp in Erfurt. They had been forced to work in an armaments factory in the northern sector of the city, but had enjoyed greater liberty than the Poles and Russians.

Korr, the hard-working but obstinate Dutch cook at the Lorenz house, had one day met two of her young countrymen in the street and talked with them for a long time. That night she had explained to Frau Lorenz that in Holland it was the custom for servants to receive their friends in the kitchen in the evenings. She told *Mevrouw* that she intended to do the same here. In the future every Thursday evening a few of the Jongs from the camp would come and see her. They needed a place to go to. In Holland they had simply been taken off the streets, packed into trucks, and sent off to Germany without even being able to let their relatives know what had happened to them. And *Mevrouw* simply couldn't imagine how uncomfortable it was for the poor lads at the camp. Obviously Korr was expecting a refusal and was willing to fight for her rights.

"But with the greatest pleasure," Frau Lorenz had answered, although she had no doubt that it would be another black mark against her from the Party if she received foreign workers in her home. "Of course your friends may come here."

After she had discussed the matter with her husband, she proposed to the cook that she should receive the Jongs in the doctor's waiting room, which was free in the evenings and was next to the kitchen in the basement. The chairs there were more comfortable, she told Korr. But Korr disdained the offer, as if they had insulted her by offering her alms, when after all it was a question of her "rights." "Nay!" she replied. "They be my guests; the kitchen is my proper place, and it's in the kitchen I'll have them."

And so the Jongs had come to the Lorenzes' house every Thursday evening. Korr presided over these gatherings like a queen at her kitchen table; she darned socks, sewed, stitched on patches, and the young men sat at her feet, a dozen or more of them. They turned the kitchen into a real London fog with their pipes, in which they smoked everything but actual tobacco, and their shouts of laughter penetrated to the living room above. The pieces of cloth for patching their worn-out trouser seats Korr accepted as gifts from *Mevrouw*, because it was impossible to buy such things. Emboldened by this, Frau Lorenz one day ventured to offer her a can of sheep's milk and a pudding mix. Proudly independent as she was, Korr could not refuse something so good for her hungry friends; eventually an unspoken agreement was reached by which the guests, whenever possible, received some slight refreshment or the remains of dinner. In return they helped Korr to stone plums and to strip beans in summer, saw to it that she always had a good supply of kindling for her kitchen stove, and anticipated her every wish. For the first time in her life she was surrounded by admirers, and in her withered heart there arose maternal and also jealous feelings. Frau Lorenz had the understandable desire to make the young men welcome in her house, so one evening she appeared in the kitchen with Karin to exchange a few friendly words with them. But that was contrary to Dutch etiquette. The next day Korr told her in no uncertain manner that it wasn't done. In the evenings after work the kitchen was reserved for the cook and her friends. Only Till and Bluebeard were sometimes allowed, by special invitation, to spend half an hour at the evening reunions, for Korr had a soft spot in her heart for both of them; but the rest of the family, including Nurse Ottilie, were just "them" to her.

Nevertheless, there were meetings with the young men whenever one of them needed a doctor. The doctor whom they had to consult at the factory did not enjoy their confidence. They preferred to come to Dr. Lorenz with their complaints and their occasional wounds.

And now here was Jan bringing messages from Franz Lorenz. "Day before yesterday Pieter and me, we just look in, see how things go by you after the occupation, *Mevrouw*," he explained. "We always had good times by you in kitchen. But only doctor and nurse was there. Remember, *Mejongfrouw* Karin, the way he fixed up my finger that was near chopped off, and you help him, and *Mevrouw* after she give me a glass of the brandy, eh?"

"Don't keep my mother on tenterhooks, Jan!" cried Karin.

"Is my husband all right?" Carola asked. "Oh, Jan, you're

an angel to bring us news! Tell us all about it quickly, Jantje, dear Jong!"

Jan beamed all over his broad, shining face. "Everything well!" he assured her. "Nothing happen. Only a little fire in roof, and *Minher* and the big *Meisje*, nurse, put out quickly. Nay, all things top-hole. Only, I think *Minher* very lonesome. But pass, no. Absolute no, says Yanks. I say, lend me bike, *Minher*, and let me go Eberstein. We slave laborers now big people, can do, can go. Let me go see *Mevrouw* and kids, I say, tell *Minher* O.K. So come on bike, *Mevrouw;* your man he send many kiss, and soon Yanks make *deutsch* pass, *Minher* fetch you."

"Oh, Jan, how shall I ever thank you?" said Carola. And now Karin took him by the hand and introduced him to everyone simply as "Jan from Holland," because she didn't know any other name for him.

"Sit down on my chair," she said. "I'm going to put on some water for tea, because Korr told me that in Holland tea is offered night and day whenever a visitor appears. And what tea, Jan! Real black tea from America. Wait till you taste it!"

Till sat down beside Jan on the arm of his chair. "You grown up a fine fellow, Till," said Jan. "What you do all time?"

"Land work," said Till importantly. "Maybe I'll be a farmer; then I won't have to take any final exam at school."

Karin came in with the tea and a few sandwiches and cookies, which Jan demolished without any effort. He said the tea made him feel homesick, and as soon as he had gone back with the news about his family to Dr. Lorenz, he would set off with a few of the Jongs for Holland, even if they had to go on foot. His father had a small tulip nursery near Haarlem, and if he hurried, he'd get back while the Darwin tulips were still in flower. There was certainly no finer sight in the whole world. Later all the Lorenzes would have to come and visit him in Holland.

But now Carola brought out two bottles of Rüdesheimer wine, and for that the Rhinelander willingly forgave her earlier remark about Russia. American whisky was all right, he said, but nothing could beat a good Rhine wine, and for the last six years not one drop of it had passed his lips. "This could almost make me change my decision to stay here in Thuringia and bring my family out here."

"Don't you want to go back to the Rhine?" Lobelius asked in astonishment.

"My comrades and I have our own reasons why we want to stay on here. I am a metal worker and could find work here."

"Do you think it possible that Thuringia could come under Russian occupation?" Karin asked, alarmed.

"I can say nothing about that. A good deal was agreed upon at Yalta, which will only come out later."

Thanks to the wine, the rest of the evening's talk took a less political turn than the men from Buchenwald had intended. As the evening wore on, a quiet contentment made itself felt, and in the gentle warmth of this friendly atmosphere the differences of opinion were forgotten for a while.

It was after eleven when the guests took their departure. Till and Jan went to sleep in the barn with Bluebeard, and it was obvious that they would be talking half the night. Early next morning the Dutchman wanted to set off back to the city on Doctor Lorenz's bike.

Carola and Karin had another talk that evening. "Do you really want to go to Buchenwald with Frau Wöllner, Mutti? I think you don't realize what you will see there. I've had a foretaste of it, anyhow."

"Yes, and one only has to look at you to know what you felt about it. Maria Wöllner will need me on this difficult trip.

Even if I didn't feel so relieved and thankful as I do today, I would go with her. The worse it is, the more reason why I cannot let her go alone."

The next morning the parsonage was like a transit camp. The wife of an SS man appeared and begged the pastor to destroy the documents concerning her family's renunciation of the church. They had done it only under compulsion; he must surely understand that. Two others brought five-year-old children to be baptized and wondered if the pastor would be so kind as to back-date the baptisms a few years. The teacher, who had been there once already, came again to try and convince Lobelius that he had always been "at bottom" a good Christian.

In the hall, Martha and Karin listened to the pastor's voice rising in Old Testament anger. When it was a question of telling the truth, there was no compromise possible for him.

Then two ladies appeared who wanted to talk to him about starting the Women's Guild and the Young People's Fellowship again. And the men wanted their own evening devoted to political and social discussions with the pastor.

"What sort of private life can a pastor possibly have?" Karin asked, after Martha had told her about the various requests.

Martha smiled. She knew all about that from her parents' house. "For a pastor his profession is the Alpha and Omega," she said evenly. "My mother once said that a pastor's wife was justified in letting herself be called Frau Pastor, for she carries at least half the burden and more than half the renunciation of life's pleasure on her own shoulders. Still, I think it's the most wonderful thing in the world."

"Do you?" Karin said, and looked at Martha's simple, strong face searchingly.

Slowly the blood rose in Martha's fair skin from the throat up to the brows. "I certainly do," she said with complete frankness.

The last visitor that morning was an old lady whom neither Martha nor Karin knew. But Lobelius knew her, and when she came into his room, he stood up and held out his hand. It was Lotte's mother.

"Is your daughter back home again, Frau Henrich?" he asked. "I know how hard it will be for all of you to forget the past and to forgive, but with love and patience it can be done."

The woman sat there and said nothing. Her work-worn hands lay in her lap, clutching a letter. She had led a blameless life; the neighbors had respected her and perhaps feared her a little because of her strictness, for when anyone did something that was not right, she didn't spare her criticism. She was proud of her righteous ways and of the well-kept farm, proud of her pretty daughter who was a good girl and whom any of the farming families in Eberstein would have welcomed as a daughter-in-law. And then it had happened—her daughter's disgrace—and perhaps it could only have happened because she had been too sure of herself. After that she could no longer show her face in town. When she had to go out, her old acquaintances turned their heads away and did not bid her good morning. There were even some who spat in front of her. And the ones who showed pity were the worst of all. Her husband took to drink. They could get no help on the farm. Lotte, who had worked as tirelessly as her parents, lay in the hospital, and who knew what she would be like when she came out. Well, now all that was over, and perhaps Stani would come back and marry Lotte. Then there would be a young man on the farm, for Stani was a farmer's son, and in time all the bad things that had happened would gradually be forgotten.

She sat opposite the pastor, shaking her gray head with the severely pulled-back hair and saying not a word. Lobelius waited patiently, as if he had nothing else in the world to do.

How often he had experienced the healing strength of this silent readiness!

At last the woman held out the ragged sheet of paper to him, and it was as if she tore it from her heart. He slowly read the clumsy handwriting and the clumsy German.

"Dear Lotte," it ran. "I'm still alive and this is to let you know. Now I go home to my former bride. I am much homesick and cannot live in land where people so bad. Am sorry, dear Lotte, and will not forget good people there also. Remember your faithful Stani."

The woman had not taken her eyes away from Lobelius's face while he was reading the letter. Now he handed it back to her, gently touching her hand. "How has Lotte taken it?" he asked.

"She just sits there with her eyes boring a hole in the wall and says it would have been better for her if she had drowned that time in the millpond."

"I'll call on you this evening," said Lobelius. "I wanted to talk to Lotte to see if she wouldn't come and be a choir member again, now that she's feeling better. Frau Wöllner says she has such a pretty voice. And I need you, too, Frau Henrich. The Women's Guild will start again soon, and you were always a pillar of strength in that. The stream of refugees from the east is unceasing; among them there are children who have no parents and for whom we must find homes. Really, we can't do without your experience and devotion."

And then the old woman, who had never shed a tear since the disaster had come upon her, suddenly began to weep. She wept long and silently, as old women weep. Again Lobelius just sat there and waited. When she had gone, he hoped that with those tears she had made her first step forward into life again.

Lobelius looked tired when after the long morning's work he went for a short walk with Karin along the riverbank. The mayor had asked them to come to the town hall in the afternoon. He had to speak to the colonel about something that had plunged the whole of Eberstein into grief and anger: three Poles had stabbed to death the eighteen-year-old daughter of the pharmacist. Why? Because of a golden chain she wore around her neck and had refused to give them. The girl had been on her way to an outlying farm with some medicine. The three men had waylaid her, at first possibly only to frighten her. But then their rage had broken out when the girl had resisted them, and it had happened.

Now there would be a tense interview with the colonel in the afternoon. Karin silently hoped that kind Lieutenant Mackenzie would be there, for she wanted to ask him for advice about Armin. Perhaps he knew of a way to send news to Freiburg or to have Armin himself sent home.

"When we've finished at the town hall, I'll drop in at the Henrichs'," said Lobelius. "I promised Lotte's mother earlier this morning. Stani won't be coming back. That's what happened to the great love that had to be proved."

"Yes," said Karin sadly.

They walked hand in hand through the grass that was still wet with the preceding night's rain. "I'll go up to the camp," she said after a while. "The Yanks sent two medical orderlies, but they can't make the people understand them. The women sent word asking if I could go back and see them."

"I won't let you go alone," said Lobelius. They were both thinking of the pharmacist's daughter. But Karin touched her neck; she did not wear a golden chain or anything else worth stealing. "They know me and will not harm me," she said, gazing at the raindrops that hung like little crystal balls on every leaf and blade. "Till rode over to Herr Franke's sister's to help her out with something," she said. "When he came back, he told me that the first violets are out in the beech-wood."

"The first violets," said Lobelius, lost in thought. Then he stopped and kissed her.

"As long as I am with you, I can do without violets," she said with a little smile. "But it's so hard to understand that in this year, as in every year, there should be violets blooming and trees putting out new leaf. After what we heard yesterday, oughtn't the earth to be withered and bear nothing but thorns and thistles, as the Book of Genesis says?"

"And to think that all this has been going on for years and we didn't know about it. . . . I'm haunted by the thought: What is wrong with us Christians that all those things *could* happen? When in a predominantly Christian land and people a whole class degenerates and becomes a bunch of raving butchers, then there must be something wrong with us all. A healthy body doesn't produce such a plague of boils—and I mean by that Christians everywhere. Two thousand years! And we have to start all over again."

"But what can one man do?"

"A very little, and also a lot," he said. "He can offer himself up, renounce his own desires and plans, believe and serve. It will always be individuals who are called upon to do that, but there is no other way for them."

She stood there with lowered head. Sunlight and shadow played together on her shining hair. Her light dress was reflected in the calmly flowing waters of the river. "Let me look at you while you're still here," he said, and lifted her face. He smiled into her eyes and laid a finger on her lips. "No, don't say anything now. Or rather, yes, say something, dearest, but nothing that will make us sad."

"I love you," she said.

He took her in his arms and kissed her more tenderly than he had ever done. "Dear heart," he said. "I know."

✦ *Chapter Ten* ✦

All at once the parsonage had become a house of silence, at least for a few hours every day. No one had asked for it in so many words, but as long as Max Wöllner lay in the deck chair under the elderberry bush, protected from the wind by the wall of the barn, no doors were slammed in the house, little Josef and Edgar were not allowed to play with their drums and tin trumpets, Frau Merkel and Frau Lübzin lowered their voices when quarreling, and the two old ladies from East Prussia, who continued tirelessly to weed and plant on their vegetable plot, abstained from talking because, as they were both hard of hearing, it was not possible for them to indulge in a *quiet* conversation.

Maria Wöllner and Carola Lorenz had brought Max Wöllner back with them from the concentration camp at Buchenwald. After much searching, questioning, and roaming around they had finally found him, under another name, in the t.b. ward. Until now they had said nothing to anyone about what they had seen on their visit to the place of horrors—not even to Lobelius.

The American doctor who had at last given them permission to enter the section reserved for tubercular patients informed them of the state of Wöllner's health. His escape to this part of the hospital had indeed saved him from death in an extermination camp, but had exposed him to the almost unavoidable danger of infection. Immediately after the liberation of the camp the American Red Cross had taken on the care of the sick until they could later be transported to hospitals or sanitariums. There were many for whom, despite the greatest care, there was no hope left. But the young t.b. specialist did not consider Wöllner's case to be hopeless. A more reliable prognosis would have to wait until a general increase in his strength could be achieved through a few months of nourishing food and rest. Meanwhile, the patient would be best off where he was.

But while Maria Wöllner was sitting with her husband, Carola had another private talk with the doctor, who after further consideration agreed to let Wöllner go. But only under the understanding that in Eberstein he would have either a single room in a hospital or a bed in the t.b. ward.

"I am certain that we can get that for him," Carola said confidently. "Frau Wöllner has worked with the sisters in the hospital at Eberstein; they will do everything possible for her. Then she can bring her husband every day to rest in the fresh air of the parsonage garden, where we live."

"Very well, but keep other people, especially children, away from him; partly because of the danger of infection and partly because of his mental state. He must rest as much as possible and in the open air when he can. There would be nothing against his taking a short walk each day, very slowly of course, and never for longer than half an hour. I think you're right when you say that the presence of his wife would be a decided help in bringing him back to health. I shall give you a card certifying that you are to receive extra rations, and I shall see to the provision of an ambulance for your transportation."

Now Maria Wöllner brought her husband every morning along the short path from the hospital, across the churchyard, to the parsonage garden, made him comfortable in the deck chair, and sat beside him or left him alone. She sensed how difficult it was for him to grope his way back to life. She, too, belonged to this life that had become utterly foreign to him after six years of separation—six years that could not be measured by ordinary standards of time. They had a long way to go back to one another, a way that led through ruins and tears, through anguish and horror, and through the icy wastes of solitude.

If only he gets well again! thought Maria Wöllner time and time again in those early days; if only we can stay together now, I won't ask life for anything more.

Carola and Karin had had the idea of moving the piano into their bedroom, where the windows opened to the garden. There Maria played for her husband every day, an hour or more, for music was their common language, in which they could tell each other more than they could with words. He never said anything when she rejoined him; only by the brightened look in his eyes could she tell that she had done him good. One day she was improvising, and she chanced upon a theme that she had not thought of playing before. It was the passage in Gluck's *Orpheus in the Underworld*, where Orpheus is playing his flute to lead Eurydice, freed at last, step by step out of the world of shadows into the light of day. Maria herself listened as if she were hearing the well-known melody for the first time: that sweet and yearning strain summoning toward life, struggling against the dark, alluring beckoning of death, and that in the end is defeated. Oh God, she thought, why that defeat? Because love was impatient, because it could not wait, because there was not enough strength to make that last sacrifice. When she went back to sit by Max, he still said nothing, only took her hand, slowly tracing with one of his fingers each single one of hers, as if he, the musician, had to discover all over again this other musician's hand. At last he said, "You know there was something he was forbidden to do?"

Startled by the urgency in his voice, she asked, "Who?"

"Orpheus."

"Orpheus? Oh yes, to look back."

"Remember," he said.

She bent over him to hide her wet eyes, brushed his forehead with her lips, and said, "We shall look forward only." Then she went to bring him his glass of sheep's milk.

All the people in the house were vying with each other to do everything they could for the man who had risen from the dead. Carola insisted that he drink only the creamy sheep's milk. Every day Till brought a little gift for the first Jew he had ever met; he couldn't remember the Jewish friends who had been frequent visitors at his parents' house before the war.

"Why was he in a concentration camp?" he asked Karin.

"Because he's a Jew."

"But he can't help that!" Till still couldn't understand that people were persecuted, imprisoned, tortured, and murdered, even though they had done nothing wrong. Now he brought Max his little presents as peace offerings: a piece of bread and butter that he had saved from his breakfast at the Frankes; a few violets that he had picked; a spray of larch for the blue vase in Maria's room. Every morning Frau Wöllner found something outside her door, often without knowing who had put it there. The two eggs could have come from either Carola or Frau Merkel; the first lettuce or the bunch of primroses from the East Prussian old ladies or from Frau Lübzin's plot; a thick slice of homemade liver sausage (much too heavy for the sick man's shrunken stomach) from Frau Franke or Dorle. The bar of American chocolate certainly came out of Karin's honorarium as a translator; the book from Lobelius; and the soft cross-stitch cushion bore the unmistakable imprint of Aunt Ulrike's handiwork.

As a matter of fact, Karin's supplies of chocolate benefited not only Max Wöllner. Bluebeard had an uncanny way of sniffing out chocolate, in the same way as hunting dogs smell out game or bloodhounds track down criminals. One fine morning, he sat down expectantly, tail wagging, head tilted to one side, next to the deck chair, and graciously allowed Maria to scratch his head; but obviously that was not what he had come for. When Wöllner saw him, he looked from the dog to his wife and back to the dog again. "Is it Puck?" he asked incredulously.

"Not actually," said Maria with a smile. "Perhaps a reincarnation."

Bluebeard now came every day for his piece of chocolate and then lay quietly for a while beside Max Wöllner.

Armin no longer needed a wheel chair to get from the hospital to the parsonage; he even occasionally took a stroll through the town on his way there. But every day when the weather was fine, he dutifully lay for two hours under the weeping willow by the pond, though it was becoming increasingly difficult for him to lie still for so long. Only when Karin kept him company was obedience easy, or so he said. There was always so much for them to talk about. He liked to read her passages from the book he was studying at the moment. Recently it had been Plato's *Phaidon*. She would sit on the grass beside his chair, her arms clasped around her knees, and listen to the words that the condemned Socrates spoke in prison to his friends before his death. "The philosopher has no care for his own body, Simmias." She smiled to herself; Helmut might have said exactly the same thing. He sometimes reminded her of that ancient Greek scholar. There was the same indifference toward worldly things and toward his own person, the same imperturbable passion for truth. Then that wonderful dialogue about death and the immortality of the soul. Karin thought there was nothing more persuasive than that in Christian teaching. But then came the passage that describes how Socrates sent away his children with his womenfolk, among whom must have been Xantippe, his own wife, apparently so that he might be left to die undisturbed. It suddenly occurred to Karin how hard it must have been for Xantippe to live with the philosopher. At least he might have parted from her on more affectionate terms! And, as if he had guessed her thoughts, Armin said, "I've always felt sorry for poor Xantippe. My school friends often teased me for defending her. But just think of the character she is usually given: that of the nagging wife with no understanding of the higher thoughts indulged in by the great sage she is married to. But this great man leaves her and his children to starve, literally starve! And then she is depicted as a shrew, who drags her great husband down to the level of her own pots and pans. What woman wouldn't turn cantankerous if there was nothing to put in those pots and pans because her husband sits with his friends conducting endless philosophical discussions? Not that I have anything against philosophy, but after all, I believe that even a philosopher must look after his own family."

"Funny, I was just thinking the same thing about Xantippe."

"The really funny thing is that no one has seen it in that light before. How deeply she must have loved him to stand all that from him! I even suspect that, in his own queer way, he must have loved her too, for he was clever enough to realize that he needed that sort of wife: someone who'd look after the material things of life for him, as far as she could; who saw to it that he didn't go about in rags; who kept the home together, despite bitter poverty, for the children's sake, leaving him free to go off to his symposia and pursue truth. Just you wait; one day, when I'm a teacher, I'll read my students a defense of Xantippe and inculcate a little more respect for the woman who had the hard luck to be the life companion of a barefooted philosopher!"

"And yet," remarked Karin, "she wouldn't have changed with any other woman in Athens."

"Maybe, but that was precisely because she couldn't help being herself: a splendid woman, strong both in anger and in love, and as single-minded in her devotion to her family as he was in his to truth. Without her he would have died of starvation. If she hadn't lost her temper with him from time to time, she would have been a colorless, washed-out, poor sort of creature. Because she was not, she is now held up to scorn. I call that the height of injustice!"

"When you get to Greece, lay an olive branch on the steps of some temple in memory of her—and in homage from me."

"I'll remember that," he said, shut the book, and looked past Karin's profile to the hills beyond. There was a lengthy pause, then he said, "I still haven't told you that Tünnes came to see me yesterday. Till wouldn't given him any peace until he had done so. Now he's going to speak to the Americans and make quite clear to them that I didn't belong to the SS clique in Buchenwald."

"That's very decent of him, as he can hardly hope to convert you to his own political beliefs."

"Nobody bothered about that sort of thing in the camp, when it was a question of helping a friend. I've already told you how all the decent fellows up there stuck together like members of a secret society. Even among the SS men, especially among the younger ones, there were some who could be trusted. I only had two brief encounters with Tünnes in the office. Once I was alone and he asked me to lend him an official stamp. We made no mention of the fact that such a thing was forbidden. But after that he knew what side I was on."

Karin had a hundred burning questions to ask, but she refrained. "Don't let Till keep pestering you with questions," she said. "You must first get your strength back before you begin to talk about such things."

"Sometimes I *have* to talk to him about them. Till now

wants to get everything quite straight about what he has been believing so passionately all these years. What a child he is still in many ways!"

"He trusts you completely. . . . I've already spoken about you to Lieutenant Mackenzie. His unit will probably be leaving here in the next few days, but he has promised me that he will deal with your case before he goes. We gave him a detailed account of everything that happened, and he knows we wouldn't try to put anything over on him. If Tünnes also speaks for you now, and if you fill in your questionnaire correctly—I have one upstairs for you—the lieutenant will give you a permit to return home. How and when you will get there is another matter. But in any case, if you have this permit, neither the French nor the Americans nor the British will put you in a prisoner-of-war camp. Perhaps the best thing would be for you to accompany us back to Erfurt when my father comes to fetch us."

"Thank you, Karin," he said. "That's a good idea. I'd have a better chance of finding transportation to the southwest in Erfurt than out here at the back of beyond."

"Karin!" someone called from the house. She stood up. "I must go and see what they want. Perhaps I'll have to go back to the camp."

But it was something else. Stina Möller had called and invited Lobelius and the others to come and listen to Goebbels' speech for Hitler's birthday on the battery set; it would start in a few moments.

Hitler's birthday! thought Karin, as she sat with her mother, Aunt Ulrike, and Helmut in the tiny parlor of the gravedigger's house. Hitler's birthday, and Karin had forgotten about that fatal date completely, the day on which in former years the streets had been hung with swastika flags. But these had now been burned, and here in Eberstein they had thought they would hear no more of that demonic empire whose voice now rang from the radio once again.

At the last minute Till came in and sat down beside Karin. While the voice filled the little room with its bellowings, he exchanged only one shocked glance with his sister, and then for the rest of the speech sat silently staring at the ceiling.

"Our Lord God shall stand by us until the victory of our rightful cause is won!" cried the voice from the chancellery bunker across the wounded, burning, devastated land. "As long as we have our Führer, we cannot be defeated. His unshakable faith shall lead us safely and victoriously out of the direst calamities, if only we do not weaken and lose faith. It is with a pure heart, with clean hands and a clear conscience that I offer our beloved Führer today the warm good wishes of his entire people."

No one said anything when the speech was at an end. Even the Voice of the People remained silent. Till left hastily. Aunt Ulrike just sat there and stared dumbly at her hands folded on her lap.

What could they have said? Two-thirds of Germany was in the hands of the Allies; towns and villages lay in ruins or in infernos of fire; thousands of men and half-grown boys were daily being sacrificed to a lost cause or being shot or hanged by SS patrols if they no longer were prepared to offer up their lives; hundreds of thousands of refugees from the eastern provinces had perished on the long journey through snow and bitter cold; the remainder had hoped to find security in central Germany. Now they were dying on the choked highways from the machine-gun bullets of low-diving planes; dying in the conflagrations caused by fire bombs in the cities; dying under the pitiless skies of a strange country whose stars were extinguished by the tempest of flames. "As long as we have our Führer, we cannot be defeated!" screamed the voice from the radio, striving even in these final moments to drag the rest of the living down into the swamp of total defeat.

It's like the old woodcuts of the Dance of Death, thought Karin, shuddering: the skeleton is fiddling us all into our graves.

But we want to live, they all wanted to live, and why are *we* among those who have survived? What's the sense in it? Or is it pure chance? Why, for example, am I one of the survivors, when I don't even know yet what to do with my own life?

That night she lay awake for a long time and thought of the separation Helmut and she had to face. They had both known it must come since their evening walk by the river, and perhaps even before that.

I love him, and yet I have to leave him, she thought. How little she had known when she had first arrived here, imagining that life in a country parsonage was one long, romantic idyll. But the simple life was not as simple as she had thought; and just because you loved a man, it didn't mean that you were the right wife for him. Everything was just beginning for her; there was so much she had to see and learn and experience before she could both give herself to a man and take him as her husband. She was no longer even certain that the church was the right refuge for her, the harbor where she could lie safely at anchor for the rest of her life. She doubted and questioned and rebelled all the time; but the wife of a pastor would be expected to be a tower of strength, an example, in her life and her faith.

If we were to wait another year or two, she suddenly thought, if Helmut would give me time to grow and ripen? Perhaps then if I came back here, I would be more prepared for him and for the task his wife must take on?

She must have given way to a sob at one point, for she felt her mother's hand reaching over to her, and after a while she heard Carola say, "Don't worry so, darling."

It was good not to be altogether alone in her great need. "Do you think things might work out differently if I waited a few years and then came back to him?" she asked.

"Who can say?" her mother replied. "And who knows, your paths might then be even more widely separated than they are now. One thing I do know: Helmut must get married *soon*. He needs a wife, and the whole of Eberstein is expecting him to take one soon, for Eberstein also needs a pastor's wife. But if he has just the faintest glimmer of hope that you may come back again, he won't marry the woman who would be just right for him, and you know who she is."

"Yes, I know," Karin said under her breath. "But we love each other so deeply; why must we hurt one another so?"

"My dear child, there is no love without sadness and without hurt for others," said Carola. "And if the sadness comes at the beginning, it is better than later, when it will bring remorse and bitterness. Love is the most beautiful and the most terrible thing that human beings have been endowed with, and even the happiest love remains a risky and a fragile bridge across the abyss that separates soul from soul, as two can never become one. But the fact that love is given us, love with its unavoidable pains and sorrows, is in itself a grace, and there are not many who experience it to the full. Therefore, you must be grateful for it, even though it hurts you now, for neither of you would have wanted to miss what you have known with each other, isn't that so?"

"I wouldn't have missed it for the world," said Karin. "And neither of us will ever love another person quite as much."

"I wouldn't wish that for you," her mother replied. "Rilke knew all about it, when he wrote:

" 'Ever and again, and even though we learned by heart
    Love's landscape, and the small graveyard with the plaintive
        names,
    Ever and again we go from thence, together . . .' "

Things had quieted down in Eberstein since the death of
the pharmacist's daughter. It was as if this innocent sacrifice
to hatred and greed had opened everyone's eyes at last. The
commandant had finally let himself be persuaded to order
the MP's to watch the camp more closely.

Armin received his permit to travel home, something that
in those days was worth more than its weight in gold. "You
give it to him," said Lieutenant Mackenzie when he was saying
good-by to Karin and Lobelius. "We're leaving tomorrow, as
soon as our relief arrives. I've been asked by the colonel to
express his thanks to you and the pastor for your help to us
and in the camp." He thought for a moment, then said, "Are
both your homes in Thuringia?"

"Pastor Lobelius lives here," said Karin, "but I think my
father will be coming soon to take us back to Erfurt."

"I know as little as you do about the final distribution of
the occupied zones," said the American. "But if it should
happen that you would prefer to live further to the west, then
please remember that I'd gladly do all I can to help you, as far
as it is in my power. In any case, I'll give you this army address, which will always find me. Any American forces' office
will forward your letter to me if you say that you worked for
us here. We badly need women interpreters in our military
government of occupation. I could certainly get a job for you.
Good-by and all the best!"

"We also want to thank you, Lieutenant Mackenzie," Karin
said warmly. "Both for your kind collaboration and for your
friendly offer of help to me."

They shook hands. "Good-by," Lobelius said.

That evening a new detachment of American troops rolled in. They had brought their own interpreter with them, a pretty, elegantly uniformed young woman with very red lips and fingernails painted the same shade. The girls of Eberstein turned up their noses at her, but the men's eyes popped out of their heads.

A Polish-American doctor had come with them and took over the care of the sick at the camp with the help of two nurses and an orderly. They appeared there next morning just as Karin was putting a cold compress on a child with fever. The nurses, clad in snow-white uniforms and with every conceivable medical aid and appliance, gazed in pity at the shabby paper bandages in Karin's first-aid kit.

"So I'm out of a job," she said, with a mixture of relief and regret, when she passed the camp gates with Helmut. "And now we're going to take a leisurely stroll back home through the meadows. Not along the main road and not through the town, where we'll meet nothing but people wanting something from you. I need some green to refresh my eyes, and I want to have you to myself just for a little while."

"That's fine with me." Lobelius smiled. "Only we'll have to swim across the river."

"Didn't you hear Till and Krischan hammering away last night? Early this morning Till told me the bridge is now as good as new, and they would like you to be the first to cross it—a kind of inaugural ceremony. They always choose a high dignitary for that sort of thing, you know."

"And so they hit on me?"

"Who else? But if it's a swim you're wanting, we can do that this afternoon. Martha has called a meeting of the Women's Guild for half-past four, in order to discuss what evening in the week would suit them best. It'll take them a good hour to decide, and during that time we can both escape and do a little swimming, then relax somewhere along the riverbank where no one can find us, and do nothing, just gaze up into heaven and be glad that we're still together."

So it worked out. They crept out of the house in the afternoon with their swimming things under their arms and with the precious feeling of two children playing hooky. They undressed in the shed, walked along by the wall through the now deserted garden down to the river, dipped their feet in the water swollen with the spring rains, and then dived in. The same little waves played over both of them like shy caresses; they moved their arms in time, and their breathing had the same rhythm as they swam upstream without speaking; only their eyes, when they met from time to time, suddenly brightened. When they had swum far enough, they turned around. A few patches of sky hung above the now thickly leaved trees as pale blue as the eggs of the song thrush. There were clouds driving up rapidly from the west, like a herd of gray sheep running before a sheep dog. Rain suddenly drummed on the leaves and made a pattern of rings on the water. Fickle April was weeping like a spoiled child, but after a few minutes she was laughing again. Karin and Helmut climbed out on the bank to enjoy the last few heavy drops of the shower. Then they lay down in the meadow opposite the Frankes' farm; the grass was already lightly veiled with the lilac umbels of lady's-smock. The two lay hidden beneath a willow, amidst the humming of insects, the chirping of crickets, the whirring of a dragonfly's glassy wings. The frog concert sounded faintly from the parsonage garden, and from the roof of the barn came the evening song of the blackbird.

A horse neighed somewhere on the farm; shortly after they saw Till riding chestnut Lola into the water. The horse and rider clambered out of the river barely ten feet from where they were lying without noticing them. The horse had neither saddle nor bridle. Till had twisted the long mane around his hand, his bare heels dug into the horse's dripping flanks, and now they were trotting along the path through the meadows. The ground shook with the heavy horse's hoof beats, and Till sang at the top of his voice.

Karin's head was lying in the crook of Helmut's arm.

"Don't be sad," she said after a long silence.

"Not sad, just grateful," he said.

The blackbird was singing; the wet grass smelled sweet. "When I get to be a very old woman," said Karin, "I think that even then I shall still live through this Eberstein spring every year when April comes. I shall remember the frogs and the blackbird and how we lay here together. How we sat in the cellar of the town hall with the captain telephoning nearby —I still seem to hear it quite distinctly: *Jawohl*, Herr General! And then how the American fire bombs began falling on the town and we thought it was all up with us and we were afraid. At least, *I* was afraid. And then how we walked toward those American tanks and I was so scared I waved with my absurd little handkerchief. But all the same it was wonderful. And the way we brought Armin back from the wood. Always the two of us together. In the camp with the sick children and the drunken man with the frightful hole in his head. Poor Ivan! And to think that the ruffian made me a bracelet of birch bark. Your first sermon after the occupation; I think that was the most beautiful thing of all. Oh, there'll never, never again be a spring like this one."

"So lovely, despite grief and death," he said quietly.

Karin sat up, propped herself on her hands, and gazed into his face for a long time with contracted brows, as if trying to imprint it firmly on her memory. "It was our spring, ours alone, with all its beauty and all its sorrow. Promise me . . . promise me that you, too, will never forget it, later, when you are perhaps . . . married to some other woman."

"Forget . . ." he said.

They both suddenly shivered and stood up quickly. The

cool damp air of early evening was already rising from the meadows. "Karin!" he said, and laid his hands on her shoulders. If he kisses me now, then I'm done for, thought Karin. And yet she was hoping that he would; there was nothing on earth she longed for more. But he let his hands slip down her arms hanging motionless at her sides, then took a deep breath and dived into the water. They swam slowly back to the parsonage garden.

"What will you do when life gets back more or less to normal again?" he asked her as they walked toward the house.

She shrugged her shoulders. "I don't know yet. Perhaps I'll study medicine. Or first spend a year as a nurse in a clinic, until the universities get properly under way again. I've often thought that the most important thing to do would be to attack the evils of our time at the very roots—hatred, distrust, impatience. Try to help people to understand each other a little better. But how to begin? No, I still don't see my way clear, Helmut. I only know that I want to do something worth while. But first I must find myself, make something of myself."

"Be sure to let me know always what you are doing. And promise me that if we come under Russian occupation here, you will go over to the West."

"If that happened, I think my parents would leave everything here and start again, right from the beginning, building up a practice somewhere else. When we were once discussing the possibility of being conquered by the Russians, my father said he would rather be poor in the West or in some other land than allow his children to grow up under another totalitarian rule. Of course I would have to work, and perhaps I would serve for a while as translator for the Americans or the British wherever we went to. That, too, might be some contribution toward international understanding. But what about you, Helmut; what will you do?"

"I shall stay here," he answered. "The occupation can't last forever, and if the Russians take over, we shall have to do what we have been doing all through the twelve years of the Third Reich: help to preserve what we believe in and strengthen the faith of those for whom we are responsible."

"Don't let's think about that now," said Karin.

That evening it so happened that she was alone with Martha in the kitchen washing the dinner dishes.

"What would you do, Martha, if the Russians came here?" Karin asked, as she put the spoons away in the drawer.

Martha held a plate in her hand, gave it another wipe with the cloth, and put it down slowly on the well-scrubbed oil-cloth top of the kitchen table. Then she raised her eyes and looked at Karin with a strange smile playing on her lips—a smile that might express utter frankness or unsounded depths of thought. "Why do you ask that?" she said. "You surely know the answer."

"Yes," said Karin. "You'll stay with him. But don't think that he will forget me quickly."

Martha went on smiling, though a little sadly now. "I can wait," she said. "There is nothing I couldn't do, where he is concerned. Even give events a little push forward in the right direction, if that would be for his own good."

"And do you think it's for his own good if I go away and you stay here?"

"You must admit that I have done nothing to push *that*."

"But it is what you've always wanted, for me to go away."

"Yes, that *is* what I hoped," said Martha, and laid her hand gently on Karin's shoulder. "Not just for selfish reasons—please try to believe that. Perhaps in time you'll be able not to grudge him to me."

"I believe you," said Karin, and the words seemed to choke her. She walked quickly to the door while Martha cleared the table in order to begin pressing Helmut's Sunday trousers. There was still enough heat left in the little black iron stove to warm the old-fashioned iron. With her hand on the latch of the door, Karin turned around. "I know that you will be a better wife for him and a better pastor's wife for the parish than I could have been," she said.

"Thank you, Karin," said Martha Born.

On Saturday the electricity suddenly came on again. The water supply was resumed; the women laughingly shouted the good news to each other across garden walls and from windows. The radio came to life once more. Now in the evenings they all gathered in the room of the general's widow, who had the one good radio in the house; it was impossible to get the BBC on the small People's Sets of the Third Reich. Without admitting to each other how anxious they were, they listened intently for some news about how the occupation zones would be divided. But there was still no word of that. It could only mean that what they had heard up to now was mere rumor, for wasn't it unthinkable that the Western powers would let the forces of Communism penetrate so deeply into the heart of Europe? Their hopes rose again.

Whenever Karin went through the little town with Helmut, they saw bleeding-hearts flowers in the neatly raked beds of the gardens, along with bold ranks of tulips and blue forget-me-not borders. The fresh bright colors stood out clearly against the gray walls. Pear and plum trees were scattering their blossoms everywhere. In a corner of the miller's garden the first cherry tree was in full bloom, reflected like a white cloud in the dark waters of the millpond. For Karin, Eberstein had once more become the picturesque old town that had so enchanted her on her first visits; a place out of another age, seen in passing. Its narrowness was not depressing any longer, because she knew that the ancient town gates beneath their plump towers were still open to the outer world. Everything was already in the past for her—a lovely memory, a bright picture

on a dark background, an April day, overclouded with passing
sadness, irradiated with a tranquil gaiety.

Till was making plans with Armin. He was to share his holidays between Armin in Baden and the Frankes in Eberstein,
since now he wouldn't be able to live at the parsonage. "Because Dorle says that the pastor isn't going to be my brother-
in-law after all," he said, then swiftly clapped his hand over
his mouth. "Gosh, I should have kept my trap shut; it's the
first time I've spoken about it. But if nothing's going to come
of it . . ."

"I see," said Armin. "So that was how it was. What an idiot
I am, never to have noticed anything! Karin and Lobelius. And
now you say it's all come to nothing?"

"*I* don't say so," Till answered cautiously, "because, to tell
the truth, I don't know the ins and outs of these things. Dorle
says so, and she says she's really sorry, because it would have
made quite a change to have an elegant, pretty pastor's wife.
It's going a bit far to call her pretty. Do *you* think my sister's pretty?"

"Yes, I think you could call her that," Armin admitted.

"The pastor's a nice fellow. I shouldn't have minded at
all having him as a brother-in-law. Obviously Karin is too
young for him. That's understandable, isn't it?"

"Yes," said Armin.

"But on the other hand, maybe he is too old for her. Because
he really must be pretty old, mustn't he?"

"Yes."

"Well, anyhow, it's none of *our* business."

"No."

"Well, I'd better get back to my cows . . ."

On Wednesday of the next week, as Karin and Carola were
together in the shed for the evening milking, Carola suddenly

leaned her head against Schirin's fleecy side and said, "Now I am really fed up with it!"

"With what?" queried Karin.

"Waiting like this. Tomorrow morning I'm simply going to set off for Erfurt. On foot, because I never did learn to ride a bike, and a humble pedestrian would be quite safe, having nothing worth stealing. I'll put my oldest things on, and everyone will take me for a poor old refugee woman. No, keep quiet and let me finish speaking. Of course I'll go by unfrequented field paths. It's longer than the main road, but on the first day I could get as far as Dittelstedt and stay there overnight with Helmut's friend. Then on the second day I could easily make my way to Erfurt."

"I haven't heard anything so crazy for a long time," cried Karin. "Forgive me for saying so, but I'm ready to bet that while you're plodding along the country lanes, Father will be on his way here by the main road, because he must come with a cart, and then when you reach home, there'll only be Nurse Ottilie's open arms to receive you."

"I can't understand why he's so long in coming!"

"What can he do when they don't give him a travel permit? Or maybe he has to wait for a baby to arrive; you know how often women get the date wrong. Sleep on it for another night at least. Then let's talk it over again tomorrow morning."

"All right, I'll wait until tomorrow," said Carola, gazing thoughtfully at her five lambs. "I was thinking we'd leave the two male lambs here, one for Aunt Ulrike and one for the Wöllners. Dorle would surely be willing to feed them for another two or three weeks, and then her father can kill them. We'll be only too glad, as always, not to have to eat our own lambs."

They went upstairs to tidy themselves up for the evening meal. From the road came the sound of wagon wheels. Horses' hoofs rang out. Then everything was quiet again. Next a voice was heard in the hall. Karin cast aside her brush and ran to the door. Carola sat down on the bed and put her hands over her face. Her legs had suddenly become as heavy as lead. She sat there unable to move a finger, and with a great roaring in her ears. Then someone gently pulled her hands from her face, and there was Franz sitting beside her on the bed, Franz in his old brown leather coat, and they were alone together in the room, alone together in the world.

The next morning the cart was waiting at the gateway of the parsonage yard—the same cart that had brought Frau Lorenz and her children here more than three weeks ago. This time Herr Krummbein was not there. Dr. Lorenz had left without a travel permit, and Krummbein had not dared to accompany him. Nurse Ottilie, too, had advised him not to go. But Franz Lorenz said for his part he'd had quite enough of being separated from his family, and as they had told him the day before at the commandant's headquarters that he shouldn't come back to ask for a permit before another two weeks, he had decided to set off without the necessary documents. There was still chaos on the main roads, but no one had stopped him, and the much-feared foreign workers hadn't given a second look at the heavy old peasant's cart.

It might be another thing on the way back with the cart heavily laden, but how could anybody live in these times without taking risks of some kind.

Till was harnessing the horses; he did it as carefully and skillfully as an experienced farmer. Had the boy grown since his father had seen him last? At any rate, he had changed; his movements were more coordinated; he was no longer like a young colt that doesn't know what to do with his legs. Krischan Möller helped him and Dr. Lorenz to load the dismantled beds, the chests and boxes. Karin and her mother chained up the sheep, fastened in the hens, and popped each of the lambs into a sack tied around the neck, so that only their astonished, loudly complaining heads peeped out. Bluebeard was enthroned on top of the piled-up boxes and well-roped mattresses, keeping a watchful eye on the whole proceedings.

Carola and Franz sat up beside Till on the driver's seat. Behind on the cart Karin and Armin kept an eye on the animals. All the inhabitants of the house had gathered at the door of the parsonage. They waved as the cart moved slowly forward over the cobbled square in front of the church. The Frankes and Dorle and of course Stina and Krischan Möller had also come along to speed the departing guests. In the foreground, on the lowest step, stood the two who felt the departure most keenly, Aunt Ulrike and Helmut; on the step behind them Martha.

"Good-by! Good-by! *Auf Wiedersehen!*" came the farewell cries. There were no tears at this departure; they had all been shed already. Even Aunt Ulrike stood there straight and composed, although she saw a fond hope vanishing as the cart slowly rolled away. . . .

Karin kept looking back as long as she could see Helmut standing there. He waved. The morning wind was blowing through his rumpled hair. Then the cart turned the corner, and it was all over. At that moment Karin felt that her life was all over too. But deep inside her she knew already that it was not really so, that she would have to go on, that there must be some meaning in life since it had not been taken away from her.

After the cool, rainy night a radiant spring day gradually rose out of the morning mist. A few small white clouds were sailing over the high blue heavens, just as they had on that morning of Easter Monday. A whole lifetime seemed to lie between then and now.

They passed the churchyard, went through the town and out of the south gate on to the main road. There lay the barracks of the camp, the chimneys of the factory, the high barbed-wire fence. For a moment they could see, over on the other side of the river, the parsonage garden and the white gable of the parsonage roof. Then these, too, disappeared. They had left Eberstein behind. Along the edge of the road cherry trees were blooming like reflections of the flying clouds. The fields spread out toward the hills in green and brown stripes. Till pointed to the Frankes' fields with his whip. "Those are ours, Father."

"Are you quite comfortable?" Armin asked Karin. He really wanted to say something quite different. He would have liked to comfort her, she was looking so pale and serious.

"Yes," she replied. "Yes, thank you."

She sat there alone with her grief; but Armin's heart was heavy too. He had read passages from his favorite books to her, they had discussed all kinds of things—Greece, Germany, Socrates, and what the young people of today could do to make sure that in the future the world would be a happier and cleaner place. This was the girl who had fetched him half-dead out of the wood; a thing one couldn't easily forget. But it was not just that. There was much, much more. And she had been thinking all the time about the old pastor with his black eye patch and his untidy hair; she had simply not been aware of him, of his shy adoration. Well, that's the way life goes.

"Lean back against me," he said. And Karin leaned on his shoulder as if it were the back rest on a park bench.

"Here!" she exclaimed. "You're the one who should be taking it easy. Good heavens, the way Till's rattling along. . . ."

"It's all right. I'll have to make worse journeys than this before I reach home. But, Karin, what will happen to you if the Russians come here?"

"We'll have to wait and see if they *do* come."

"Well, old Tünnes seems to think they will, even if he hasn't said it in so many words. But I really can't believe it.

247

If they occupy Thuringia, you'll come to our Black Forest house, won't you? As soon as I get home, I'll write and tell you if our house is still standing and if my mother is all right and all that."

"How will you send your letter, though?"

"Yes, you're right. What a crazy world! But isn't it wonderful to think we're still alive? It's spring, and we're both young and . . . and you mustn't be so sad, Karin."

"No," she agreed. "But just look at what humanity has done to this beautiful spring!"

Wrecked tanks lay at the edge of the road and in the fresh green grass of the meadows. In the villages were ruins blackened by fire, the charred roofs of barns, shattered houses. Then there were undamaged farms again; fenced fields with young calves; a flock of sheep wandering up a hill with a shepherd and his dog; a crowd of children singing and dancing around a flowering tree.

But the road that passed through all these scenes was a seething mass of movement, like a poisoned vein swollen with bad blood. Till had to exercise the greatest skill and care to get them through it all without accident. He did it so well that his father left him to it without attempting to take over the reins. He and Carola had so much to tell each other that they were glad not to be interrupted.

American jeeps kept dashing past; Russians, Poles, Frenchmen, Belgians from the labor camps were traveling along on every conceivable kind of vehicle. Mothers with their children who had fled out into the countryside during the bombing of the towns were now making their way back in the hope of finding their homes still more or less habitable.

After Dittelstedt a cyclist hung on to the back of the Lorenzes' cart for a while; he was obviously exhausted and trying to get a little rest. "Come up on the cart," said Karen, when they stopped for a moment at a crossroads, and she and

Armin helped the man to clamber up and haul his bike after him. When Karin gave him a few cigarettes, he began to talk. He had been on the road from Breslau for three weeks, passing through German, Russian, and American troops; it was a mystery to him how he had come through without being captured or shot. He wanted to get home to his family. Everybody wanted to get home after five years of war and separations. But how few would find their homes undestroyed; how many would seek in vain for their relatives in the indescribable confusion, where it was impossible to get news or information! Some had fled from their homes because of the bombs, others because of the Russians, still others because of the Americans or the British—their one idea was to get away. Children were sent off into the country while their mothers had to work in the armaments factories. How would they ever trace one another again, how would they ever get to know which members of their scattered families were still alive? How were the women to find out whether their husbands, sons, and brothers had been killed or wounded or taken prisoner?

Armin, who had pricked up his ears at the southern German dialect of the cyclist, asked, "And where do you belong?"

"Lörrach," was the reply.

"Why, then, you'll have to pass through Freiburg!"

"Yes, indeed! I'll stay a night there if the folks I know are still alive."

"Will you spend this night with us at Erfurt and go on tomorrow to Freiburg with a letter from us?" said Karin, turning to her mother, asking her, "We can put up another guest for one night, can't we, Mother?"

"Yes, easily," her mother called back, turning her radiant face toward the stranger for a moment. "There's room enough. You are welcome."

Now they were drawing near Erfurt, and the press on the roads became even greater. It held them up, but it was also an advantage. In this inextricable confusion there was not much danger of an American patrol asking Dr. Lorenz for his travel permit. In fact, they entered the city from the north without any difficulty.

After the peace of Eberstein, almost untouched by bombs, the northern suburbs of Erfurt looked like a landscape on the moon. On the main road into the city a track had been cleared, but on either side lay tottering ruins and yawning craters. Fragments of ripped curtains hung at dark blank windows. Twisted pipes, tangled wires, fallen girders lay around bombed factories like the metal guts of monsters. Walls that had once been homes protecting human beings from the elements were no longer standing. They had contained joy and grief, strife and love, birth and death—all the intimacies of private lives; and now everything lay open and abandoned to the cold gaze of strangers. A radiator still hung between heaven and earth on the blasted wall of an upstairs room. A child's cot balanced precariously over the abyss. Every gust of wind raised clouds of dust and smoke from the smouldering gray heaps of stone and lath and plaster and charred wooden beams. The cart could only move forward at a walking pace now, so the whole desolation passed by them slowly and in ghastly detail. Here and there was a patch of bright color.

"Flowers?" Karin asked.

"For the dead," Armin replied. Tied on a doorpost, all that remained of a vanished house, was a piece of cardboard. "Rudolph, I am at Nelly's in Friedrich Strasse" read the message written there in big, clumsy capitals.

Karin could hardly recognize her own home town, especially the northern suburbs. What street was that? What square? The center of town was not quite so bad. They had to make a long detour following the park. When they finally reached the western suburbs, they heaved a sigh of relief.

There was the Lorenz house, its front showing rusty brown

traces of a fire bomb. But it was still standing; it was safe and sound! Behind the garden wall white and yellow narcissi were blooming on the lawn, as they did every year at this time. The chestnuts were already bearing their first candles of blossom. The old lime tree was still there, festively flourishing its new green leaves. "Thank goodness you got here safely," said Nurse Ottilie, as she went to meet them. "Herr Krummbein has inquired twice if his horses and cart have gotten back yet. Welcome to you, one and all! Welcome home!"

"Thank you, Ottchen!" they chorused, grateful for her unsentimental approach. With so much to be done, there was no time for emotions. A few women patients were waiting to see the doctor. The cart had to be unloaded, the animals attended to.

"There's a whole crowd of new names for the files, Karin!" Nurse Ottilie shouted from the dispensary. "Could you give the lentils a stir, Frau Lorenz? Set the table, Till."

Immediately after lunch Armin and Till took the cart back to Herr Krummbein. Carola and Karin set up a bed for Armin in Till's room. The man from Lörrach would sleep in the waiting room.

Not until evening did Karin find a minute for herself. She sat at the little writing desk in her own room and gazed around her. The pictures looked so pretty on the ivory-yellow wall; the furniture had been made by skillful craftsmen, each piece in quiet harmony with the rest. There were her books on the open shelves. Armin would be pleased to see them.

She didn't know how long she had been sitting there when the door opened and her father came in.

"Good to be home?" he asked, in his deep, kindly voice.

"So good!" Karin nodded.

Through the darkness came shouts and cries from a distant street. "They're still looting," her father said. "It's the same every night."

"And what's going to happen now?"

"Nobody knows." They were both thinking the same thing: that perhaps they must soon leave this beloved house and become, like millions of others, homeless—refugees in some strange city. Once more Karin looked around her room, tenderly, already taking leave of it. But even such a difficult separation would be nothing to what she had gone through.

"We'll manage!" she said. "The main thing is that we are all together again and have survived the deluge. If we go to the west, I can get a position as an interpreter with the Americans."

"Let me look at you," her father said, lifting her face. "You're thinner."

"It doesn't matter," said Karin, trying a smile that didn't quite come off.

Her chin has lost its childlike contours, thought her father. The line from the temples to the cheeks has become softer, more womanly. There is a new strength, somehow . . .

She looked at him with clear and serious eyes.

"I still have a lot to tell you," she said.

"Later."

"Yes. Later."

He took her hand and for the first time touched it with his lips, like a woman's hand.

"My grown-up daughter!" said Franz Lorenz.

A few weeks later, the Allies gave Eastern Germany to Russia.